PRAISE FOR THE
STEEL BROTHERS SAGA

"Hold onto the reins:
this red-hot Steel story is one wild ride."
~ A Love So True

"A spellbinding read from a
New York Times *bestselling author!"*
~ BookBub

"I'm in complete awe of this author. She has gone and
delivered an epic, all-consuming, addicting, insanely
intense story that's had me holding my breath, my
heart pounding and my mind reeling."
~ The Sassy Nerd

"Absolutely UNPUTDOWNABLE!"
~ Bookalicious Babes

FLAME

FLAME

STEEL BROTHERS SAGA
BOOK TWENTY

HELEN HARDT

WATERHOUSE PRESS

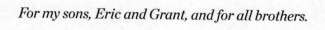

For my sons, Eric and Grant, and for all brothers.

PROLOGUE

Callie

I knock softly on Rory's door when I get home. "Ror? You awake?"

The door opens, and a yawning Rory looks back at me. "Cal? What are you doing up this late?"

"I just got in. Sorry to wake you."

Another yawn splits my sister's pretty face. "S'okay. What's up?"

I walk into her room and close the door behind me. "Some shit's going down."

"Like what?"

"I ran into Pat Lamone tonight."

Rory wipes the last of the sleep from her eyes and widens them. "Shit. How?"

"He's back in town, apparently, working the evening shift at the Snow Creek Inn."

"How can he be back in town?"

"Hell if I know. I had to act all innocent with Donny, like I hardly remembered him."

"Did he buy it?"

"I think so. He was more angry about other stuff."

"Like what?"

"I think..." My heart hurts. It hurts so badly for the man

I love. "I think he and Dale must have gone through some serious stuff before they came here. Like really bad."

"I guess we always suspected."

"Maybe you did. I didn't give it a thought, which makes me feel about an inch tall right now."

"Damn, Callie. You're in love with him, aren't you?"

I nod, sniffling back tears.

She pulls me into a hug. "It'll be okay. We'll work it all out."

"How can we? Why is that jerk back in town?"

"I don't know, hon. But I'll find out." She sighs. "I have some news myself. It's not good."

I pull back. "What? What happened? Is it Talon Steel?"

"No, no. He's still fine, as far as I know. It's Raine."

"Oh my God. What happened?"

"She's fine, as well, but she's decided to stay in Denver. A former colleague offered her a partnership in his new day spa. She'll be in charge of the salon. It's too good an opportunity for her to pass up."

"Ror, what are you going to do?"

Rory pauses a moment. "I don't know. Except that I think I do."

"I wouldn't blame you if you wanted to get far away from this place."

"But the family. The fire. They need me. And you, Cal. If Pat Lamone is back in town, you and I need to stick together."

I gulp audibly. Rory's right, but I can't be selfish. "Raine needs you too."

"I don't think she does, Cal. I don't think we're in that place."

"But you live together."

"We do. Or did. But lately..."

"What?"

"Things have been a little tense, like I told you. She can't seem to get over the fact that I'm bisexual and she isn't. Plus, apparently Willow White has offered to buy Raine's business here, so other than me, there's no reason for her to stay."

"You're a pretty big reason."

"I shed a tear or two earlier tonight, but I feel okay now. I think our time has passed. We weren't each other's forever."

I say nothing. I'm not sure what to say.

"Have you found your forever?" she asks.

I simply nod. I have. Whether Donny feels the same way after tonight is up in the air, but at least he loves me. He said it, and I believe him.

One silly fight doesn't change that.

But it does bring the current issue back to light.

"I'm sorry about Raine," I say, "and Donny and I will work through our issues. But Pat Lamone..."

"Right." Rory nods. "I guess we gather the group together."

"Some of them don't even live here anymore."

She nods. "Carmen Murphy is still here. And Jordan."

Carmen Murphy. Brendan's cousin, born to his unwed aunt, Ciara Murphy. And Jordan Ramsey, Rory's and my cousin, who was in Pat Lamone's class at school.

Pat Lamone.

There were others, but he was the worst.

He tried to destroy us.

He failed.

But now he's back.

CHAPTER ONE

Donny

I'm chilled yet numb as I stand in front of my mirror to brush my teeth.

So much to process for one evening.

God, my head. I'd swear Paul Bunyan is inside swinging his ax through my skull and into my brain.

Ibuprofen will ease it. Maybe.

I pull open the mirrored door to the hidden medicine cabinet—

What is that? I pull out a glasses case. I don't wear glasses. Never have. I do wear sunglasses, but I've never left the case inside this cabinet. Besides, I don't even recognize this brown leather case.

I unsnap it and open it.

Nestled inside the black lining is a key.

A key to what?

The key chain has a number and address etched on it. A bank in Denver.

This is a key to a safe-deposit box.

And I don't have a safe-deposit box.

It's settled, then.

I won't be sleeping tonight. At all.

★ ★ ★

My alarm blares at me. Six thirty a.m. Did I sleep? It was four a.m. the last time I looked at the clock.

And now ... work.

First a quick call to the hospital to check on Dad. I don't want to disturb Mom at this hour.

My phone rings then. Mom. This early? Is something wrong?

"Mom?" I say into the phone, trying not to sound too frantic.

"Donny"—her voice is ... different—"your dad had a rough night."

Icy shards hit the back of my neck. "Is he okay?"

"Yes. He is now, thank God."

"What happened?"

"His blood pressure dropped really low, and he spiked a fever. The doctors thought he might have an infection, but they got it under control and have him on another course of antibiotics."

"Do they know what caused it? If it wasn't an infection?"

"No."

"Not good enough."

"I agree, but all they can tell me is that these things sometimes happen during recovery from major surgery."

"Not good enough," I say again. "Do you want me to drive into the city?"

"More than ever," she says, "but you can't. I need you covering things in town at the city attorney's office."

"Mom, Snow Creek will survive without—"

"No, Donny," she interrupts. "Please. Take care of things

in town. I can't have another worry on top of everything else."

"Okay, Mom. Maybe Dale can go to the hospital."

"Diana's here. Dale has his Syrah to look after, and Bree has classes. I'll be fine."

My mother *will* be fine. She's as strong as they come. But she depends on me. I'm her rock when Dad's out of commission. And Dale, Diana, or Brianna can't take my place.

I'm ready to jump in the car in my pajama pants and rush to Grand Junction.

The same way I rushed back to the ranch when she asked me to become her assistant city attorney. I'll do anything for my mother.

She's right, though. I have to take care of things in town. Life doesn't stop just because of a tragedy. I know that better than anyone.

"All right, Mom," I say. "But if you change your mind, I'll be there."

"I know you will."

"You want me to call Dale and Bree?"

"No, I'll take care of that, or I'll get Marj to do it. You get into the office and make sure things run smoothly while I'm gone."

"You got it. Anything for you, Mom."

"You're a wonderful son, Donny. I love you."

"I love you too. Give Dad my love."

"I will. Bye, sweetie."

I heave a sigh and stare at my phone for a few minutes.

I can't lose my father. He means the world to me. And damn ... It would be ten times harder on Dale.

Dad is fine now, according to Mom. She wouldn't sugarcoat anything where Dad's well-being is concerned. If she were more worried, she'd want me there at her side, even if it meant no attorney were in the office in town.

I rise, finally, and stumble into the shower. I make it a cold one as I need to wake up. I hate cold showers, but they do the job—for waking up, at least. Not for blue balls.

Damn.

Blue balls.

Callie.

Callie and I and our fight.

It wasn't a fight so much as . . . .

I'm not sure what it was.

I know only that I'm in love with Callie Pike, and she's in love with me.

This should be a time for happiness, joy, euphoria.

Instead?

It's a time of doubt, of wondering if my father and uncles have been lying to us our whole lives, of knowing mysteries surround our family, the biggest of which is—who shot Talon Steel?

Secrets. Secrets and lies—and it could all come crashing down when we least expect it if I don't figure out what's going on.

I turn off the shower and shiver as I wrap myself in a bath sheet. I towel off my hair and open the mirrored cabinet above my sink.

The glasses case.

The safe-deposit box key.

I don't wear glasses. I don't have a safe-deposit box. How the hell did it get here?

I don't have time to go to Denver today, but I sure as hell won't send anyone else.

Mom and Dad have an alarm system. No one could have gotten into the house unauthorized. What is the name of the company that surveils the house? I have no freaking idea.

I give Dale a quick call.

"Yeah, Don?"

"Hey, do you happen to know the name of the company that monitors the main house? I need some information."

"Yeah, it's Monarch Security. What do you need?"

"Someone got in . . . and into my room."

"What?" Dale grits out.

Already I feel the anger rising in my brother. I share it. Who was in our house?

"Yeah. I found a glasses case in my medicine cabinet."

"You don't wear glasses."

"Very good, genius. There weren't any glasses inside, but there was a key to a safe-deposit box in a bank in Denver."

"You sure it's not yours?"

"Of course I'm sure. I don't have a safe-deposit box."

"You don't? Maybe you don't remember opening it. You lived in Denver a long time."

"For God's sake, Dale. I'd remember renting a safe-deposit box."

"Okay, okay. I just thought maybe you had one for client documents or something."

"My firm took care of all that stuff. Who the hell got into the house?"

"I don't know. Check with Monarch. They should have video surveillance."

"Video? It's not just an alarm system?"

"No. Dad told me about it a while ago when you were still in Denver. The house used to belong to Grandma and Grandpa

Steel, as you know. Grandpa Steel had everything installed, and Dad had it updated shortly before you and I arrived at the ranch. All state of the art."

"Why?"

"I didn't ask. I just assumed because of our monetary situation."

"Yeah. Okay. I'll give them a call. Then I need to go to Denver and find out what the hell's in this safe-deposit box."

"Yeah. Let me know when you do that."

"I will. I'm not sure when I can. So much is going on here in town."

"You need to make the time."

He's right. I mentally add it to my huge-ass to-do list.

John Lambert is serving the Murphys with papers this morning—papers that tell them to leave their building for three days so a potential gas leak can be investigated and, if necessary, repaired by the city. Dale and I need to search the place during that window.

I ignore the surge of acid in my stomach, or at least I try to. I hate that I did this. I hate it with a passion. But was there any other choice?

I swallow down the disgust at myself. No time. The key. Denver. It will all have to wait.

Who the hell has been in this house?

CHAPTER TWO

Callie

I arrive early to work.

Why not? I didn't sleep at all. Between thoughts of Pat Lamone's return to Snow Creek and how Donny and I left things...

Sleep wasn't going to happen, and it didn't.

I stop at Rita's for some black coffee. Ava's bakery sits across the street, fresh almond croissants in the display case.

They're not even the slightest bit appetizing.

My appetite has gone on hiatus.

Freaking Pat Lamone. Already back to his old games, spreading lies about Rory and our family. How long has it been? Ten years?

Yeah, ten years. Aren't people supposed to mature after ten years?

I guess we got complacent. We thought those times were gone forever.

Well... we chased him out of Snow Creek once. We can do it again if we have to.

Though I'd really like to catch a break. Just once. One break.

The fire. Our vines—gone. Law school—gone.

And now... Pat Lamone. If only he could be gone as I thought he was.

I sigh and sit down at a table in the café. I don't have to be at work for a half hour yet. I take a sip of coffee and rub my forehead.

This will be a long day.

★ ★ ★

Being invisible has its perks. Sure, my sister's the homecoming queen and all, and my brother was the big man on campus four years ago—the best quarterback our small town has ever produced.

But Caroline Pike is invisible.

She's the one who earns the good grades, always makes the honor roll, and who, no matter how hard she scrubs her face, always has one or two zits to show for it.

I stare into the mirror in the restroom at Snow Creek High. The stench of stale cigarettes makes breathing a chore, but I'd rather be in here than out chatting in the hallway with all the others. Even the smell of marijuana doesn't drive me away, and frankly, it smells like a skunk to me.

Jeannie Maguire, our school's most notorious pothead, stumbles out of a stall, her blue eyes glazed and bloodshot. "Pike. What's up?"

"You okay, Jeannie?"

"I'm great." She smiles and leaves the bathroom.

I tried pot once with Jeannie and my cousin Jordan. I didn't feel a thing, and I certainly don't relish the idea of looking anything like Jeannie Maguire, walking around in a stoned haze.

But what else is there to do in Snow Creek?

Jeannie's a townie.

I'm not. I live on my parents' ranch, and there's always something to do. My brother, sisters, and I don't dare ever say we're bored or Dad will put us to work.

I don't mind helping out, but I never get bored. When I'm not busy with something else, I read.

My nose in a book.

Being invisible has its perks.

★ ★ ★

"Hi, Callie."

I'm jolted out of my flashback by Donny's voice.

He stands next to my table. His long and muscled legs are clad in black pants, and he wears a white button-down with a perfectly Windsor-knotted burgundy-and-blue striped tie. In his fingers, he crumples a black suit jacket. His hair is slightly unruly, but it only adds to his charm.

My heart starts to pound.

"What are you doing here?" I ask.

"Same as you, apparently. Coffee run."

"I could have gotten it. Why didn't you text me?"

"Because I'm perfectly capable of getting my own coffee, Callie."

He looks tired. Gorgeous, as usual, but tired. His eyes are heavy-lidded and slightly bloodshot.

He didn't sleep any better than I did.

"Come on," he says. "I'll walk with you to the office."

I drain the last of my coffee.

"Can I get you another?" he asks.

"Yeah. It's a three-coffee kind of morning."

"You too?"

I nod. Our disagreement last night is part of the issue, but only a bit. Donny doesn't know about my past with Pat Lamone, and I'm hoping I can keep it that way. Rory and I will figure something out. She's going to reach out to Carmen and Jordan today. The four of us will get together as soon as possible and put this to bed for good.

I hope we can.

"Cal . . ." Donny says.

"Yeah?"

"I'm sorry about . . ."

I smile weakly. "Yeah, me too."

"So much is going on," he continues.

You don't know the half of it.

I simply nod. "I know."

"My dad had an episode during the night."

My jaw drops. Here I am feeling sorry for myself, when Donny's father is still not fully recovered. I vow to get over myself. "Is he okay?"

"Yeah. His blood pressure dropped, and they thought he might have an infection, but it looks good now."

"I'm sorry, Donny."

"It's all good." His tone doesn't indicate belief in his words, though.

"Shouldn't you be at the hospital with your mom?"

"Yeah, I should be, but she wants me here, making sure the city runs smoothly." He shakes his head. "This tiny town, and she's worried about it. Go figure."

"Did you sleep at all?" I ask.

"I think maybe an hour? You?"

"Maybe an hour. Maybe not." In fact, not.

"Look," he says, "we'll work this out. I love you, Callie."

"I love you too."

"There's just a lot of shit going on in my life right now. I don't want it to touch us, but how can it not? I've brought you in on it. I need your help."

"I understand." I want to help. I'm thrilled he trusts me with what he's doing.

Do I dare trust him with what's coming back to haunt me?

I trust him to take a bullet for me.

But this... Pat Lamone... It goes so far beyond high school drama.

It's in the past. I'd truly thought it buried. Why has he shown up back in Snow Creek?

"Come on," Donny says. "Let's get to the office. Lots to do."

I rise and follow him to the counter where he orders another coffee for me. Then we head to the office.

The city attorney's office.

Where justice is served.

Hot or cold.

My own thought makes me shudder.

CHAPTER THREE

Donny

Troy has Callie working on some research, so I leave her to it. That's what she wants—to actually do real work pertinent to her interests. I can't pull her off to do Steel bidding. There will be enough of that to come.

Ten o'clock comes and goes. Nothing from Lambert yet.

I fully expect Brendan and his dad to come to me once it's done. They'll think I can intervene or something.

This is a state issue. I have no control over it.

Yup, I already have my canned speech ready, despite the self-loathing in the pit of my gut.

I thread my fingers through my hair. Man, I need some shut-eye. Except all I'd do is toss and turn, as I did for the few hours I was even in bed last night.

Fuck.

Buzz.

I nearly jump out of my chair.

It's done. Want me to stop by your office?

I text Lambert back.

Yeah. Maybe you should. To make

the whole thing look legit, as if
you're letting me know.

Got it. Be over in a minute.

The last thing I want is to see John Lambert, but I'm in too deep to back down now. May as well make it all look good. Ten minutes later, my phone buzzes.

"Donny," the receptionist downstairs says, "there's a Mr. Lambert from the state energy board here to see you."

"Send him up."

A knock on my door a few minutes later.

"Come in."

The door opens, and John Lambert's bald head peeks in. "Hey, Don."

"John, good to see you," I say for show. "What brings you by?"

"I wanted to give you a heads-up on a situation here in your town," he says.

"Sure. Come on in. Close the door."

Once he's seated across from my desk, I ask, "How'd it go?"

"He's not happy, but it went fine."

"Good."

"He wanted to know why it's just the bar and not the whole block. I told him there was a specific gas line under his place that was at issue. Not sure if he bought it."

"He doesn't have to buy it if you had the paperwork."

"I did."

"Good. Thanks."

"I'll be thinking about how you can repay me."

"I know you will, John. For now, enjoy the rest of your stay at the Carlton."

"Will do." He salutes and stands. "Anything else?"

"Not at the moment. I'll keep in touch, though. Make sure you're available if I need you."

"Absolutely."

"And John?"

"Yeah?"

"I don't have to remind you how important it is that no one knows about our agreement."

"No, you don't. It's my ass on the line too. See you, Don." He leaves, closing the door behind him.

I drop my head into my hands. What have I done?

Less than a minute later, another knock.

"What is it?" I yell, more harshly than I mean to.

"Never mind."

Shit. Callie's voice.

"I'm sorry," I say loudly. "Come in."

She eases the door open. She's so beautiful. She's wearing black leggings and a burgundy tunic today. Comfy clothes, and she looks delectable.

"What do you need?" I ask.

She clears her throat. "You told me to come see you when I was done with any work from Troy and Alyssa."

"Already? You're efficient."

She smiles halfheartedly and closes the door. "I'm not sure there's any need for the city to be paying me. There's just not enough work."

"We've been through this, Callie. My mother wouldn't have hired you—"

"Yeah, yeah, I know," she interrupts me and then sighs.

"I'm sorry. I'm just . . ."

"I get it. Lack of sleep. We'll get through this."

She nods numbly, and I wonder why she's so bothered. Sure, I asked her to keep a secret, but it has nothing to do with her.

"Is there something else disturbing you?" I ask.

"No."

"Are you sure?"

She drops her gaze to the floor. "Yeah."

Classic tell.

"Callie," I say. "What is it?"

She looks up. "It's nothing, Donny. I'm just tired."

"You know what? You should just go home. Take the rest of the day. Get some rest."

"That's kind of you, but no, thank you. I'm here to do a job, and I'm going to do it."

"You're no good to anyone without sleep."

"Oh? And you are?"

I can't help it. I give a scoffing laugh. "You got me there."

"What have you got?" she asks. "I want to—"

The door to my office jerks open, and a red-faced Brendan Murphy stands in the entryway holding up a paper. He looks taller than he is, and his blue eyes are full of fire. "What the fuck is this, Steel?"

Callie jerks around. "Brendan?"

"Stay the fuck out of this, Callie."

"Whoa," I say. "Ease up, Brendan. Don't talk to her like that."

"This is bullshit," he says.

"I know all about it," I tell him. "A guy from the energy board was just here to fill me in."

"Then you can take care of it, right? It's crap."

"I'm sorry," I say. "It's a state issue. I have no control over it."

I'm going to hell. I'm so going to hell.

Brendan rubs his temples, shoves his free hand into the pocket of his jeans. "They can just come in and shut down my business for a week?"

"Yeah, I'm afraid they can."

"What's going on?" Callie asks.

"What's going on?" Brendan mimics. "The state of Colorado thinks we have a potential gas leak under our property. That's what's going on. Have I smelled gas? No. Have I had any issues whatsoever? No."

"I'm sure the energy board has its reasons," I say as calmly as I can.

"Of course. It's all written down. An issue with the material used in this particular pipe that just happens to run under our property. They can't access it from anywhere else."

"I'm sure it's for your own protection," Callie says.

Oh, God. Now I've made a liar out of Callie. At least she doesn't know it.

Brendan doesn't respond to her.

"They have to check it out," I say. "It could be nothing, but they're required to do their due diligence. Take a week off. Go to the mountains. To Denver."

"Fuck that," he says. "I'm going to be watching these guys like a hawk while they're on my property."

Great. That's just great.

"Brendan," Callie says, "if there's a potential gas problem, you probably shouldn't be anywhere near the place."

Nicely done, Callie. I'll pay you back later.

"If I were you," she continues, "I'd take Donny's advice. Take a vacation. When's the last time you got out of Snow Creek?"

"Some of us don't have the money to go jaunting around the globe," he says.

Callie's cheeks redden. "Now just a minute . . ."

"Sorry, Callie," he says. "I meant to get *him* with that one."

"Murphy," I say, "I have no control over this."

The lies are bitter. Bitter and acidic and nauseating.

"You're the damned city attorney!"

"*Acting* city attorney," I say, "emphasis on the word *city*. This is a *state* issue. They outrank me."

"Surely you can make a phone call."

"I could, but it wouldn't do any good. Besides, if there's a potential issue with the gas lines under your property, you should want this, Brendan. What if a line springs a leak? Would that be good for business?"

Brendan draws in a breath, holds it for a few seconds, and then exhales. He says nothing.

"Look," I say, "if I could help, I would, but it's out of my hands."

"I'm sorry," he finally says. "I'm just pissed as all hell. A week's income lost."

"Let me look into that," I say. "The state is probably required to reimburse you for lost income if they shut down your business through no fault of yours. Okay?"

"Yeah, they should do that."

"I agree. I'm sure there's a regulation somewhere. I'll find it."

"All right. Thanks, Don. And sorry . . . about all of this."

"Don't worry about it. I understand. Take a vacation. Tell

you what. I can set you up at one of our places in Aspen for the week. You can take your parents and Ciara if you want. Get out of town and forget about this headache."

He pauses. Is he considering it? *Please, consider it.* I'm well aware I'm offering to make myself feel better about the whole thing. When did I become such a good liar?

Then, "That's kind of you, but no. I'm not going anywhere." He storms out.

Callie bites her lip. "What's up with him?"

"He's pissed. Who can blame him?"

"Yeah, but if he'll be reimbursed and there's a potential problem, he should be glad it's going to be taken care of."

I nod.

Right.

This is so fucked up.

CHAPTER FOUR

C a l l i e

I don't get it. I never thought Brendan Murphy was a hothead. Who wouldn't want a potential gas threat fixed?

Unbelievable.

"Let's get out of here," Donny says.

"And go where?"

"Lunch."

I check my watch. It *is* nearly noon.

"Okay. Where do you want to go?"

"The winery. Dale has a tasting today. They serve lunch."

"You want to go all the way to—"

"Fuck." He rubs his forehead. "No. Of course not. I just want to get the hell out of here!" He claws at his tie, loosening it. "I feel like I'm back in a damned cage!"

My heart drops into my stomach. His words shock me. Not so much the words as *one* word. Back. *Back* in a damned cage. I swallow the lump in my throat, or try to, anyway. I suppress the shivers that want to take over my body.

Back. *Back* in a damned cage. Power propels his words—a haunting power that exudes from him like the scent of alcohol exudes from pores after drinking too much.

I feel numb. I even wiggle my fingers to make sure I can. That's how frozen I feel.

Donny Steel knows what it's like to be in a cage.

What happened? Why were he and Dale adopted by the Steels?

So much I don't know.

So much that no one knows.

"Let's go." He grabs his suit jacket and jams his arms into it.

"To the winery?"

"No, of course not. To . . . I don't fucking know. Anywhere. Let's just get the hell out of here."

I bite my lip. "Okay. We can go over to Lorenzo's. Or Rita's. Or Ava's."

"I'm not hungry."

Good enough. Neither am I. I'm not sure I'll ever be hungry again. My life is a mess, and apparently so is Donny's. He's got his issues, some of which I'm privy to. A lot of which I'm not. I don't want to pry, but I love this man.

Back in a fucking cage.

My God. My poor Donny.

All of a sudden, Pat Lamone and my own past seem inconsequential to me. What has Donny been through? How did he end up at Steel Acres Ranch?

I won't pry. I can't. I don't even know where to begin with something this big.

I clear my throat. "All right. Where do you want to go?"

"Honestly, Callie? I want to go somewhere and fuck the daylights out of you, but where the hell is that? I don't want to go back to the Snow Creek Inn. I don't want to go home. I don't want to—"

His words ignite a flame inside me. Perhaps this is what we both need at this moment.

"Here," I say. "Fuck me here."

My command doesn't surprise me in the slightest. I want to escape from the thoughts plaguing my mind as much as he does. Here is good. Anywhere is good, but here is *now*.

"In the office? With Alyssa and Troy right outside?"

"They'll go to lunch in a few minutes." I walk to the door and open it. "Troy's already gone."

"And Alyssa?"

"She's gathering her purse." I walk a few steps out the door. "Hey, Alyssa. Heading to lunch?"

"Yeah. Can I get you anything?"

"No thanks."

"Okay. See you in an hour."

I walk back into Donny's office and close the door. "All clear."

"Fuck," he growls and rips off his jacket once more. "Get undressed."

I freeze. He wasn't kidding around. He wants to fuck, and he wants to fuck now. No undressing me. No foreplay.

It's going to be like that first time in the library.

And you know what? I'm okay with that.

I shed my clothing, attempting to go at a reasonable pace but ending up racing Donny to the finish. His clothes strewn about, he stalks out from behind his desk, his erection raging, his hair a mess, and his eyes on fire.

An electric current skitters across my flesh. My nipples are hard and aching, my pussy erupting in flames.

Donny grabs me, turns me away from him, and bends me over his desk. "God, Callie, I can smell you. You're wet. Already so wet." He swipes his fingers through my folds and groans low in his chest. "Damn."

Then his cock is inside me, and he's thrusting, thrusting, thrusting. I revel in the completion, the end of the empty ache. I want it to go on and on forever.

"Fuck, Callie," he grits out. "Want to last. Want to make it good for you. Want to— Fuck!"

He releases inside me, and I'm so on edge, so sensitive, that I feel every single contraction of his cock inside me.

So it didn't go on and on forever. This is good too. Really good.

He stays still for a moment, embedded in my body. I melt against his desk, releasing the tension in my body and laying my chest on the mahogany wood. A few pens and a pad of Post-it notes dig into me, but I don't care.

This is where I want to be. Where I'm meant to be.

Sex with Donny is a beautiful thing, even when it's fast and furious. Even when I don't come. With Donny, it's not the climax that I crave. It's him. Pure and simple. My body craves his in a way it's never craved anyone before.

He pulls out then. "Damn. I'm sorry."

"For what?" I ask, my cheek against the edge of his blotter.

"I'm not very good at satisfying you. Pleasing women is my specialty, Cal, but with you… I don't seem to have any control."

I rise then. The Post-it notes stick to my abdomen with my perspiration. I peel them off. "I don't recall complaining."

"You're a good sport."

I let out a soft laugh. "You think it's really about me being a good sport?"

"No. Hell, I don't know what I think."

I push a stray hair off his forehead, which is slick with sweat. "Okay, fair enough, but here's what *I* think. I'm kind of glad you don't have any control with me. I like that I have that effect on you."

"Oh? You don't miss the orgasms?"

I laugh again softly. "I won't say that. Doesn't everyone love a good orgasm? But I'm not all about the climax, Donny. I'm about the experience."

"You must like your experiences instantaneous, then," he says.

"It wasn't instantaneous."

"Damn near."

"It was a release. You're on edge, and frankly, so am I. I get it."

He rakes his fingers through his already disheveled hair. "I should have never involved you in this."

"I want to be here for you."

But he doesn't know the other part of why I'm on edge. Sure, I feel what he feels. I'm worried for him and his brother and sisters and what they might uncover. Even more, I'm concerned about what this man went through as a child—what brought him to Snow Creek and the Steels.

And though that thought outweighs anything else, I'm also freaked about my own problems.

Pat Lamone.

It could be nothing.

But already I know it's not nothing. He lied to Donny at the motel. Said Rory had slept with him. Said I'd been next in line. Said we were easy. We were gold diggers.

In truth, *he's* the gold digger. We have proof. I'm guessing he found out about my relationship with Donny and thinks he can make money by threatening to expose Rory, me, and the rest of us.

He can think again.

We took care of him once, and we'll do it again if need be.

Man, I wish I were as strong as those thoughts...

"Callie?"

I jerk toward Donny's voice. "Yeah?"

"You okay? You got a...weird look in your eye for a minute."

I force a smile. "I'm fine."

"Good," he says, "because I'm going to take care of *you* now."

CHAPTER FIVE

Donny

Callie's low ponytail is sagging, and strands of her brown hair have come loose. Her amber eyes are on fire, though, and I know I can pull two or three orgasms out of her easy.

I didn't get to prove that she isn't "one and done" while we were in Aspen because Dale called about Dad.

I'll prove it to her now.

I lift her in my arms and set her on the edge of my desk. Then I spread her legs. Most guys I know won't go down on a woman after they come inside her. Me? I take every opportunity to go down on a woman. Usually I'm wearing a condom, though, so the semen-in-pussy thing isn't a problem.

With Callie, I don't care. I want her to come, and going down on her will make that happen.

She's beautiful—swollen, pink, and wet. I flick my tongue over her clit and shove a finger into her. I don't have to get her ready. She's already there.

She gasps at the intrusion, and I look up at her. Her eyes are closed, her cheeks pink, her lips parted just a touch. I want desperately to move upward and kiss her—that's how beautiful her pink lips are at this moment.

But not before she comes.

And comes again.

I swirl my tongue over her clit again before clamping my lips around it and gently sucking. I find her spongy G-spot, add a second finger, and then do the patented Donny Steel scissor finger move while tugging just so on her clit.

Each woman is different. Some are very sensitive to clitoral stimulation. Some need a damned bulldozer.

Callie is perfect.

She takes just enough pressure, doesn't make me work too hard.

And I'd gladly work harder than ever to please her.

She moans above me, threads the fingers of one hand through my hair as I lick and probe her.

Then—

"Yes, Donny, yes!"

She clamps around my fingers, releasing. I ease up on her clit, licking it softly now, just enough to keep her going.

She moans again, and when I look up at her gorgeous face, her teeth are clamped down on her lip.

She's trying not to shriek.

We *are* in the office, after all.

One and done? Let's see about that. When her spasms slow, I begin again.

But—

My phone. My fucking phone is buzzing. Callie's eyes shoot open.

I withdraw my fingers. "I'm sorry. It could be about Dad."

"I know." She cups my cheek. "It's okay."

As hot as I was a second before, my body is now cold as ice. Still naked, I reach for the phone on my desk. It's Dale. Damn.

"Yeah?" I say into the phone.

"It's me, Don."

"I know. Is Dad okay?"

"Yeah, yeah. He's fine. I just talked to Diana. That's not why I'm calling."

"For Christ's sake, I'm in the middle of ... lunch."

"Since when do you care if I interrupt your lunch? I purposefully called so I wouldn't interfere with your work."

I heave a sigh. "Never mind. It's all good. What's up? I thought you had a tasting luncheon today."

"I do, but Ashley's handling it for me. I wanted to get the scoop on the Murphy thing. Did the papers get served?"

"Yeah. He's not happy."

"I never labored under the delusion that he would be."

"I'm doing some research into whether the state will reimburse him for lost income. An eminent domain kind of thing."

"And if they won't?"

"They will," I say.

"Meaning ... ?"

"You know what I mean." I stay coy as Callie's listening intently.

"You mean we'll take care of it."

"Bingo."

A pause. Then, "Agreed. We need to clean up our messes."

"True story," I say before ending the call.

And then I wonder at my own words.

This is *our* mess. The fake gas leak. The thing that's making my stomach do somersaults and my conscience feel like shit.

But what of the rest? The messes our parents may have left for us?

Who will clean *those* up?

I know the answer.

The only ones who can.
We will.

CHAPTER SIX

Callie

Donny throws his phone back down on the desk. "Now...
where were we?"

But my orgasm has ceased, and for now, I'm done. I love
Donny Steel, but he won't get another climax out of me for at
least an hour, and—I eye his cock—he's far from ready to screw
me over his desk again.

That phone call turned him nearly flaccid.

"Donny..."

"Yeah?"

"It's okay. I'm done."

He opens his mouth—presumably to argue the point—but
then closes it. After a pause, "All right. But I'm going to prove
you're multiply orgasmic eventually."

"Not in the next hour, you're not."

"Fair enough." He walks behind his desk, opens a drawer,
and pulls out a box of tissues, handing them to me. "Not a warm
washcloth, but it's all I have here."

"It's fine." I take a few tissues and discreetly take care of
myself before tossing them into his wastebasket. Then I grab
my bra and panties and begin to dress.

Donny is busy pulling on his boxer briefs and slacks, when
his phone buzzes again. He visibly tenses up, and a subtle

shudder racks through him.

I get it. Each call could be something about his dad.

"Yeah?" he says.

Pause.

"I'm on it." He ends the call and tosses the phone back onto his desk.

"Who was that?" I ask.

"Nothing important."

"So your dad's okay?"

"Yeah. As far as I know. I should check in with Mom."

I finish dressing. "I understand. Do you have anything for me to do?"

He shakes his head. "Go ahead and take your lunch break."

I nod. Whatever's going on, he's not going to share it with me. I won't pry.

Seems I think that a lot lately.

Would I be more prone to prying if I didn't have my own shit to deal with? I don't know the answer.

Once dressed, I walk out of Donny's office and hightail it to the ladies' room to make sure I don't look like I've just been ravaged. A quick fix of my hair and lip gloss, and I look like a normal person again.

Now what?

It's lunchtime, but I'm far from hungry. Still, I need to eat. I won't be any good to Donny, Rory, or anyone else who needs me without strength, and that requires fuel.

Rory's in town today, teaching voice and piano in her little studio next to her former apartment and above Raine's hair salon. Soon to be Willow White's hair salon. Will Rory be able to keep her studio there?

I walk down the stairs, out of the building, and then two

blocks to the salon. It's closed now, since Raine's out of town and Willow hasn't opened yet, but Rory's studio is accessible by a staircase in the back alley. I ascend and open the door. Lonnie Jefferson, a young woman who works at Rita's part time, is sitting in the small waiting area, and through the wafer-thin walls, I hear the keys of a piano plunking.

"Hey, Lonnie," I say. "Is Janae having her lesson?"

"She is. Almost done, I think. How are you, Callie?"

"I'm good." Big lie there, but I'm used to it.

"Your family getting along okay?"

The pity. Here it goes again. I force a smile. "We're all fine. Thank you for asking."

"If there's anything Jerry or I can do, please let us know."

"Of course. That's kind of you. But we're getting along fine."

She smiles. "I'm glad to hear that. I'm sorry to hear about Raine and Rory."

My, good news certainly travels fast in this small town. I should be used to it by now, but I'm not. I'm a private person.

"They're both in a good place," I reply.

"That's good to know, and"—she flashes a toothy smile—"you and Donny Steel, I hear?"

Lonnie is a nice person, but I never knew her to be the town crier. When a Steel is involved, though . . .

"We're seeing each other," is all I give her.

"I'm thrilled for you."

I'm not sure how to reply, so I'm thankful I don't have to. Six-year-old Janae barrels out of the studio. She's an adorable knobby-kneed first grader, and Rory says she has a lot of potential on the piano.

I'll take her word for it. All I heard was plinking of single keys.

"How'd it go, sweetie?" Lonnie asks her daughter.

"Good! Miss Rory says I passed all my songs."

Rory smiles. "She's a natural, Lonnie. You wouldn't believe how many students can't find middle C after ten lessons. She got it the first time."

Janae smiles, cute with one of her front teeth missing. "Thank you, Miss Rory."

"Not at all. See you next time, Janae!"

Janae and her mother leave the studio, and I turn to my sister.

"How are you holding up?"

She sighs. "I'm good. Just worried. Not just about the Pat Lamone thing, but about my livelihood. Raine's already drawing up the paperwork for Willow to buy this place. Willow may not want amateur pianists and vocalists making noise above her salon."

"You can see your students at home. Mom and Dad won't mind."

"Who wants to drive a half hour to a lesson when they're used to walking a few steps outside?" Rory shakes her head. "Won't work."

She's right, of course.

Things are changing for the Pikes.

And not for the better.

Still, I have happiness in my heart because of Donny.

I almost feel guilty for it.

Then I remember those words. *Back in a fucking cage.*

I can't. Can't allow myself to go there. Donny wouldn't want me to pry. Would he? I love him so much. I don't want to take any chance of losing him.

Besides, if Donny finds out about the whole Pat Lamone situation . . .

"We should talk, Ror. Have you reached out to Jordan and Carmen yet?"

"Not yet. Jordan's in as big a mess as we are with the fire. Uncle Scott and Aunt Lena don't even own the property. They just live on it and make a living. That fire has screwed us all. And then Raine. And Willow White. Not to mention that asshole Lamone." Rory's eyes cloud up.

"Hey, we'll get through it." But even *I* don't believe my words.

"Cal..."

"Yeah?"

"You don't suppose Donny would..."

"Would what?"

"Never mind."

"Oh. You were about to ask if he might be able to..."

"Yeah. Forget I even thought it."

"I won't lie, Rory. It's crossed my mind. But I'm not asking my boyfriend for money. I can't do it. Would you ask Raine?"

"It's not comparable. Raine and I aren't together anymore." She paused. "But...no. I wouldn't."

"See?"

"But it's hardly comparable, as I said. Raine's a hair stylist with a modest income. Donny Steel's a freaking billionaire. He can afford to save all of us. It's pennies to him."

"I know. And trust me, it's crossed my mind, but that's not how we're wired, Rory. We don't take charity. I can't stomach the idea."

"Normally I can't either, but this Lamone thing has me on edge. Big time."

"Me too. You want to grab lunch? I've still got a half hour."

"Not hungry."

"You think I am?" I shake my head. "Not in the slightest. But we have to eat, Ror. If we don't, we risk becoming weak, and we can't be weak right now."

She sighs. "You're right. What sounds good?"

I scoff. "Nothing. But Rita's is the cheapest, so that's my choice."

"Good enough." Rory follows me out of the studio and locks the door behind her. "We need to talk about how to approach Jordan and Carmen, anyway. I'd rather we do it together."

I nod.

My sister's right.

The problem? I don't want to talk about Jordan and Carmen. Or Pat Lamone. Or the fire and what it's cost us. Or Raine and Willow White.

All I want is to run.

Take Donny Steel and run.

CHAPTER SEVEN

Donny

I told Callie the phone call I got right before she left my office wasn't important. In the grand scheme of things, perhaps it isn't.

Except that it is.

It was John Lambert. He's thought of a way I can pay him back, and he wants to meet me for lunch here in town.

I'm headed over to Lorenzo's. I'm steering clear of Rita's—where the sheriff and his officers lunch nearly every day—and Ava's—where I'll run into my cousin and probably other family members who may be in town for the day.

Lorenzo's is a safe bet.

Well...the safest Snow Creek has to offer. If Murphy shows up, I'll feign that I'm working with Lambert to get Murphy reimbursed for the damages he'll suffer by being closed for a week.

The week is a boon. I asked Lambert for three days.

I'm not unhappy about the extra time, especially with all that's going on with Dad's hospitalization. More time is good.

Ugh. If only my stomach would settle.

I walk into Lorenzo's. Lambert's already here, at a table in the back. The owner, Lisa Lorenzo, is at the hostess stand today.

"Hey, Donny. Just you today?"

"Actually, I'm meeting someone. I see him in the back."

"The guy from Denver? Okay. I'll send your server over."

"Thanks." I walk to the table and take a seat. "John."

"Hey, Donny." He cocks his head. "You're looking a little glum."

"Just don't like owing people favors, man."

"I feel you. I don't either, which is why I'm glad I'm on the receiving end this time. You've bailed me out enough."

True enough. "What's it going to take, John?"

"Ease up, Steel. Let's order. Have some lunch. We can get to details later."

"I'd be more comfortable getting to details now." I can't eat anyway, so I'd rather know exactly what the cost will be for John's help with the Murphy situation. I'm hoping it only costs dollars. I've spent enough of my ethics already. I'm really in debt there.

"Nah," he says. "I'm starved." He waves at a young woman. "Debbie, we're ready over here."

Are we? I haven't even looked at the menu. Doesn't matter. Whatever I order will taste like sawdust anyway.

Debbie hustles over, pad in hand. "Hi, Donny." She gives me a smile. "You gentlemen ready?"

"We are," Lambert says. "I'll have Lorenzo's feast."

"You've got a big appetite," Debbie says.

Indeed. Lorenzo's feast is a hunk of lasagna, chicken parmesan, ravioli, and a side of spaghetti with a giant meatball.

"Donny?" Debbie lifts her eyebrows.

My standard *I'll have the same* is replaced with, "Just a small plate of spaghetti marinara, please."

"Since when does a Steel boy *not* order the feast?" She laughs.

"Had a big breakfast," I lie.

Damn, I'm a good liar. Who knew? Even this little white lie makes me hate myself.

"Good enough." Debbie pushes her pad into her apron pocket. "I'll get this started."

"So"—I raise my brow at John—"don't leave me in suspense."

Lambert takes a sip of his water. "We forgot to order drinks."

"I don't drink during the workday."

"I'm not talking alcohol, Don. Jesus. I was thinking maybe an iced tea?"

I wave to Debbie, and she rushes over.

"Yeah, Don?"

"My companion would like an iced tea."

"Sweet or unsweet?"

"Unsweet," Lambert says.

"And you, Don?"

"Water's fine."

"Good enough. So sorry about that." She hustles away, clearly flustered that she didn't ask us about drinks.

I couldn't care less.

"Let's get to it," I say.

"Ease up," Lambert says for the second time. "Can't a couple of old friends enjoy a meal?"

A couple of things are wrong with Lambert's statement. First of all, we're not friends, so we're hardly *old* friends. He was a client when I practiced law in Denver, and I got him out of several scrapes, the most notorious being a defamation lawsuit. Second, I won't enjoy any meal while all this is going down. I feel like complete shit about what I've caused to happen, but Lambert?

He doesn't seem to care in the least.

How can I enjoy a meal sitting across from a person of such questionable ethics?

I laugh aloud—a soft scoff.

Who the hell am I to judge? Lambert breached his ethics big time, but he did so at my request. I'm the king of ethics breaching. I put this plan in motion, and I'm going to break and enter someone's property to search for documents involving my family.

Who the fuck is the worst?

It's not the man sitting across from me.

And that stark realization has me wanting to unload the contents of my stomach right onto the table.

CHAPTER EIGHT

Callie

Bonfires at Snow Creek High School were all the rage. The town stopped allowing them after my sophomore year due to fire hazards—at least that's what they said—but when Rory and I were in school, they were the bomb.

They were supposed to be, anyway.

The school sponsored one after each football game, and it was at one bonfire during my sophomore year—Rory's senior—that things got out of hand.

Someone had brought alcohol, of course. That in itself wasn't out of place. Someone always sneaked alcohol in. This time, though, it was laced with something.

The party line was—and still is—that the culprit was never caught.

He was, though. Just not by the police.

He was caught by Rory and me. And four others.

We were ready to turn him in for the reward money. The Steel family offered a huge bounty because one of their sweethearts, Diana Steel, got caught in the cross fire. She attended the bonfire her freshman year and ended up in the hospital with alcohol poisoning—which turned out not to be just alcohol poisoning, but alcohol poisoning *plus* something else. The records were sealed, so to this day, we don't know what else was in that mixture that someone called hairy buffalo.

We only know that it made those who drank it pretty stoned out of their heads. I still remember watching Carmen stare into the flames of the fire as if she were ready to walk into them.

Then there was Rory. She'd been crowned homecoming queen at the game, and on a dare, she drank a red plastic cup full of hairy buffalo.

Big mistake.

I warned her, but she was high on life that night. She was the Snow Creek homecoming queen—the most beautiful and popular girl in school.

She drank it down, and to this day, she still says it is the sweetest concoction she's ever tasted. Thankfully, she didn't drink any more of it, or she might have ended up next to Diana in the hospital.

That was the start.

We found out who'd spiked the hairy buffalo.

Pat Lamone.

And he tried to destroy us for it.

Rory's staring out the window from our table at Rita's. I have no doubt she's replaying the same episode in her mind.

In the end, we didn't turn Lamone in, for reasons that seemed valid at the time.

Now he's back.

"Diana Steel," I say. "Funny how I'd forgotten her part in all this."

"She didn't play a part," Rory says. "She was a victim, like I was. Like Carmen was. Like many were."

"Yeah, I know. I just mean, Donny and all... His sister.

Maybe..."

"No," Rory says flatly.

"He could help."

"The only way he can help is to pay off Lamone, and you won't ask him to do that."

She's not wrong.

"I wonder," I say, "how the Steels handled it back then. You and I were so involved in our own issues that we didn't pay any attention to Diana and what this cost her."

"Other than a few days in the hospital, it didn't cost her anything. She's far from the first young girl to get alcohol poisoning."

"It wasn't just the alcohol."

"True." Rory sighs. "I wonder what it was."

"There's one way to find out."

She shakes her head. "If he wouldn't tell us then, he's sure not going to tell us now."

"I'm not talking about Lamone," I say. "I'm talking about Diana's hospital records."

Rory's eyebrows fly upward. "Callie, you're the legal scholar. You know hospital records are confidential."

"Of course I know that," I snap without meaning to. "But there are ways."

"Oh my God..."

"It's just a thought, Ror."

"I know. It's the thought of a desperate person. I get it." She takes a drink of her soda. "Why the hell is he back?"

"We could have destroyed him then," I say, "just as he could have destroyed us."

"So the only reason he'd come back..."

"Is if he knew we couldn't get to him," I finish for her.

"Which means . . ."

"He got hold of the evidence?" Rory's knuckles go white around her glass. "How could he have? It's in a safe place."

"Is it? When's the last time you checked?"

Rory bites her lip. "I haven't. I hate going there."

"Me too, but I don't think we have a choice."

She sighs. "Yeah. We don't. Tonight?"

"I guess. In the meantime, we need to bring Jordan and Carmen in on this."

"Do we? I know we said we would, but you and I are the ones who . . ."

She doesn't finish, and I don't blame her. She doesn't like to even think the words, let alone say them. I get it. I'm the same way.

And for the first time, I actually consider bringing Donny in on this. Maybe Rory's right. He could wave his magic wand of money and make this go away. But I've never depended on anyone other than myself to get out of scrapes, and I'm not going to start now.

"I can't take a day off to drive to Denver," I say.

"We shouldn't have to, if everything's still in place."

"I suppose not. Why the *hell* is he here?" I say more loudly than I mean to.

"Why is *who* here?"

I jerk at the voice that comes from behind me.

Rory's eyes widen. "Carmen," she says.

Carmen Murphy, red-haired like all the Murphys and beautiful to boot, holds a cup of coffee. "Can I join you guys?"

I can't help myself. I look around. We were talking about Jordan and Carmen mere minutes ago, deciding to leave them out of this, and then Carmen shows up. Is the universe trying to tell us something?

"Sure," I say. I'm sick of talking about Pat Lamone anyway. I give Rory a side-eye, hoping she'll know it means to stay silent on Lamone.

Until—

"I've been meaning to talk to you guys," Carmen says. "Pat Lamone is back in town."

CHAPTER NINE

Donny

Lambert revels me with tales of his latest conquests from a strip club in Denver while we wait for Debbie to bring our lunch. When she finally does—service at Lorenzo's isn't great, especially for a new place—he dives right in.

The man's determined to make me sweat.

I twirl my spaghetti on my fork, forcing each bite into my mouth. I normally love any kind of Italian food, but the sauce is like battery acid today. It's eating away at my mouth and throat. I swallow, each time more difficult.

Seriously, I want to puke.

I swallow my last mouthful, chase it with the rest of my water, and glare at him. "Enough, already. What the fuck do you want, Lambert?"

"Sure you don't want a drink? A real one?"

"I told you I don't drink during working hours," I grit out.

"Fine, fine." He dabs his red cloth napkin to his lips. "I came across your sister a week or so ago in Denver."

"Oh?" I sure don't like where this is going.

"She's a pretty little thing."

"No." My voice is strong. Direct.

"You don't even know what I'm going to ask."

"I'm not pimping my sister out for a favor, John. Not

in this lifetime or any other. You can go to the police if you want. I'll lose my license, my career, possibly my freedom. I'll do it gladly if my sister's at stake."

"Christ, Don."

"Make no mistake, though. I'll take you down with me. So you'd best tread carefully here."

"For God's sake," Lambert says, "Diana's not even on my radar."

"Then why'd you bring her up?" My nerves are on edge, my body tensed.

"I want a new house, Steel. I want her to design it."

I raise an eyebrow. I'm not buying. Not even slightly. "She's an intern, John. An intern. They'll never let her design on her own."

"That's what I want. A Diana Steel original. You can make that happen."

"John, I can get you the best architect in Colorado, okay? As much as I love my sister, she's not it."

"I want the Steel name behind my new house," he says. "It'll increase the resell value a hundredfold."

"There is no Steel name in architecture yet," I tell him adamantly. "Dee's good, sure, but she's brand-new. Fresh out of school."

He looks down at his empty plate. "That's what I want, Don."

I eye him, trying to figure out his angle. Whatever it is, I hate it. "And you're telling me this is to increase resell value, not because you want to bed my sister."

"She's way too young for me."

"You can say that again." Lambert's in his forties and Dee is twenty-five. "Something doesn't jibe with this, Lambert."

HELEN HARDT

He raises his head and meets my gaze. "Don't read something into this that's not there, Steel. This is what I want. A home designed by your sister."

"You don't want me to build it for you? Buy it for you?"

"Are you offering?"

"I'm offering you the world on a platter, John, which is why I don't understand your request."

"Maybe I want to get her started on the right foot. In the world of architecture. Take my request for what it is. There's no hidden meaning."

I resist an eye roll. I'm still not buying, not for a minute.

"Something else," I say. "What about a design by Dee once she's up and running her own firm? Or when she's established?"

"Nope. I want it now."

"How about a new house, then? Not designed by Dee but to your specs, and I foot the bill?"

"It's tempting, but I've thought a lot about this. This is what I want."

"You're not getting into my sister's pants."

"That's not my plan, but should things progress to that, I'm pretty sure she doesn't need her big brother's permission."

I stand, my plate still a quarter full of spaghetti. "We're done here. Take me down if you want. I don't give a fuck."

"Sit down, Don. People are looking at us."

He's not wrong. I take my seat. I certainly don't want to bring any unnecessary attention to our lunch. Someone from the Murphy family could walk in, and though I could play my part, I'd still rather it not happen.

"This is what I want," he says again. "It can only help Diana's career."

49

Again, he's not wrong. But, "I'm not dragging my sister into this. Nor any other members of my family. That's not negotiable."

"Everything's negotiable."

"Not my family," I say through clenched teeth. "I've told you. Take me down if you want. It's a small price to pay for leaving my family out of this mess."

I'm bluffing, of course. I don't want him to take me down. And I'm betting he won't, because I'll take him with me, and he has a hell of a lot more to lose.

"Have it your way," he finally says. "I guess I'll keep thinking on how you can repay me, then."

"You do that." I pull out my wallet and throw some bills on the table. "This will cover lunch. Have a good day, John."

I rise and walk swiftly out of the restaurant, still holding back puke.

Only now I'm angrier than I was when I walked in.

I didn't think it was possible.

One thing's for certain—Lambert's request has some kind of hidden motive. I've a hunch he's hot for Diana, which is probably accurate, but there's something else behind the request. Something more sinister.

I don't know what it is, but if it's more sinister than bedding my little sister, it's bad. Really bad.

I head back to work and glance through the window into Rita's. Callie sits at a table with Rory and Carmen Murphy, Brendan's cousin.

That can't lead to anything good.

Callie still doesn't know about the fake gas leak. Carmen's probably filling her in. Without thinking through my actions, I open the door to Rita's. The bells jingle as I walk in.

"Hey, Don," the sheriff greets me.

"Sheriff, Officers." I nod and head to Callie's table.

"Donny."

I turn back toward the sheriff's voice. "Yeah, Hardy?"

"Come here for a minute."

"What?" My voice is harsher than I mean it to be. What does he want with me? I already texted him this morning asking about the investigation into my father's shooting. He said they'd hit a bunch of dead ends.

"Sit down. I'll buy you a coffee."

I sit. When the sheriff tells you to sit, you sit. You respect law enforcement and the military. Straight from the Talon Steel Father's Handbook.

Hardy Solomon went to school with Dale, though they weren't close. Dale wasn't close to anyone. Hardy's a good guy, but Mom has always said he's a lazy sheriff and that her office does more investigating than the police do.

"How's Talon?" Hardy asks.

"He had a rough night, but he's okay. Do you have any good news?"

Hardy trails his fingers over the grip of his pistol in his waistband holster. "Afraid not. Dead ends, like I told you."

"What did you want to talk to me about, then?" I ask.

"Just wanted to check on your dad. That's all." He moves away from his gun and brings his fingers to his chin, where he massages his prematurely gray stubble.

Right.

As if I don't have enough to think about, now the sheriff is acting strange. I glance at the other two officers sitting with Hardy. Neither meets my gaze.

"Thanks for asking," I say. "Have a good day."

"You too, Donny." Hardy's fingers go back to his pistol grip.

And something slimy slithers up my spine.

I push it to the back of my mind and head to Callie's table.

She puts down her drink and gives me a radiant smile. "Donny, hi. I saw you talking to Hardy. Is everything okay?"

"For now, I guess. Hi, Rory, Carmen. Enjoying your lunch?"

Callie clears her throat. "Uh...yeah. Do you need me back at the office?"

Time for an attitude adjustment. I trample over the thoughts of John Lambert and Hardy Solomon and concentrate on the lady I love. A smile spreads across my face.

"No. Just thinking that when I see three beautiful ladies dining alone, I want to be a part of it." I grab a chair, turn it around, and straddle it, still smiling...and thinking about what Callie and I were doing a little over an hour ago.

I swear to God, I can still smell her over the dark roast coffee.

"You want anything, Donny?" Rita calls from the counter.

"No thanks, I'm good. So, ladies ... What brings all of you here?"

"Lunch?" Rory says.

Without thinking, I grab Callie's hand.

Carmen raises her eyebrows. "Are you two ...?"

"You mean the good news hasn't gotten to you yet?" Callie smiles coyly as a blush spreads across her cheeks. "Lonnie Jefferson told me at Janae's lesson."

"Wow! Congratulations, you two. Snagged a Steel, huh?"

Callie gets redder. "We're just..."

"In love," I say boldly. "We're in love."

Callie's jaw drops.

"What?" I ask. "Is it a secret?"

"No, of course not, but it's still so . . . new."

"I'll say," Carmen says. "Tell me the scoop."

"I'll stay out of the gossip." I rise and kiss Callie's cheek. "See you back at the office. No hurry."

I walk out of Rita's and back out onto the sidewalk. Callie's still blushing like a lobster through the window. What the hell? Why shouldn't the whole town know we're in love? It'll give them something to ponder while Dale and I do our digging. If there's one thing the town of Snow Creek can't resist, it's gossip about the Steels. I'd rather they be gossiping about Callie and me than about why Murphy's is closed down.

Mission accomplished.

CHAPTER TEN

Callie

"How'd you hook a Steel?" Carmen demands. "Not only a Steel but one of the Three Rake-a-teers."

My cheeks are about to burst into flames. "It kind of just happened."

"I guess I saw the two of you getting cozy at Dale and Ashley's wedding reception," Carmen says. "But then all hell broke loose when that woman's poor husband collapsed."

I twist my lips. It feels funny to talk about this, but I'm not sure why. "There's not much to tell. Donny just told you. We're in love. Now, about Pat Lamone . . ."

"Screw Pat Lamone," Carmen says. "This is much more interesting."

Rory clears her throat then. "Carmen, as distasteful as it is, we need to discuss this."

Carmen takes a long sip of her coffee. "I know. I just don't want to."

"Trust me, neither do we," I tell her. "But we don't have a choice."

"Why is he back?" Carmen asks.

"I need to do some research," I say. "The statute of limitations on his crimes has probably passed, in which case he can't be brought up on charges for what he did back then."

"Stalking? Drugging people?" Rory shakes her head. "Sometimes the law sucks, Cal."

"I know it does. But statutes of limitations exist for a reason. Evidence deteriorates with time. Eyewitnesses forget. A memory isn't infallible."

"Sounds like they just protect criminals," Carmen adds.

"They protect defendants," I say. "But yeah, it sometimes amounts to the same thing. We do have due process in this country, though. That's a good thing."

"Blah, blah, blah . . ." Rory says.

"Hey, if you were accused of a crime you didn't commit, you'd be pretty darned happy about due process."

Though I believe those words with all my heart, I'm hating the idea of statutes of limitations at the moment. Without the charges, we have less to bargain with. Lamone probably knows that.

"All I'm seeing at the moment," Carmen says, "is that we know one criminal who is guilty who isn't going to pay."

"That was our call at the time," I remind her. "We could have gone to the police."

"We had our reasons." Rory looks into her lap.

"Ror, I know we did. I don't regret anything. I'm just saying we have to put our thinking caps on because some of the leverage we had then may not exist now. But come on. The three of us have more brainpower in our little fingers than Pat Lamone has in his head. We can do it."

The problem? I'm not sure I believe my own words.

Sure, Pat Lamone may have the brainpower of a tomato, but if we no longer have his previous crimes to hold over his head, we don't have much.

He can attempt to ruin us all over again.

FLAME

"You and I need to confront him," I say to Rory.

"What about me?" Carmen asks. "I was a victim too. I drank the shit."

Rory meets my gaze. We didn't let Carmen, Jordan, and the others in on everything, and I'm not about to get into it now in the middle of Rita's.

"I have to get back to the office," I say.

Rory rises as well. "I have a lesson, too."

I don't know if she does or not, but I know the two of us have to talk before we say anything more in front of Carmen.

"You guys want to meet for a drink after work?" Carmen asks.

"I can't," Rory says. "I have rehearsal with Jesse and the band tonight."

"I'm ... seeing Donny," I lie. Though maybe I will be. Who knows?

"Let's do it soon, then," she says. "We should talk about all of this."

"Yeah, you're right," I tell Carmen. "We'll be in touch."

Rory and I leave Rita's. Once outside, Rory says, "I take it back. We don't need to bring Carmen and the others in on this."

I regard my sister. She's seriously spooked. "Ror, what's going on?"

"It's just all coming back. Like a fucking steamroller. I never let myself think about those times, Cal, and now ... I have to think about it. Jesus, we were kids. I'd handle things so differently now."

"I know. We all would. I don't let myself think about it either. I had to completely immobilize my body when I ran into Pat at the Snow Creek Inn with Donny. One false move

56

and I felt like Donny would be able to read my mind. What would he think?"

"If he knew?" Rory shakes her head. "Probably nothing. I mean, the man loves you." She sighs. "I'm glad I never told Raine about any of this. She wouldn't have understood. And that right there tells you exactly why our relationship wasn't cut out for the long haul. I love her and I miss her, but it's more like missing a close friendship. You know what I mean?"

I scoff. "No, I don't. I've never been in an intimate relationship with a friend."

"I suppose it's different for a bisexual person. Everyone I meet is a potential intimate relationship. Another thing that Raine never got. She's girls only, all the time."

"I get it, Ror."

"You think you get it, but you don't. My only hope, I guess, is to meet another bisexual person, whether it's a man or a woman, and fall in love."

"I think you're selling the human race short," I say. "Just because Raine couldn't handle your bisexuality doesn't mean all straight and gay people can't."

"Raine isn't the only one. Remember Lucia Vasquez? And Tomas Revere? Both of them could have been serious relationships for me—they were great people—and both ended them because of my bisexuality."

"I'm sorry." I'm not sure what else to say.

She sighs. "No biggie. Honestly, it's better that I'm alone right now. I don't want to drag anyone else into this drama we're facing."

I bite my lip.

Her words ring true.

I can't drag Donny into this, especially not while he's facing his own family crisis. His father was shot, for God's sake.

"You up for going over tonight?" Rory asks.

"I don't see how we can't. We'll make sure everything's still there. If it is, we're good—at least until I know for sure the statute of limitations has run out."

"I'm not sure the statute of limitations matters, Cal," Rory says. "We still have the evidence. We can still pin it on Pat. He may not stand trial, but he can still be chased out of town."

"True," I tell her, "but don't forget. He has shit on us too."

CHAPTER ELEVEN

Donny

Callie sticks her head into my office. "I'm back. Do you need anything?"

"Yeah, actually. Check with Troy and Alyssa first. If they don't have anything for you, come back and see me."

She seems a little off.

Or maybe I'm a little off.

This is a such a mess.

A minute later, she peeks in again. "They say I'm all yours."

I'm all yours.

Her words give rise to ideas in more ways than one.

But with Alyssa and Troy right outside the door, I can't pin her against the wall and fuck her again. So it's work. God knows there's enough of it.

"Come on in. Have a seat."

My gaze never strays from her as she closes the door, strides forward, and sits her perfect ass down in one of the chairs facing my desk.

I clear my throat. "I want an in-depth title scan on every business property in Snow Creek."

Her eyes pop into circles. "O . . . kay."

"We're looking for liens—any liens—but most specifically any liens held by the Steels."

"By the Steel Corporation? Or by individual Steels?"

"Anything. I'll give you a list of all my family's holdings. Look for all of them."

"Just businesses? Not residential?"

"For now," I say. "Once you're done with the business properties, we'll start on residential."

Again with the wide eyes. "You think your family really does own this town."

I gaze at the ceiling. A watermark. It's big and reminds me of the shape of the state of Florida. Crap. One of the pipes must be leaking. I should call—who? Who's in charge of maintenance around here? I don't have a clue. It would serve me right if the whole ceiling fell right onto my head.

I drop my gaze and stare into Callie's amber eyes. "I never believed it, but rumors start somewhere. Take any rumor, and there's usually a tiny grain of truth behind it. That's how they start."

"You mean you actually believe—"

"I don't believe anything. Not until I see evidence. And as an attorney, I'm able to interpret the evidence to fit my narrative."

"Donny..."

"Sorry. I know you understand how evidence works. I guess I'm already getting ahead of myself."

"You're assuming that the Steels *do* own this town."

"I guess I am. Callie, I've found things out in the last week that I never could have imagined. I've found out my family has been hiding information. Important information. Information that could affect the property rights of my siblings, cousins, and myself."

She gulps. "What if..."

"What if what?"

"What if it *does* affect those rights? Will you...?"

I shake my head. "I won't lose everything. We all have massive trust funds that are untouchable. But there's much more that the family holds beyond trust funds."

"Can I ask why, then?"

"Why what?"

"Why go digging into the past? You have a great life. Why mess with it?"

"Because what if my great life is built on lies? I need the truth, Callie. What is my life without the truth?"

"You're right," she says noncommittally.

"Why would this bother you?" I ask. "Is there something you're not telling me?"

"Of course not," she says quickly. Almost too quickly. Then she smiles. "I'll get right on this. Anything else?"

"No. Let me know when you find something. This will take you a while. Days, weeks."

"I understand."

"And Callie?"

"Yeah?"

"I love you."

Her cheeks pink. "I love you too, Donny." She leaves and closes the door behind her.

Why go digging into the past?

Her words.

It didn't escape my notice that her last smile was forced, and that her words may have a meaning other than her concern for me.

Why go digging up the past indeed?

Except I get the feeling she wasn't talking about *my* family's past.

She was talking about something else.

★ ★ ★

Callie and I didn't make plans tonight. I gave her a chaste kiss at six when I left the office and told her to leave for the day as well. She stayed in town to see Rory for dinner, and I drove home. The house is empty while Mom's in Grand Junction with Dad, and I could easily bring Callie over and fuck her until morning.

Instead, I call my brother.

"Yeah, Don," he says into the phone.

"Hey. You get the guys ready?"

"Yeah. I've got five men, suits rented. With the two of us, that'll make seven. A good show for anyone who's watching."

"What are they going to do while we're pulling up floorboards?"

"They'll help. They're being paid very well for their silence."

"And you trust them?"

"I do. They come highly recommended."

"By whom?"

"Not Uncle Joe or Uncle Ry. Don't worry. I called in a favor and had them vetted."

"And the suits?"

"Our faces will be completely obscured. No one will know it's us."

"You sure?"

"For God's sake, Donny. Of course I'm sure."

"Okay, okay. Sorry. My nerves are totally on edge. I wish we could just do this at night."

"No one in town will believe government workers are working at night."

"I know, I know. I'm not sure how I'm going to leave the office with Mom in Grand Junction."

"You'll come up with something."

"I've cleared the calendar for the next couple of days, and I've got Callie working on an assignment that will take quite a while. That plus what Alyssa and Troy give her will keep her busy while we're doing our thing. I just need an excuse to be out of the office."

"How about a city attorney seminar in Grand Junction?"

"Where Mom is? I don't think so."

"You'll come up with something."

"Maybe..."

"Yeah...?"

"If I bring Callie in on—"

"No. No one else gets in on this."

"Hear me out, Dale." Somehow I've got to tell him that I've already brought Callie in. "I'll be in the office. That'll be the party line, but I can't be disturbed because of a daylong phone conference. Callie will watch the office and make sure no one goes in. I'll keep it locked."

"Just keep it locked, then. There's no need to bring Callie in."

"Yeah. Maybe. It'd be good, though, to have someone who can—"

"No, Donny. We already decided to keep this between us."

"Right."

"So we begin," he says. "On Friday. Day after tomorrow. That's when the guys are set. We'll work through the weekend during the day. If it's a gas leak, that'll fly."

And sometime between this evening and then, I have to break it to Dale that I've already told Callie some of this stuff.

"In the meantime," I say, "we owe Uncle Joe a visit."

"We do?"

"Yeah. He's the only person who seems to know about that half brother of our grandfather's. I want to know why."

"All right. You want to go over there tonight?"

I sigh. "Yeah. I guess so."

"What about Aunt Mel?"

"I don't know. I'm not sure I want to call first, because he may not want to discuss any of this with us."

"Right." He sighs. "How do we handle it, then?"

"I don't know. Let's figure this out. Tonight. Can you come over here? To the house? It's empty except for Darla, and she's off duty."

"Don..."

"I know you're a newlywed and all, but Willow's there to keep Ashley company."

"Yeah, yeah, yeah. All right. I'll be over in thirty."

CHAPTER TWELVE

Callie

My older sister's eyes are heavy-lidded. She's...sad? Frightened? I can't get a read on her.

"Ror?"

"I'm okay. I just... All afternoon I've been replaying those past events in my mind. It sucks. It sucked then, and it sucks even more now. We should have—"

"Don't go there. Don't play the what-if game, Rory. We felt we didn't have a choice at the time, and we did what we did. There's no going back. Only forward."

"Right." She sighs. "You want to drive, or should I?"

"I'll drive." I eye the Snow Creek Inn down the street. "You think he's working tonight?"

"I don't know," she says. "Don't care. I don't want to see him."

"Neither do I. Let's go."

My car is parked in back of the courthouse. We walk to the space and get in. I turn on the ignition.

Then I sit there.

"Cal?"

"Right." I throw the car into reverse and pull out.

We buried the key right outside town limits. We considered burying it on our own property but ultimately decided against it. We didn't want the rest of our family to ever be implicated.

A little over an hour later, after we drive home, change clothes, and sneak supplies into the trunk, we reach the ending of the dirt road that leads to our destination. I stop the car.

"Here goes nothing," Rory says.

"A half mile down the path, if I recall."

"Six-tenths, to be exact." Rory pulls a pedometer out of her purse.

"Does that thing still work?"

"Hell if I know."

"Maybe we should have gotten a new one."

"I'll know the spot. Trust me." Rory opens the passenger door and exits the car.

I follow, clicking the doors locked and opening the trunk at the same time. Two shovels. Two pairs of leather work gloves. Kneepads. Yeah, we came prepared.

Rory says nothing, just dons a pair of gloves and kneepads, picks up a shovel, and starts down the path, watching her pedometer.

Finally, she speaks. "Looks like it's working."

"Good."

Silence then, for a half mile. I couldn't speak if I wanted to. My entire throat has constricted to the point I'm not sure I'm getting enough oxygen. But of course I am. I'm breathing, not even close to losing air.

Still, it's like a noose is tightening around me. I touch my neck, feel the rapid cadence of my pulse.

We walk.

Then, as we close in—

Rory stops, her body seeming to freeze.

"Ror?"

"I ... I can't. I can't do this."

"We don't have a choice. Only forward, remember?" I try to sound calm despite the pounding in my own chest.

No response.

"Breathe, Rory. Come on."

She inhales. Exhales. Inhales again. Is her throat as tight as my own?

"Good?" I ask.

"Not really, but I'll make it."

We buried the key all those years ago at the base of a ponderosa pine after we'd carved a tiny symbol into its trunk to mark the spot. It was a simple half-moon made to look like an animal could have scratched it into the bark.

We needn't have bothered. Neither of us would ever forget this spot. It was carved into our minds as the half-moon was carved into the trunk of the tree.

"Now or never," I say under my breath. I dig my shovel into the hard earth.

Rory joins me, neither of us saying a word. We buried the key in a metal file box about four feet deep. The dirt is packed tightly after ten years. Colorado is known for its hard clay soil.

It's difficult work, but Rory and I are used to difficult work. You don't grow up on a ranch without learning how to dig efficiently.

Thud, go our shovels each time we make another dent in the earth.

Thud.

Thud.

Thud.

Until—

Clank.

"Eureka," Rory says sarcastically when her shovel hits metal. "I probably dented it."

"Doesn't matter."

We both continue shoveling the dirt away until we can retrieve the soiled metal box. Green metal. An old file box we found in the basement of our parents' house. It was empty, so we figured it was okay to take. No one ever said a word about it.

"Your arms are longer than mine," Rory says.

I nod and reach down to retrieve the box.

"Now or never," Rory says.

I click the box open.

And I gasp.

It's empty.

The key is gone.

CHAPTER THIRTEEN

Donny

Dale and I pull into Uncle Joe's driveway at eight p.m. We exit the car and knock on the front door. It opens, and Brock stands there.

"Hey, guys," he says. "What's up?"

Brock. Just what we don't need.

"Is your dad here?" Dale asks.

"He's out in the pool, having a swim. Mom's still in Grand Junction with Aunt Jade."

Aunt Mel being gone is an unexpected boon, but Brock being here? So much for any of this getting done tonight. We can't bring Brock in.

"You going to invite us in or what?" I say.

"Since when do you need an invite? Get your asses in here. I'm about to join Dad in the pool. Is everything okay? Is there news on Uncle Talon?"

"Nothing new," Dale says. "He's doing fine. Should be released tomorrow or maybe over the weekend."

"What about who did it?"

"Nothing," I say. "I saw Hardy today. They're still looking into it."

"Don't tell me," Brock says. "The two of you are going all vigilante to try to solve the crime yourselves. Which is why you want to talk to my dad."

Dale and I meet each other's gazes in an understanding glance ... *Good idea. Let's go with it. Uncle Joe's known to be a hothead. This will work.*

"The thought crossed our minds," I say slowly.

"Mom'll have a cow if Dad goes off all half-cocked," Brock says. "I'm staying here with him while Mom's in Grand Junction, at her request."

Great. So no chance of getting Uncle Joe alone.

"Come on out back. We can go for a swim and talk to my dad. And you can tell me the scoop on Rory Pike," Brock says to me.

"Rory? You mean Callie. I'm with Callie."

"I know that, assface." He laughs. "I heard Rory broke up with Raine."

"She did. Don't tell me you—"

"Have designs on the hottest woman in Snow Creek? Uh...*yeah.*"

"She's bisexual," Dale adds.

"So? Last time I checked, bisexual means she likes guys too. Also, last time I checked, I'm a guy. Plus, the whole thing is pretty hot if you ask me."

I resist an eye roll. "She's four years older than you."

"My mom's two years older than my dad. You're six years older than Callie. Ashley's ten years younger than Dale. So what? Besides, I'm not saying I'm interested in marrying her."

"Don't," I say.

"Why not?"

"It would upset Callie if you screw her sister and then disappear."

"Who said anything about disappearing?"

"For God's sake," Dale interjects. "Dad has been shot and the two of you are bickering about women."

He's right. "Sorry, bro. Let's go see Uncle Joe."

"Did you guys bring your trunks?" Brock asks.

"Of course not," I retort. "Normal people don't travel with swim gear everywhere they go."

Brock chuckles. "No one ever accused me of being normal. No worries. We have lots of extra."

"I'm not wearing one of those package-baring Speedos you wear," Dale says dryly.

Brock shakes his head, scoffing softly. "We've got regular trunks too. For God's sake."

★ ★ ★

Thirty minutes later, Dale and I are suited up, and I've completed ten laps across Uncle Joe's pool. I've got to admit, it helped take the edge off.

"I know why you're here." Uncle Joe eyes me.

He's thinking about the midnight visit I made to him a few days ago.

"About Dad," I say. "We want to find out who shot him."

Uncle Joe nods, seeming to understand. "And you don't trust the police to get the job done."

"I just think we, as a family, may have resources the police don't."

"We do. I've already been talking to some of the people on our payroll."

"And . . . ?" I cock my head toward Brock.

Has Uncle Joe told his son his theory that he, not my father, was the target of the shooting? I'm not sure, and I can't get a good read on Uncle Joe. He's always a hard one to pin down . . . until he goes red.

Uncle Joe pulls himself out of the pool, sits on the concrete, his feet dangling in the water. "Hand me my towel, will you, Brock?"

"Sure, Dad."

Brock, with dark hair and eyes, looks exactly like Uncle Joe. Right down to the muscular swimmer's body. Bradley, Joe's older son, has the dark hair but the green eyes of his mother, Aunt Melanie.

Uncle Joe towels off as I pull up next to him and push my hair back.

"Sit down, Brock, if you want to be a part of this," Uncle Joe says.

"A part of what?"

"We're going to find out who shot my brother and make sure he pays."

"Dad, I want to put the guy away as much as the rest of you, but—"

"Then stay out of it, son," Uncle Joe says. "Go inside."

"Stay out of it? Are you serious? I love Uncle Tal. We all do."

"Your mother would kill me for dragging one of her precious babies into this," Joe says.

"But she'll be okay with you dragging her precious nephews into it?"

Brock has a point. Both Dale and I are very close to Aunt Mel. She saw to our therapy when we first came to Steel Acres. She and Dale are even closer than she and I are.

"Touché," Uncle Joe says.

"And with all due respect," Dale adds, "Donny and I are

already in."

"Sit down then, Brock." Uncle Joe nods to the white wrought-iron table that sits poolside. "We're about to go on a manhunt to end all manhunts."

A manhunt to end all manhunts. I glance at my brother. His eyes are narrowed, focused, and angry. He's with Uncle Joe all the way.

I'm all in too, of course, but has Dale forgotten that we have other things to dive into as well? Say . . . like whatever else is hidden in Murphy's Bar?

Joe rises and takes a seat at the table. "Come on. Let's get to it." Uncle Joe sends a text, and within a few minutes, his housekeeper brings bottled water, wine, and a martini—Uncle Joe's favorite.

"Don, Brock, you want something different?"

"I'll stick with water," I say.

"I'll have some of Dale's wine," Brock says.

"Good enough. Thank you, Patrice."

"Not a problem." Patrice walks back to the house and enters, leaving the four of us alone under the setting sun.

We're heading into November, and a chill spikes the air. Uncle Joe has heaters set up around the pool, though, so we're comfortable.

"Son," Uncle Joe says to Brock, "Dale, I've already enlightened Donny with my theory. Well, Ryan's and my theory. We think *I* was probably the target of the gunman."

Brock's jaw drops. "You? Why?"

"We're not sure why, but Talon and I look very much alike, and Talon was on the north quadrant property, where he almost never goes but where I am on the daily."

"Still, that doesn't—"

Uncle Joe interrupts Brock with a hand gesture. "Talon doesn't know this theory, and we're leaving him in the dark until he's fully recovered."

Dale furrows his brow.

"You don't agree, Dale?" Uncle Joe says.

"No, I do agree. I just don't like keeping things from my father."

"I get it. I don't like keeping things from my brother." Uncle Joe clears his throat. "But we all want him fully recovered before we bring him into this."

"Why would anyone want to shoot you, Dad?" Brock asks.

"The Steels have all kinds of enemies," Uncle Joe says. "We have for nearly a half century."

"Enemies?" Brock drops his jaw once more. "Why would we have any enemies?"

Dale and I say nothing.

Brock, who's very observant—part of why he's so great with the ladies—notices right away. "The two of you don't look overly surprised."

"Dale," I say, "shouldn't we confer—"

"No, Donny. Let's let him in."

Okay. Then he can't be angry at me for letting Callie in. Or can he? Brock is a member of the family. Callie is not. Though I sincerely hope she will be someday. In the immediate future, though, I have to deal with this other bullshit before I can begin a life with the woman I love.

"Okay, Brock," I say, "here goes."

CHAPTER FOURTEEN

Callie

I'm numb.

Numb, except for my heart, which is racing like a thoroughbred at the Kentucky Derby.

Rory scrambles, digging her fingers around the metal box frantically, totally ruining her manicure. Her days of free manicures are probably over now that she and Raine are no longer together. And why I think of that at this moment defies all logic.

"Ror..."

"Maybe it fell out," she says, breathless.

"Of a latched file box?" I shake my head. "It's no use."

"It has to be here. No one knew we were here. Not even Carmen and the others."

"It's possible someone saw us bury the box." Though I don't believe my own words.

"No way. We were really careful, and Jordan was the lookout."

Jordan.

I don't want to think about my own cousin betraying us, but she's the only one who knew where we were and what we were doing that night.

"I wonder..."

"What?" Rory asks.

I don't respond right away.

"Callie, for fuck's sake. Don't keep anything from me now."

"Do you think Pat got to Jordan?"

Rory stops digging with her fingers. "I didn't think that until this very second."

"How would he know?" I ask. "That she was with us that night? That we were anywhere that night? We were careful."

This time it's Rory who doesn't reply.

"I suppose someone could have seen us, but Jordan . . ."

"She doesn't have eyes in the back of her head," Rory says dryly. "We should have brought someone else that night."

"Stop with the 'should have' game. It doesn't matter anyway. Forward, right? We deal with the situation as it is now. It's not like we have a choice anyway."

Rory says nothing. Simply nods.

"Let's get out of here," I say. "The key's not here. It didn't escape a latched box."

"We should have locked the box," Rory says.

"Then whoever took the key would have just taken the whole box and sawed it open later. Didn't I just say to stop the 'should have' game?"

"Shut up, Callie. I get so sick of your sanctimoniousness sometimes."

"Sanctimoniousness? Just because I say we need to deal with the here and now and not the past, which, Rory, we can't change, so why bitch about it?"

She says nothing.

How can she? I'm right, and we both know it.

I begin filling the hole with the dirt we dislodged, and

Rory relents and helps me. We don't speak as I take the box and Rory takes our two shovels back to the car.

We don't speak as I click open the trunk and we throw the shovels and box inside.

We don't speak as we drive home.

It's nearing ten o'clock, so both Rory and I drop our jaws when we walk into the house and see our mother in the family room reading.

She looks up, and her eyes widen. "Where have you two been?"

"In town. Having a drink," I say quickly.

"And did an avalanche of dirt fall onto you?" Mom asks.

Rory and I meet each other's gaze. Then I look down at my hands. My manicured nails are ruined just as badly as my sister's are. Dirt is lodged underneath them. My clothes are filthy as well. Rory doesn't look much better. In fact, her hands look worse from scrambling in the dirt to try to find the nonexistent key.

I'm usually good at coming up with an explanation on the spur of the moment.

In fact, so sure am I of my ability to do so, that I open my mouth, thinking the words will come.

They don't.

It's Rory who saves the evening.

"We're a mess, I know," she says. "We were at my place— well, Raine's place—to pick up some conditioner from the stock—and we heard this squeaking in the alley behind the salon. It was a rabbit. The poor thing had gotten its leg stuck in an old drainpipe. It took both Callie and me to get it out. The little thing wasn't exactly cooperative."

Mom's eyes widen. "It could have bitten you! What were you thinking?"

"We were careful," Rory continues. "That's why it took both of us. And we didn't get bitten."

"Is the rabbit okay? Was it hurt?"

"It hopped away," I say. "In fact, it couldn't get away fast enough. So it's okay. Or it'll be okay after it lies low for a few days. We just couldn't bear its squealing. We had to help it, Mom."

"Of course you did. You girls always did both love animals. I suggest you both shower before you go to bed. I changed all the sheets today."

"Yeah, of course," Rory mumbles.

"We're adults, Mom. We know to shower when we get dirty."

Mom smiles. "I know that. But a mother is always a mother. You'll both find that out someday."

"Good night," Rory and I say nearly in unison.

We head down the hallway to our respective rooms, but Rory comes into mine first. "I hate it when she does that."

"Does what?"

"Says I know what it'll be like to have kids. She knows damned well I may end up with a woman."

"And on what planet does that mean you can't have kids?"

"I know. It's just..."

"Mom loves Raine. You know that. Have you even told her...?"

"Yeah. I mentioned it because Willow White is buying the salon. She said she's sorry, but deep down I think she's relieved."

"Because Raine's a woman?"

"She'd rather see me with a man."

"She'd rather see you happy, Rory. You know that."

"Yeah, I know." She sighs. "I suppose I'm just trying to find something else to ruminate on to forget the fact that our lives are tumbling into a big void."

I shake my head. "You're so overdramatic! You and Jess both. It must be a performer thing."

"Don't tell me you're not worried about this."

"Oh, I am. Great save with Mom by the way. I never knew you had it in you."

"It kind of just popped out. When you didn't say anything, I knew I had to."

"Well done. I kind of froze."

"I know. That's totally not like you."

I sigh. "Life has gotten . . . weird."

"You're telling me. Except while my relationship is ending, yours is just beginning. So you have that to be happy about."

"What if . . ."

"What?"

"What if Pat Lamone tells Donny everything?"

"So what if he does? We didn't do anything wrong."

"That's not exactly true, Ror."

Rory sighs.

Silence for a few moments before Rory heads toward the door. "You take the first shower, Cal."

I nod. Our water heater can't handle two showers at a time, so if I go now, Rory can go in a half hour. We're used to it.

I head into the bathroom I share with my sister. Our bedrooms are on either side of it. Mom calls it a Brady Bunch bathroom or a Jack and Jill bathroom. I turn on the shower and then open the mirrored door to the medicine cabinet. Already I feel a headache coming on, and I need a few ibuprofen.

As I open it, an image pops into my mind.

It's me. Opening Donny's mirrored cabinet, and finding . . .

Finding . . .

A glasses case holding a safe-deposit box key.

A key that—now that I think about it—looks very familiar.

A key that resembles what Rory and I hoped to find buried inside that metal file box.

No.

No way.

Donny did not take that key.

I didn't look at it too closely. Already I felt guilt at nosing through his stuff.

But I did think it was rather odd that a key was stuffed inside a glasses case.

Why there?

Why a glasses case?

Why not hidden in a dresser drawer under his socks? Or elsewhere?

One thing's for sure. I have to ask Donny about it. And if I ask him, he'll know I was snooping.

Damn.

"Stop it, Callie!" I say aloud.

"Stop what?" Rory's voice comes from her room on the other side of the door.

Shit. She heard me over the shower?

I unlock the door to her room and peek in. "You decent?"

"Yeah."

"Remember when we went over a few days ago to help Darla? And I cleaned Donny's bathroom?"

"Yeah."

"I found a safe-deposit box key in a glasses case in the

cabinet over his sink."

"So?"

"It was from a bank in Denver, and now that I think about it..."

Her eyes widen. "Donny has the key?"

"Donny has *a* key. Assuming it's our key goes pretty far."

"Was it from the same bank?"

"I think so. I didn't think about it at the time. It was before we knew Pat was back in town, so there was no reason to be thinking about any of this stuff."

"If it's still there, you can get it."

"Sneak into his bathroom and steal his key? It might not even be ours."

"True, but if you can get a good look at it, you'll know. Isn't the box number on the key?"

Is it? I rack my brain. "I... I don't know, Rory. Do you recall?"

"No." Rory shakes her head. "I don't. I kind of put that to bed the night we buried the damned thing. Lamone was gone. It was over. I never thought it would come back to haunt us."

"Neither did I."

"I don't suppose you can... You know. Get into the Steel house and check. Jade's still in Grand Junction, right?"

"Yeah."

"So you get Donny to take you there, and then you use his bathroom. Easy enough."

Right. Easy enough to put something over on the man I love. Not a great way to begin a relationship.

"For God's sake, Rory. It's probably not even our key."

"Probably not. But why would Donny Steel use a safe-deposit box in Denver? The Steels have actual safes."

"He did live in Denver for ten years."

Rory twists her lips. "Right. I wasn't thinking."

"So it actually makes perfect sense for him to have a safe-deposit box in Denver."

"Wouldn't he have cleared it out before he moved back here?"

"In a perfect world, maybe. But maybe he didn't have time."

"I suppose," Rory says. "Still, you can easily check."

I sigh. "Yeah. I suppose I can." I close the door and listen to the shower running. It's fogged up the mirror by now, and the humidity in the bathroom erupts on my skin.

I shed my soiled clothes and step into the warm stream of water.

And for a moment, I imagine that it's not only cleansing my body, but cleansing all the rest of this shit away.

CHAPTER FIFTEEN

Donny

For the first time in his life, Brock Steel appears to be speechless.

Plus, he's shooting flaming darts with his eyes ... toward his father.

Then he looks at Dale ... at me.

And his expression is ...

"We're okay," Dale says.

"But ... my God."

"Diana and Brianna don't know about this," I say. "We're counting on you. Our sisters ... They wouldn't be able to take it."

"And you think I can?" Brock rises, paces around the concrete pool deck.

"It was a long time ago," Dale says.

"Yeah? Well, to me, it's five minutes old."

Uncle Joe interjects then. "Brock, son, with all due respect, this didn't happen to you. It's not yours to own."

"Really, Dad? It doesn't kill you to know what Dale and Donny went through? What your brother went through?"

"Of course it does, but I've known for twenty-five years. It's over. It's dead and buried."

"Except it's not," Brock says. "None of this is. Our past is coming back to us. And Uncle Talon almost paid the price."

Uncle Joe's countenance goes dark then.

We all know what that means.

"We're going to figure this out," he says. "I couldn't protect Talon all those years ago, and I've failed yet again. He took the shot meant for me."

"We don't know that, Uncle Joe," Dale says.

"Ryan and I know," he replies. "And we're right. I guess I need to let him know that the three of you are now in on this."

"Which means the two of you should help Dale and me go through the Murphy place."

Uncle Joe shakes his head. "I disagree. It's better to only have the two of you unaccounted for. Four of us would be much more noticeable."

"Good point," Dale says. "Don and I will handle it. I've already got decoys set up as well. We'll be seven altogether, and the other five will handle security. We go in Friday."

"Not tomorrow?" Uncle Joe asks.

"I need to get covered at city hall, with Mom out of town." I haven't told Dale yet about Callie's involvement. Doesn't seem like the right time.

"I'm feeling like I should be doing something," Brock says.

"There is something you can do, son," Uncle Joe says. "While Dale and Donny are searching Murphy's, you can be at the main house while Jade is in Grand Junction."

"Doing what?"

"My father left a ton of old records in the basement crawl space. Talon, Ryan, and I went through a lot of them twenty-five years ago. They are ultimately what led us to the truth behind Talon's abduction, and they led us to Dale and Donny. But I have a feeling we haven't yet scratched the surface of what may be hiding in those boxes."

Brock nods. "All right. And you, Dad?"

"One of us has to be at work. If it's not me, it has to be you, my right-hand man."

"Maybe you should do the research," Brock says. "You know what you're looking for."

Uncle Joe pauses a moment. "I see your point, but I'm an old man now. Hunching in a crawl space is a job for a twenty-four-year-old, not a sixty-three-year-old."

"Fair enough," Brock says. "I'll keep my eye out for anything suspicious."

"You're looking for documents dated fifty years ago," I tell him. "This all started with our grandfather, possibly our great-grandfather, and I'm betting there's a ton of stuff we don't know about."

Brock wrinkles his forehead. "This is a lot to take in."

"I know, Brock," Uncle Joe says. "I understand. God, your mother's going to have my head on a platter, but you're the one I always knew I could count on."

"Of course, Dad. But you can count on Mom and Brad, too. They adore you."

"They do, and I love them both like you can't imagine. But you and I are cut from the same cloth. We always have been."

Brock nods.

I look toward my brother. He is to Dad what Brock is to Uncle Joe. What I am to Mom.

Dale's father was shot with a bullet meant for Brock's father.

There's no stopping the two of them now.

And I realize how necessary I am to this whole equation.

Without me, the two of them *will* go off half-cocked.

Fuck.

That's a lot of responsibility on my shoulders.

I rise. "We need to go, Dale. It's nearing midnight."

He darts me a glare but then joins me. "Yeah. Right."

Dale, Brock, and Uncle Joe could easily spend all night talking, strategizing, getting angrier and angrier. Dale's still a newlywed, though.

"Ashley's probably wondering where you are," I say.

He nods and then gives me an appreciative gaze.

"Don't forget what's important." Then I look to Uncle Joe. "You either."

Uncle Joe's dark eyes widen for a split second, but then he nods. "I never do, despite what it looks like sometimes."

"I know. Let's go, Dale."

"Good night," Dale says. "We'll be in touch."

"We will be as well," Brock says. "And . . . I guess I should say thanks."

"What for?"

"For letting me in. Letting me help."

"Cuz," I say, "don't thank us. Trust me." *This will tear out your heart by the end.*

I don't add that last part, of course.

Perhaps I don't need to.

Brock isn't like me.

He's like Uncle Joe. Like Dale. His anger will be his fuel.

But anger doesn't last forever.

And when it dissipates, you find your heart is scarred.

I don't wish that for my cousin.

I don't wish it for my brother or my uncle.

I don't wish it for myself.

And I wonder, for the first time, if I have any business

trying to make a relationship work with a woman as amazing as Callie Pike.

What if the scars on my heart never heal?

Do I dare drag her into my drama?

Perhaps I should let go.

While I still can.

CHAPTER SIXTEEN

Callie

I sleep fitfully, and when the alarm rings at six, I seriously think about calling in sick, especially since my job at the city attorney's office is pretty superfluous.

But that's not my style.

Callie Pike is a good girl.

At least she tries to be.

Except that once ... all those years ago, that is now being dragged back up.

I'm first in the office this morning, before Troy and Alyssa even. I knock on Donny's door, but there's no response. When I try to turn the knob, I find it's locked.

Okay, then. I send him a quick text to let him know I'm at the office. Then?

Time to get to work. Donny wants title scans? I'll give him title scans. After double-checking to make sure a VPN is indeed installed on my computer, I begin.

Snow Creek, Colorado.

A small town with an apparently troubled history.

I find the relevant databases.

But where to begin?

And the answer surfaces in my mind. I'll begin with the Snow Creek High School building—the site of the whole Pat

Lamone incident. Well, not exactly the site of the incident, but where it all began.

I type in the address and order the title scan. A few seconds pass, and then documents pop up.

A *lot* of documents.

Which seems odd for a public building. A public building is owned by the government, right? That's what I thought, anyway.

But this building—this high school has apparently changed hands quite a few times in the last fifty years.

Fifty years ago, it was owned by something called the Fleming Corporation. I hastily scribble down some notes. About thirty years ago, it was completely renovated, and Fleming Corporation transferred it to the Steel Trust.

Mental Note: Ask Donny about the Steel Trust.

The Steel Trust didn't hold it for long, though. They transferred it to the City of Snow Creek, but sure enough, the Steel Trust continued to hold a lien on the building until ten years later, when the city transferred the building back to the Steel Trust. The building changed hands between the city and the trust several more times, until the last deed dated nearly a year ago. The building is now in the hands of the city again, with a lien held by the trust.

Why?

Why would the Steels continually transfer a public building back and forth?

I quickly type in the address to the building I'm in at the moment—the courthouse and administration building.

I wait another few minutes for the myriad documents to load.

More of the same.

This building—where Donny and Jade do their business—was originally owned by the Fleming Corporation. Then it was transferred to Thomas Simpson about thirty years ago. The name rings a bell.

I do a quick search.

Thomas Simpson was an attorney and mayor of Snow Creek until his death twenty-six years ago. And yes, he's the father of Bryce Simpson. Grandfather to four of Donny's cousins—Henry, David, Angie, and Sage.

Why would he have owned a public building? He was the mayor, and his office was in this building, presumably, but a private citizen shouldn't have ownership of a public building.

Then again—why would the Steels own a public building?

Upon Thomas Simpson's death, the building did not pass to his widow or his son. It passed into a trust for the benefit of Henry Thomas Simpson.

My eyes pop out of my head.

Henry Simpson. Donny's cousin.

And there it is to this day.

This building—where I'm sitting right now—is owned by Henry Simpson. Well, not technically. It's owned by a trust for the benefit of Henry Simpson. Something else to research.

And I wonder...

Does Henry even know about this? Donny obviously doesn't.

I scribble more notes and continue down the rabbit hole.

Rita's Coffee House and Café—owned by Rita Hemsworth with a lien by the Steel Trust.

Raine's Salon—owned by Raine Cunningham with a lien. Steel Trust.

Ava's Bakery—owned by Ava Steel. No lien. Interesting. But Ava's a Steel.

The Tattoo Shop—a lien.

The Antique Shop—a lien.

Lorenzo's—a lien.

Several other businesses with liens, and several housed in buildings actually owned by the Steel Trust where the business owners rent space.

By lunchtime, I've gone through nearly all the business properties in our small town, and every single one, with the exception of Ava's bakery, has some connection to the Steel Trust.

And the public properties?

Owned by the trust, with the exception of the one I'm in at the moment, which is owned by Henry, who is part of the Steel family.

So the Steels really *do* own this town.

And Donny had no idea.

And then I realize something even stranger.

Alyssa and Troy came in shortly after I did.

I was so absorbed in my work that something escaped my notice.

Donny hasn't come into the office.

And it's lunchtime.

CHAPTER SEVENTEEN

Donny

Earlier that morning...

I wake to the sound of my phone.

"Yeah?" I say without even looking to see who it is.

"Donny, thank God." Diana's voice.

My heart drops as fear hurtles through me in boundless waves. "Dee, what is it? Is Dad okay?"

"They had to take him back into surgery," she says.

All other problems in my life dissipate. Only Dad matters. "Shit. What's wrong?"

"They don't think it's serious, but he ran high fevers overnight, and they can't figure out the cause. They need to have a look inside."

"Prognosis?"

"They don't know. Donny..."

"I'm on my way. Tell Mom."

I don't shower. I pull on the first clothes I find—a pair of worn jeans and a black T-shirt—shove my boots on, and head out.

Callie.

I text her quickly that I'm going to Grand Junction. I leave out details. I have no idea what I'm rushing into, and I don't want to worry her.

Within thirty minutes, I arrive at the hospital and Dad's private room.

Diana runs into my arms. "Donny, thank God. Mom needs you."

My mother is slumped in a recliner, her hair in disarray, her eyes puffy and red. She sniffles when she raises her head, but she doesn't stand.

"Hey, Mom." I pull up a chair and sit next to her. "What can I do for you?"

"Pray," she says, gripping my hand.

"Do you have any new information?"

Mom doesn't reply. I nod toward Diana.

"Nothing," my sister says. "He's been in surgery for an hour and a half. Aunt Mel went to get coffee and make some phone calls. Is Dale coming?"

"I don't know. Did anyone call him?"

"I did, but he didn't pick up."

"If you left a message, I'm sure he's on his way. You know how close he is to Dad. What about Bree?"

"She has an exam this morning. We were texting last night. I couldn't bear to tell her this before the test."

I nod, though I disagree with my sister. Bree should know. Dale should know. They should both be here. This is Dad, for God's sake.

Dale would move mountains to get here.

Just then, the mountain rushes into the room, his long hair a tangled mass of blond waves. Diana flies into Dale's arms.

Dale kisses the top of Dee's head and then turns to me. "What's the news?"

"Nothing new. We're just waiting."

"Mom?" He nods toward our mother, who's a mess on the chair.

"She's hanging in there."

Truth be told, though, I've never seen my mother like this. She's turned into a zombie with swollen eyes and a red nose. This isn't like her. This is worse than when he was first shot, and we didn't know whether he'd even make it.

I clasp my hand around her forearm. "Mom?"

She sniffles.

"Mom, you need to snap out of this funk. Dad needs you."

Dad needs you.

Those words get her.

Her eyes widen, and then tears flow from them. "Oh, Donny."

"I told her the same thing before you got here," Dee says, "but I didn't get that reaction."

Dale shakes his head at Dee.

Dee may be of her body, but Mom and I have something the rest of her kids don't. She loves us all equally, but she and I have that mother-son bond that is unequaled by anything else.

"What can we do for you?" I ask Mom. "Aunt Mel should be back with the coffee soon."

Mom sighs. "Melanie's been a saint. I don't know how I'd have gotten through all this without her. She has a way of calming me down."

"I know." And I did know. Aunt Mel is a psychiatrist—retired now, for the most part—and helped Dale and me so much when we were kids. Dale still sees her when he needs a boost.

"Come on, Dee." Dale tugs on her arm. "Let's go see if we can find any news from the nurses' station."

The two of them leave the hospital room, which was beginning to feel pretty cramped. We Steels are not small people.

That's not why they left, though. They know Mom will respond to me.

I have so many questions, but I can't bombard Mom with them right now. Not when her husband—my father—is in surgery.

Dale and Dee don't return, so I sit with Mom. Just sit with her, my hand on her forearm.

And we wait.

★ ★ ★

An hour later, a nurse enters the room. "Mrs. Steel?"

Mom looks up. "Yes?"

"Your husband's in recovery. The doctor wants to speak with you. May I send him in here?"

"Yes, yes. Of course. This is my son, Donny."

I stand and shake the nurse's hand.

She smiles. "I'm sure your mother is glad you're here. I'll get the doctor."

A minute later, a gray-haired man enters. "Mrs. Steel, I'm Dr. Lodge. Your husband did well."

A heavy sigh of relief whooshes out of Mom. "Then he's okay?"

"Yes. He should make a full recovery, but what happened is quite . . . concerning."

"Did you figure out what was making him so sick?"

Dr. Lodge clears his throat. "We did, and it has nothing to do with an infection or with his previous injury and surgery."

"Then what happened?" I ask.

Dr. Lodge blows out a breath of air. "We'd just opened him up when the toxicology report came in."

"Toxicology?"

"Yes, from the blood that was drawn last night," he continues. "The lab doesn't normally interrupt surgery, but they made an exception in this case. A good call on their part."

Mom's swollen eyes widen.

"What did you find?" I ask.

"There's a reason the antibiotics we administered weren't working," Dr. Lodge says. "It's because your husband didn't have an infection."

"What was causing the symptoms then?" I ask.

"Toxicology showed atropine poisoning," Dr. Lodge says.

"What's atropine?"

"Technically it's a tropane alkaloid. It's used to treat heart rhythm problems, stomach or bowel problems, and certain types of poisoning when injected. It can mimic septicemia, which is what it did here. If I'd known to look, I might have noticed your husband's dilated pupils, but his eyes are so dark anyway..."

Anger rushes through me. Poison? My father was poisoned? "How did he get atropine?" I demand.

"We don't know. It's not in his chart, and it's contraindicated in his case. It's usually administered by injection, but in your father's case, we pumped his stomach as a prophylactic measure. I'm glad we did, because it helped, and we got him stabilized. He'll have dilated pupils for a few days, but other than that, his symptoms have abated."

Mom freezes.

"Mrs. Steel," the doctor says, "I assure you that we're going to investigate this. It was in his stomach, which means he ingested it orally."

"Someone laced his food or drink," I say, thinking out loud, my voice dark and harsh.

Mom is still frozen. I want to help her, but right now, I need to know all the information this doctor has.

Whoever tried to shoot my father clearly came back to try to finish the job.

Except…

If that's the case, then Uncle Joe's theory is wrong. Someone wants my father dead, and this was no mistake.

Or someone wants both of them dead.

"What the goddamned fuck?" I rake my fingers through my hair.

That spurs Mom out of her somberness. "Donny…"

"Sorry, Mom, but for Christ's sake. What the hell kind of hospital is this?"

"Mr. Steel," the doctor says, "I assure you we're—"

"Looking into it. Right. I know. But you know what? It's not *your* father lying there in recovery with two surgeries behind him. It's not *your* father who was poisoned in this damned hospital. It's not *your*—"

"Donny, please." Mom stands, finally. The fire is back in her blue eyes. "Dr. Lodge, this is unacceptable. I'd like to see my husband now, please."

"He's still under anesthesia. The nurse will come get you when he wakes up."

"I'd like to see him now," Mom says again.

"Mrs.—"

I can't help myself. I go all Dale. All Uncle Joe. All rogue. I grab the doctor by the neck of his blue scrubs. "You will take my mother to see my father now, or by God, I'll—"

"Don!"

The voice jolts me. One of only two voices in the world that have that effect on me.

Dale stands in the doorway of the hospital room—flanked by Diana and Aunt Mel—seeming to dwarf everything else. "What the hell are you doing?"

I loosen my grip on the doctor, and Mom slinks back into her recliner.

The doctor steps back. "You're crazy."

"I assure you my brother's not crazy," Dale says. "But he does want answers, and so do I."

"I wish I had some. Now if you'll excuse me, I have other patients to attend to." He leaves quickly, rubbing his neck.

"Nice work," Dale says. "You chased away Dad's doctor. Man, I looked at you, and for a minute I thought I was looking in a mirror."

His comment isn't lost on me.

A nurse comes in a moment later. "Mrs. Steel, I'll take you to see your husband now."

I help Mom out of the recliner. "You want one of us to come with you?"

"I'm sorry," the nurse says, "but since Mr. Steel hasn't awakened yet, I can only allow Mrs. Steel in recovery."

"Good enough," I say, "and thank you."

Dale grabs my shoulder. Not gently. "Bro, we need to talk."

"About what?"

"Not here."

"You mean not in front of me," Diana says.

"Yeah, that's what I mean," Dale says, "but it's not for the reason you think."

"Good. Then I'll stay." She whips her hands to her hips.

Right, Dale. Good luck getting our hotheaded little sister to let this one go.

"Sorry, Dee," he says. "This is business."

"Steel business? Last time I checked, I'm a Steel too."

"You're going to have to trust me," Dale says as he shoves me out the door. "Let's take a walk."

We walk down the hallway, past two nurses' stations, to the elevator. Dale punches the down button.

"If you think—"

"Save it," he says.

And I shut up. I listen to my big brother. Because that's what I do.

Once we're in the elevator—which is empty save for us—he starts in. "Don, you've got to get hold of yourself. This isn't helping Mom."

"Don't you try to tell me what isn't helping Mom. You don't—"

He grabs my collar—much like I grabbed Dr. Lodge. "Don't go there. Just don't. You know I love our mother. My relationship with her is different from yours, but I love her just as much as you do."

I nod—sort of—and he lets go.

"I know that. Damn." I tug my fingers through my hair. "It's just . . . It's just . . . all this shit. Sometimes I think I should have stayed in Denver."

"Dad would still be lying in that recovery room if you had, and you'd be here anyway."

"Would I? How much of this shit can be tied to me

coming home? To the two of us talking to Brendan at his place? Those documents?"

"That's a big if, Don. We can't do anything about it anyway. It is what it is. Dad was shot, and apparently someone poisoned him as well. Let's just thank God that he's pulling through and figure out what to do next."

"I fucking bribed a government official to manufacture a fake gas leak on a property so we could break and enter." I shake my head.

"And this is just *now* occurring to you?"

"No! I mean . . . No. I . . . I know there was no other choice, but just when I wrap my head around that, convince myself I *had* to do it, this goes and happens. Someone wants to off our father, and damn it, I want to know who."

"It's still possible that the target was Uncle Joe."

"And that's supposed to make me feel better? Uncle Joe's like a second dad to us."

"You've got to hold it together. For God's sake. You're the level-headed one, Don. The one I depend on. You're our voice of reason. You keep Uncle Joe and me in line."

"Get over yourself. I'm risking my career here. I'm keeping the Murphys from their livelihood just to—"

"Just to find out what our parents have been lying to us about," he interrupts. "This affects the whole family."

"Then why us? Why do we have to deal with it?"

"We're the oldest."

I regard my brother. My strong and fierce brother. And before me stands a man who's keeping his temper at bay. Who has something else to live for besides himself and his vines. Ashley. Ashley has calmed him.

It's like we've traded places.

I'm in love too. Why the hell am I going off all high strung?

"I've got a mercenary government agent who wanted me to pimp out Dee to him, dude. I'm a little on edge."

Dale's cheeks redden. "What?" he grits out.

"Yeah. Well, not in so many words. He wanted me to get her to design his new house. His party line was that he wanted the first Steel-designed house. But I read between those lines. He wants to bed her."

"Isn't he like twice her age?"

"Almost."

"Fuck." Dale messes with his mane. "Fuck it all."

"See what I mean? Our life is whacked right now. It's fucked up. And in the middle of it . . ."

"In the middle of it . . . what?"

"Callie."

"What about her?"

"I love Callie, Dale. And I have to end it. I can't drag her into this shitstorm."

"I think she's already in."

I scoff. "More than you know."

"What?" he grits out again.

"Don't even start with me. You dragged Brock in last night."

"Brock is family, Donny."

"Well . . . so is Callie. To me, anyway. Except I can't let her be. The Pikes have been through enough. I can't drag their daughter into this Steel mess."

The elevator doors open, and we zigzag through the people getting on. Why people won't let an elevator unload first is beyond me. I feel like punching each one of them in their smug faces.

I follow Dale outside and into the parking lot. "Where exactly are we going?"

"I don't know. Somewhere where I can yell the way I want to."

CHAPTER EIGHTEEN

Callie

Still no sign of Donny after lunch—which consisted of a turkey sandwich that I took two bites of and then threw away. I spent the remaining time going through more title documents.

And finding the same kind of stuff.

Steels, Steels, Steels.

They're everywhere in Snow Creek, and I want to know why.

And then...

Something occurs to me—a frightening thought.

Do the Steels have a lien on *our* property? The Pike ranch and vineyards?

Mom and Dad bought it from the Steels all those years ago. How old was I? We moved here when I was in elementary school. Was it third grade? Fourth?

The story as told to me is that the property had once belonged to another ranching family, the Shanes, but the Steels bought it from them and then sold it to us years later.

My fingers freeze, hovered an inch above my keyboard.

Do I even want to know?

Do my parents truly own their property?

Surely they wouldn't purchase an encumbered property.

Would they?

Nausea claws at me. Good thing I didn't eat much lunch.

I inhale. Exhale.

Then I start tapping keys.

The title scan begins . . .

I close my eyes. I'm not sure why. Maybe I think if I don't look, it won't be real.

Except I know I'll look. Eventually. I can't *not* look.

I open my eyes slowly . . .

. . . and let out a gasp.

We own our property. Well, my parents own it. Frank and Maureen Pike. Free and clear.

I'm holding my breath, and I didn't even know it. I exhale smoothly.

How is this possible? How do *we* own our property free and clear, but the residents of Snow Creek don't?

I bite my lip.

Actually . . . I don't know about the residents of Snow Creek yet. I only know about the business-owned properties.

I rise. I need a walk. A walk around town to think. Just as I grab my purse, Alyssa returns from lunch.

"Donny in yet?" she asks.

"Not yet."

"Any word?"

"No, and that's weird because"—I grab my phone—"I texted him earlier— Oh, God." The text is still on my phone, and it's unsent.

"What is it?"

"I forgot to hit send on the text. Where is my mind?"

"Wouldn't he have texted us to let us know where he is?" Alyssa asks.

"You'd think." I quickly send the text, adding a frantic *Where are you?*

Then I purposefully shove my phone into my purse. I don't want to be glancing at it all afternoon. I've got enough on my mind.

CHAPTER NINETEEN

Donny

Dale and I end up sitting in his truck.

"If you're going to yell," I tell him, "can you hold it down to a dull roar? We're in an enclosed space."

Dale breathes in and closes his eyes. Then he opens them. "I'm not going to yell."

"You just said you were."

"I changed my mind."

"Can I see some ID? Are you sure you're Dale Steel?"

"Listen, Don, level with me. How much does Callie know?"

"She knows about the stuff Murphy found under his floor."

"And the gas leak?"

I shake my head. "As far as she knows, that's real. I didn't tell her I'm behind it."

"Okay. Good. Good."

"What about Ashley?"

"That's different. Ashley's my wife."

"I get that, but does she know about the fake gas leak?"

He pauses a moment. Then, "No. She doesn't. I didn't want to worry her. She's dealing with her mother and all, helping her get settled in and dealing with her loss. And we'll be moving to the new house next week..."

"Really? That's why you haven't told her? Because of her mother and the move?"

"Yes, that's why."

"I call bullshit."

"Fuck you, Don."

"Fuck you right back. You didn't tell her for the same reason I didn't tell Callie. This is fucked up. I don't even like to think about it."

He doesn't reply.

Yup. Got him.

"I hate keeping things from her," he finally says.

"I know. Tell her if you want to. You have my blessing. I don't want this to screw with your relationship."

"I almost did, but I ultimately decided not to. For you."

"For me?"

"You're the one who'll lose your license if this gets out. It won't hurt anyone except you and John Lambert, and while I don't care about him, I sure as hell care about you. Besides, if anything happened to your precious law license, our mother would suffer."

I nod. He's right. My following her into law meant everything to Mom. It still does.

"I know Mom doesn't get me and I don't get her," Dale says, "but I meant what I said. I love her so damned much. I would never do anything to intentionally hurt her."

"I know that."

"Do you? Do you really?"

"Of course I do. And I know how much all this shit with Dad is killing you."

He inhales sharply and nods.

"We need help, though, Dale. That's why I brought Callie

in. I trust her. I love her, and she loves me. I know it's a lousy time in our lives to try to begin a relationship, but love doesn't always choose the best time to worm its way in."

"Don't I know it." Dale heaves a giant sigh. It seriously sounds like a gust of wind.

"We can't do it all," I continue. "Right now, I wish I were about ten people. One of me could deal with the Murphy situation, one of me could chase down the person who shot Dad. Another could investigate how the hell someone was able to poison him in a hospital bed. One of me could hold down the fort at the city attorney's office. One of me could deal with the fallout our biological father left us, and one of me— damn, the one I really *want* to be—could focus on Callie."

"It's not fair, is it? To fall in love and not be able to give it your all."

"You did."

He gives a scoffing laugh. "I fought it every step of the way."

"You had issues. The fire. Floyd Jolly."

"I did. And now you have issues as well. My best advice? If you truly love Callie—if you can see a life with her—she has to come first."

"Interesting, coming from a man who just said he's not telling his wife about our gas leak situation."

Dale exhales. "Point taken."

"Which means . . ." I pause a moment, hating what has to come next. "I have to end things with Callie."

"It doesn't mean that."

"Of course it does. I *can't* tell her everything."

"You can. If you trust her."

"Then you have to tell Ashley. Except seriously, the fewer

people who know what's going on, the better. John Lambert's word is good. If he takes us down, he goes down with us. Ashley and Callie can both be trusted."

"You're not hearing me, Don. I *do* trust Ashley. I trust her with my life. I just don't want to burden her."

"She won't consider it a burden."

He sighs. "I know."

"Look. I've struggled with this. Believe me. I love Callie Pike. But it was quick love, you know?"

"I know. It was the same with Ashley and me."

"Right. I know that, so let me ask you this. When it comes like a lightning bolt like that, how do you know it's real?"

"You just know. When I look back, I can't recall *not* loving Ashley. It hit me when we first met."

"You say that now, but what if she'd turned out to be a huge bitch?"

He laughs. "That's just it. I already knew she wasn't. Or I think I did."

"You didn't. You were attracted to her, but you didn't know she was the one until you got to know her, which you did do very quickly."

"I did. But it's real. I never doubted it, and I was ready to let her go because I didn't want to drag her into my screwed-up life."

"Then you know exactly where I'm coming from."

"God, do I. But Donny, don't give Callie up. If you love her the way I love Ashley—and I think you do. I can see it in your eyes. You can't let her go, man. Let her in."

"I want to. I just . . . I guess I just don't feel like I have the time. All this other shit requires me twenty-four seven. It's like I said. I need to be cloned about ten times to deal with it all."

My phone buzzes with a text, and my heart nearly stops. "Damn. Please let Dad be okay."

I pull the phone out of my pocket.

It's not about Dad.

It's a text from Callie.

I'm in the office. Are you coming in today?
Is everything okay? Where are you?

"Is it Dad?" Dale asks anxiously.

"No, thank God. It's Callie. But I thought I . . ." Then I see my text to her this morning. I forgot to hit send. "Jesus, fuck."

"What?"

"I texted her this morning that I was heading into the city, but I didn't hit send."

"Call her. Make plans with her tonight. You deserve it."

I've already punched in the number.

"Donny!" Callie's voice is frantic. "Where are you? Are you all right?"

"I'm so sorry," I say. "I thought I texted you this morning, but I didn't hit send."

"You're kidding. I did the exact same thing. I texted you when I got in but didn't hit send."

"I guess we both have a lot on our minds," I say. "I'm in Grand Junction. Dad had to go back in surgery this morning, but he's okay."

"Oh my God! What happened?"

"It's a long story. I'll tell you about it . . . tonight. Okay? Dinner? At my house? Mom's still here, so we'll be alone."

A short pause. She has to think about it? What's going on?

"Okay. Yeah. I'd like that, Donny. Do you want me to bring

in food from town?"

"No. I'll text Darla. See you there around seven?"

"Sure."

"Good. I love you, Callie."

"I love you too. Bye. And Donny?"

"Yeah?"

"Don't ever scare me that way again."

"I love you," I say again, intentionally not making the promise she asks for. I feel like a giant dick as I end the call.

I turn to Dale. "You and Ashley should come for dinner."

"I just heard you tell Callie you'd be alone."

"We will be. Later. But if I'm going to level with Callie, you're going to level with Ashley. We need their help."

"Don..."

"What's good for the goose is good for the gander."

"Except we're both ganders."

"Fucking semantics. Christ, Dale. For a guy who couldn't get through college, you're the smartest man I know."

"I think about that sometimes."

"About what? That you're the smartest man I know?"

He scoffs. "Hell, no. And not college, either. But you're brilliant. Look how well you did for yourself. Genetically, we're not Steels, so where did our smarts come from?"

"Mom, I guess."

"Mom was a lovely person, but she was hardly brilliant. She worked as a cashier at a grocery store."

"Circumstances. She didn't go to college, and she didn't have a rich family."

"Still, as you say, I didn't go to college either, but I'm a brilliant winemaker."

"You learned from Uncle Ry."

"True. For God's sake, Don, will you work with me here?"

"I know what you want me to say. That our birth father must have had intelligence. I'm not buying. How much is nature and how much is nurture? We grew up as Steels. We learned from the Steels. They taught us everything we know. Leave Floyd Fucking Jolly out of it."

He nods. "Good enough. I suppose it doesn't matter how we're born. It's how we live."

"Absolutely."

But I wonder . . .

How can we live with ourselves after what we did to the Murphys?

CHAPTER TWENTY

Callie

I arrive at the Steel house right at seven—after pulling over and sitting in my car for ten minutes to avoid being early.

I don't know why I'm playing this game. Donny and I love each other.

Just a lot on my mind.

I should be with Rory, dealing with Pat Lamone. Instead? I'm here, and I know where the evening will lead. Indeed, I want it to lead there.

Sex is a great escape.

The reality, though, is that there's no escape for me. Not from my past, and not from Pat Lamone.

I knock on the door, and Fred and Ginger, Talon and Jade's two labs, bound to the doorway as I peer through the side window.

Then Donny, looking particularly scrumptious in jeans and a simple T-shirt, his feet bare, walks to the door and opens it.

"Hey, sweetheart," he drawls.

Sweetheart. The endearment spears right into my heart. He's never called me sweetheart before. He's called me baby a few times, but sweetheart? Never.

"Hey yourself," I return.

113

He pulls me inside and into a hug. Different, but so comforting. Sure, he usually grabs me and plants a raw kiss on my lips, but he's in a different mood this evening. It's coming off him in waves.

And I'm okay with that.

I'm in a different mood as well.

He's got his dad on his mind. He's worried.

I've got Rory and Pat Lamone and past indiscretions on mine.

And . . . I'm worried too.

He kisses my ear and whispers, "I've missed you."

"I've missed you too," I say into his shoulder.

He releases me, kisses me quickly on the lips, and grabs me by the hand, leading me into the spacious country kitchen. "Darla made red snapper."

I gasp in mock surprise. "Not Steel beef?"

"Remember our conversation in Aspen about how I like fish as much as beef? And turkey as much as beef?"

"What about chicken and duck?" I counter. "What about tofu?"

"Chicken and duck are great." Then he makes a face. "Don't give me that vegan stuff, though."

I smile. "I actually don't mind vegan if it's done well. But I'll always be a meat and fish eater."

"You'll like tonight's meal, then. Darla bakes it with garlic and fines herbes."

Garlic? I guess if we both have garlic breath, it won't matter. I love the stuff.

"She also made us a green salad and sides of fingerling potatoes and broccolini."

I inhale. "It all smells great." Then I cast my gaze to the table.

It's set for four.

I tamp down my disappointment. "Who's joining us?"

"Just Dale and Ashley, and only for dinner. We'll be alone later."

"I didn't mean..."

"Sure you did." He cups my cheek, thumbs my lower lip. "And so do I. I want to be alone with you, Callie. I *need* to be alone with you."

I open my mouth, but nothing comes out.

"I love you," he says. "Nothing has changed."

"I...didn't think it had." And I hope to God, if he ever finds out about Pat Lamone, that it won't.

"Didn't you?"

"No. Not really. I did wonder why you didn't show up at work this morning, but I believe you when you said you didn't hit send on the text, because I did the same thing."

"Great minds..." He laughs.

More like cluttered minds. He had a lot on his this morning, and God knows my mind is cluttered with things I'd prefer never to deal with again.

"Yeah. Weird that we both did it."

Except it's not weird at all. It makes perfect sense.

"Everything's ready." He looks out the French doors. "Here come Dale and Ashley now." He pulls open the doors.

The dogs rush out in a tangle of wagging tails and panting tongues, and Dale and Ashley enter.

Ashley gives Donny a hug, and then she turns to me with her arms outstretched.

Weird. We hardly know each other, but I give her a hug.

When I pull back, she says, "You get used to the hugging thing. It was weird for me at first too."

My cheeks warm, and I can't think of a reply.

Dale doesn't hug me. Just nods and says, "Hi, Callie."

"Hi, Dale."

"Everything's ready," Donny says. "Let's sit. I brought up a bottle of something red for you, Dale, even though we're having fish."

"Red goes with everything."

"Says the master winemaker." Ashley laughs.

"It does. That white with fish thing is an old wives' tale. There's so much more variety with red wine."

"My man speaks the truth," Ashley avers. "Are you a wine drinker, Callie?"

"I'm mostly a Diet Coke drinker. Or beer. But wine is okay. I just don't know much about it."

"If you want to learn," Donny says, "I can't think of two finer teachers than Dale and Ashley."

My cheeks warm further. I swear flames are erupting beneath my skin. Honestly? I wouldn't mind learning about wine. I wouldn't mind getting to know Ashley Steel better either. She seems like a lovely person.

But I've got so much else on my mind. Might be nice to think about something else for a chance, and wine tasting fits the bill.

"What the heck?" I finally say. "Pour me a glass, and you can begin my lessons tonight."

"No one will mind if I just have water, right?" Donny says.

"Not at all," Dale says. "We already know you're a lost cause."

"I'm pretty much a blank slate," I tell them, "so go for it. What are we drinking tonight?"

Donny grabs the bottle from the counter. "This is . . .

aged Cabernet Sauvignon."

Dale and Ashley both roll their eyes. Totally in unison. It's eerie.

"Aged Cab is way too dark for red snapper," Dale says. "We need a light red. Do you have any of the Ruby in the basement? It would be perfect."

"Good thing I didn't open this yet." Donny picks up the bottle of Cab. "Be right back."

A few minutes later, he returns with a bottle of the wine Dale called Ruby.

"This is Uncle Ryan's Southern Rhône blend," Dale says. "He named it after Aunt Ruby, of course."

"That's sweet," I say.

"I agree with my hubby," Ashley says. "This will be great with the meal tonight. It's lighter and less tannic than a lot of reds. A big aged Cab is best with a robust meal, like—"

"Steel beef?" I finish for her.

"Exactly! I think you're going to take to wine just fine, Callie."

I smile. I already like Ashley. I just wish we were getting to know each other in better circumstances.

"I'll take that." Dale grabs the bottle from Donny and expertly uncorks it. "The beauty of a light Rhône blend is that it doesn't need to be decanted. We can enjoy it straight from the bottle." He pours three glasses. "Sure I can't tempt you, Don?"

Donny sighs. "What the hell? Maybe it's time I tried once more to become the wine snob my big brother wants me to be. Sure, pour me a glass."

Dale pours the fourth glass and then hands one to each of us. "Ashley, I'll let you do the honors."

"Sure." Ashley picks up her glass by the stem. "Swirl the wine in the glass, Callie. First thing to take note of is the color."

"It's red," I say.

She chuckles. "Very good. Light? Dark? Orangey? Purply?"

"Would you hate me if I said it looks like every other glass of red wine I've ever seen?" I smile hesitantly.

"Of course not. That's a normal reaction. In fact, forget about color for now. We can't accurately assess the color without having other wines to compare it with. Swirl it again and stick your nose into the glass. What do you smell?"

Ashley literally sticks her nose in the glass, almost coating the tip with wine. For real?

I swirl and do the same.

And unceremoniously dip the tip of my nose right in the red liquid.

I quickly move the glass as the wine drips from my nose.

Donny erupts in laughter. I shoot him a stink eye.

"That happens to everyone." Ashley hands me a tissue.

"Or maybe my nose is just bigger than yours."

"No, your nose is perfect. I wish mine were as nice as yours."

Ashley is beautiful, and I can't find a thing wrong with her nose. Still, I appreciate her compliment.

"Try again," she says. "Just don't go in so far."

I begin—

"Swirl the wine first," she says.

"Oh. Right. How many steps are there to wine tasting?" Frankly, I'd prefer to just drink it and realize it's still okay but I'll never love it.

"There can be many," she says. "I'm giving you the

condensed version."

"My wife is almost a doctor of wine, after all." Dale smiles.

"Try again, Cal," Donny urges. "I'll do it too." He swirls his glass and inhales.

"What do you smell?" Ashley asks.

I inhale. I try. Really I do. "It smells like wine. Like alcohol."

"It's okay. Let me give you some ideas. I'm getting strong red currant."

"I'm not sure what a red currant smells like," I say.

"Fair enough. Try strawberry. You know that scent."

I nod and smell the wine again as I swirl it. Again, I get mostly the smell of wine, but I close my eyes, determined to learn something so I don't look like a complete idiot in front of two wine scholars. "I'm getting something. I'm not sure it's strawberry. Maybe..." I sniff again. "Maybe blueberry?"

"That's black currant," Ashley says. "Excellent! Ready to taste?"

"Sure." I swirl it again and take a drink.

"Let it sit on your tongue for a few seconds," Ashley says, "and think about how it feels in your mouth."

I can't talk because my mouth is full, but for God's sake, it feels like liquid in my mouth.

"Now swallow," she says.

I obey.

"So?"

"Well... it's good." I'm not lying. It does taste nice. Better than any other wine I've drunk.

"Anything else? How did it feel against your tongue?"

"Kind of... silky? I guess?"

"Good. Very apt for a lighter red. Flavors?"

"It was tasty. To me, it tastes like wine." I take another sip and try harder. I swallow. "I guess I can taste the blueberries."

"Good. We're obviously not looking for exact flavor panels. You're never going to take a sip of wine and say, 'that tastes exactly like blueberries.' It's more of a nuance. A reminder. Kind of like the smell of honeysuckle on the breeze. Think of it that way. Just a waft of honeysuckle trailing along with the wind. It's not like you've got your nose in the honeysuckle flower. It's just a remembrance."

Dale smiles. "That's a brilliant way to put it, baby."

"Well, I *am* almost a doctor of wine." Ashley smirks.

I take another sip. "You know, I may just begin to appreciate wine."

"Great!" Dale says. "You can teach my little brother here. Maybe you can give up the froufrou drinks, Don."

"Hey, I love Mom's margaritas. In fact, I wish I had one now."

"Oh, no," Ashley says. "You promised you'd try the wine tonight. I'm going to take you through the same exercise Callie just did."

I smile.

Yeah, there's a lot on my mind, but it's hard not to smile when I'm with Donny. And Dale and Ashley are so together. So in love.

It's nice to smile.

CHAPTER TWENTY-ONE

Donny

Honestly? I taste alcohol and a touch of grape when Ashley takes me through the tasting.

"I'm a lost cause," I tell her.

"Nah, you're not. You're a challenge."

"My brother's always been a challenge." Dale laughs.

"Said the pot to the kettle." I grin.

My brother is laughing. Smiling. Even with all that's going down. That's what Ashley has done for him, and I love her for it.

I've always been the one who's able to stay jovial even in the darker times. I need to remember that now.

Part of me wishes I could go back in time and not make the deal with Lambert. I *can* call it off. I'll still owe him a big favor, and I can live with that.

Just like that, I feel better. Lighter. Happier.

How did I ever think I could breach my ethics like this and be okay with it?

Yeah, I'm calling it off. I'll tell Dale later.

For now, I want to enjoy the evening.

Except...

We brought Ashley and Callie over here to tell them what's going on. To get their help.

Oh, hell...sure, their help, but ultimately to get their blessing. What if they don't give it?

"Ready, Donny?" Ashley asks.

I jerk at the sound of my name. "For what?"

"To do the tasting exercise like Callie did."

I exhale. "No. I'm not."

She lifts her brows.

"I mean... Dale? Bro? I can't do this." I shake my head. "I just can't."

"Taste the wine?" Dale asks.

"No. For God's sake. I can't do what we're doing."

"What's going on?" Callie asks.

"Dale and I need to tell the two of you something. And Dale, I want to call it off."

"You're not thinking straight," Dale says.

"No, I'm thinking straight for the first time in a few days. This has to stop. We're not about this."

"Excuse me," Ashley says, "but exactly what are you two talking about?"

I glance at Callie. She doesn't echo Ashley's question, but she's thinking the same thing. I see it in her inquisitive eyes.

"It's a long story," I say, "and you both already know part of it. About the stuff Murphy found under his floorboards."

"Okay," Ashley says. "What else is there? I know you're looking into it."

"Yeah. We are. But..."

"Don, I don't think this is—"

"Damn it! I hate shouting at you, and I hate disagreeing with you. But I can't do it, Dale. I can't."

"It's already in motion."

"What is in motion?" Ashley demands.

Callie is still quiet for a moment, until, "This seems like a family thing. I should go."

"No. Stay, Callie. I want you here. In fact…" I rake my fingers through my hair and then pick up the glass of wine and take a long drink. Then another, draining it. Tastes the same way it always does. Like wine.

"Please, Callie," Dale says. "Stay."

I place the now-empty goblet back on the kitchen table. "Callie, you may not want me after I tell you what I've done."

"Donny, I—"

"No, don't. Just let me say this."

"No," she says adamantly. "And don't interrupt me again. This is important."

"Not as important as what I have to say."

"How do you know that?" She whips her hands to her hips. "You don't know what I'm going to tell you."

"Let her talk," Dale says.

"For fuck's sake. Fine. What is it, Callie?" Already I regret my harsh tone. None of this is her fault.

"You asked me to research property titles in Snow Creek. I did that today."

"Okay."

"And…" She lets out a harsh sigh. "The Steels *do* own this town."

Ashley's eyes pop into circles. "What?"

"Something called the Steel Trust has ownership or liens on almost all the business property in town, except for Ava's bakery."

My jaw drops. I thought I was ready for this. I knew it was coming. But in the back of my mind—that place where I keep all those things I never think about—I was hoping I was wrong.

But rumors start somewhere.

"Just a minute," Dale says. "What the hell is the Steel Trust?"

"I don't have a clue," Callie says. "I figured you guys would know."

I shake my head. "Uncle Bryce would know. He's the CFO. And Uncle Joe, of course, because he and Uncle Bryce have been tight since they were in diapers and they run the company together."

"Fuck," Dale says. "I mean, it's not weird that the family has a trust. I'm sure we have many. I just didn't think any of them owned the town."

"Technically a lien isn't ownership," Callie says. "It's a claim against a property by a creditor."

"Why the hell would our family be creditors?" Dale asks. "Is the property mortgaged?"

"Some of it is," Callie says. "Murphy's isn't, but still they have the lien."

"Which means the Murphys owe some kind of debt to the Steels?" Ashley asks.

"It's not that simple," I say. "The bar was actually sold *with* the lien, which means the trustee of the Steel Trust had to okay the sale to the Murphys."

"Who's the trustee?" Ashley asks.

"Who knows?" I say. "None of us even knew the trust existed."

"It gets weirder," Callie says. "Some of these properties are mortgaged, and not by any company that your family owns, at least not that I can tell. Which means the mortgage holder took the loan with a lien on the property. Which is really weird. Most mortgage holders won't give a loan on property that has any encumbrances."

"Except," I say, "we're the Steels."

Dale nods. "I can't believe our parents would do this kind of thing."

"It's still possible they don't know about this." Though even I don't believe my own words. Not anymore.

Mom and Dad have been lying to us since we got here. Lies of omission, sure, but still lies.

"Maybe the Steels *do* own a mortgage company," Dale says. "We could own a buttload of them for all we know."

Ashley massages her jaw. "I'm still not able to wrap my head around just how rich you are."

"*We* are, baby." Dale entwines his fingers with her free hand.

"You know," I say, "a thought occurred to me a while ago, once all this shit started in motion. It's not something I ever thought about before. I guess I never needed to. But here it is, front and center. Our main business is ranching. Beef, fruit, wine. That's how we—the Steels—make our money. We're good at what we do. We have a huge operation, but here's my question. Who the hell becomes a billionaire from ranching?"

Ashley and Callie both widen their eyes.

Dale does not.

I cock my head. "Do you know something I don't?"

"No," he says. "But your question doesn't surprise me. It's something I've been wondering myself since we first talked to Brendan about what he found under his floor."

"Do you think it's occurred to any of the rest of our cousins? Our sisters?"

Dale shakes his head. "I doubt it. They're all a lot younger than we are. Just starting their lives. Plus, they don't know about what we found at Murphy's."

"Donny," Callie says, "you're scaring me."

"I'm with Callie," Ashley agrees. "Are you insinuating that your family is into something illegal?"

"God, no," I say. "Not our mom and dad, anyway. But I can't say the same about our grandfather, Brad Steel. Seems he kept a lot of shit hidden. Shit that seems to be rolling downhill at the moment. Toward us. In fact..." My thoughts race. "I wish we hadn't brought the ladies in on this."

"Hey," Ashley says, "I stand with both of you. Always."

"I do too," Callie says, though the look in her eyes is a little haunted.

A lot haunted.

Her amber eyes, usually on fire, have dulled a bit. She's frightened.

Hell, so am I.

But the last thing I ever wanted to do was frighten the woman I love.

CHAPTER TWENTY-TWO

Callie

I should leave.

I should just walk away.

Donny's dealing with his own problems, and he's sharing them with me.

This is good. I want to help.

But my God, I have my own mess to deal with at the moment, and I'm not sure I can add his to mine.

Though isn't that what love is all about? Helping each other? Supporting each other?

I wasn't lying when I said I stand with him. I do.

Does that mean he'll stand with me?

I could tell him what's going on. Maybe he could make it all go away.

The key.

The key in the glasses case in Donny's bathroom.

I'd forgotten until this moment. That's what I'm here to find.

"Could you excuse me?" I rise. "I just need to ... you know. The bathroom."

"Sure, baby." Donny attempts a smile. "You can use the one in my room. Down the hall to your right. Though I guess you know that, since you guys were here cleaning when Dad first got shot."

"Right, thanks." I force a smile and head out of the kitchen toward the hallway leading to Donny's room.

I brush my hands over my arms to ease the chill that erupts.

I'm about to steal something from Donny's bathroom.

I don't even know if it's my key.

I gulp loudly as I enter Donny's room and close the door behind me. I don't lock it. Don't want to look suspicious. I head to the bathroom and close the door, locking it.

Then I stare at the mirrored cabinet.

I'm here. All I need to do is open it, look inside the glasses case, and take the key.

Maybe I don't even need to take it. If the box number isn't mine, I'll leave it. Donny has a safe-deposit box in Denver. He lived there for ten years. No big deal. Makes perfect sense.

I'm frozen, though. Numb. All I can do is stare at the face in the mirror and wonder who it actually belongs to.

This isn't Callie Pike.

Nice, good, invisible Callie Pike.

Except Callie Pike wasn't invisible. Not all those years ago. The sister of the homecoming queen is never invisible.

I've been lying to myself.

I was never invisible. I never had an acne problem. One or two zits at a time at most. Sure, Rory never had any, but one or two zits at fifteen years old is not an acne problem.

I stare again at the stranger in the mirror, and before me she transforms.

She's no longer twenty-six, but fifteen.

Yes, one pimple on the chin. A small one.

And she's not invisible.

★ ★ ★

"Callie," Mom calls, "Are you ready? We're going to be late."

I put the last touches on my makeup. It's silly, really. The only reason I'm the sophomore homecoming attendant is because my sister's the queen. Still, I have to be at the game, have to be escorted by a football player and ogled on the field during halftime.

It's really Rory's big night—if being crowned the most beautiful and popular girl in high school means it's a big night.

For Mom—a former beauty queen herself—it's a huge night. She's reliving vicariously through Rory.

I wish I'd gone earlier with Rory. She went over with Jesse, who's the emcee for the homecoming ceremony and the commentator for tonight's game, along with Donny Steel, who came in from Denver for the occasion. Jesse and Donny are old football rivals—if you can be rivals when you play for the same team.

Somehow, they're still rivals.

But they were both asked to do the honors tonight. I'm not sure why. Jesse, probably because of Rory. Donny? Why would he come all the way home from law school in Denver to announce a high school football game at his alma mater?

I don't know.

Doesn't matter anyway.

But I'll be there. Zits and all. Part of the homecoming court, courtesy of my big sister.

★ ★ ★

My eyes pop open. When did I close them?

Present me stares back at me in the mirror.

Donny was there.

That night.

Donny was there.

How had I forgotten?

Probably because it wasn't the biggest part of the evening. At that time, Donny Steel was a rival of my big brother's. Sure, I'd crushed on his brother, Dale, during those years, but that was only because everyone crushed on Dale Steel, even though he was so much older. He was so gorgeous and quiet and brooding... Who wouldn't crush on him?

Donny... I never gave Donny a thought during those years. He left Snow Creek when I was a mere eleven years old and was only home for holidays and major events. I never gave him a look, and of course, he never gave me a look because I was just a kid back then.

But now...

My God...

He was there.

Donny was there.

I reach toward the mirrored cabinet, my hand visibly shaking.

I open the door.

Scan the shelves.

Ibuprofen. Aftershave. Cologne.

The eyeglasses case—and the key inside it—are gone.

CHAPTER TWENTY-THREE

Donny

"I want to call it off," I say again.

"Call what off?" Ashley asks.

"Don, no. We've come this far." Dale scratches his temples. "We can't. This is too important."

"Excuse me. Call what off?" Ashley echoes herself.

I sigh. "I'll explain. But let's wait until Callie gets back. Except I wish I could protect her from this."

"She already knows some of it," Dale says. "It's up to you. I can tell Ash later, and you don't have to—"

Callie walks back into the kitchen, her face paler than usual.

"Baby, you all right?"

"Fine."

"You don't look fine."

"Just a little bit of an upset stomach," she says.

"Do you need anything? An antacid?"

She shakes her head. "I'm good. Really."

I'm not sure I believe her, but what can I do? We're all in now.

"Callie," I say to her, "I'm going to give you a choice right now."

"What kind of choice?"

"To walk away."

Her jaw drops. "From you?"

I rub my forehead, trying—with desperation—to ease the ache that's forming. Any minute now, I'm sure it will explode. "From . . . all of this. And unfortunately, that includes me."

Her eyes widen, and her lips curve downward into a frown. "You're dumping me? In front of your brother and sister-in-law?"

"God, no! I love you, Callie. I love you so much. This isn't what I want. It's about what's best for you."

Ashley grabs Dale's hand. "We should go."

"No," I say. "Stay. We need to deal with this. I'm just giving the woman I love a chance to escape what's coming. Because, Callie, baby, a shitstorm is coming."

"What if I have a shitstorm of my own coming?" she says.

I look at her then. I really look at her. Her white pallor. Her slightly trembling lips. The goose bumps on her forearms.

She's frightened.

And it's not because of what's going on with my family.

"What is it, baby?" I ask. "I'll make it go away. Is it the fire? What do you need?"

She blows out a breath. "Right. The fire. We're fine. I just worry sometimes."

I don't believe her. She's struggling with something, but I can't force her to tell me. Maybe later, after Dale and Ashley go home.

"Callie, I don't want to drag you into this mess, and I promise I won't think less of you if you want to leave."

"I won't leave you," she says. "I love you."

"I know that. It doesn't have anything to do with loving me. Or me loving you."

"Donny, I want to be here for you. Help you any way I can. I'm not leaving."

I cup her cheek. If possible, I think I just fell in love with her even more. I just hope she doesn't run away screaming when she hears what I've done. "There's another reason I want you to consider leaving. Once you know, you can be considered an accessory."

"You've committed a crime?" Ashley says, her eyes wide.

"Not exactly."

"For God's sake, Don, let's just spit it out. It was my idea, anyway."

Ashley's jaw drops. "You guys are really scaring me now."

"It's okay, Ash," Dale says. "We'll protect you. You haven't done anything, and Donny hasn't committed a crime."

Callie meets my gaze. She doesn't say anything. Doesn't ask. Doesn't say she's scared. Though she is. Her wide eyes tell the tale.

But she doesn't look any different from how she did when she came back from the bathroom.

I inhale deeply, hold the breath and gather my courage, and then exhale. "Here goes."

The story tumbles out of my mouth in a monotone voice.

How I called in a favor with the energy board, got the Murphys to vacate their property while a potential gas leak was investigated.

How Dale and I are going in tomorrow with some decoys.

When I finally stop talking, Ashley and Callie are both staring at me.

"Is that all?" Callie says.

"Yeah. So far, anyway."

"Thank God. I was afraid you'd done something awful."

"I did."

"You did something dishonest," Callie says. "Unethical."

"Unlawful," I say. "At least it will be when we trespass."

"On property our family has a lien on," Dale adds.

"I understand," Callie continues, "but this isn't something unforgiveable. No one will be hurt in the long run."

"See?" Dale says. "Your lady understands. Murphy wants the lien off his property, and once we check everything out, we can do that for him."

"You're sweet, Cal," I say, "and I suppose you're technically right, but—"

"You said yourself you and Dale will reimburse the Murphys for any lost income. This isn't a huge deal. You're doing what you have to do to uncover the mysteries of your family."

"You may not even find anything more," Ashley says.

"In which case, we shouldn't have done this at all," I retort.

Ashley shakes her head. "I agree with Callie. Do I like this? Of course not, but it's clear the two of you don't like it either. Your friend at the energy board won't rat you out. He has a lot more to lose than you do."

"I know that. I just wish . . ."

"You wish it hadn't come to this," Callie says. "I get it."

In her eyes, I see not only love.

I see understanding.

She *does* get it.

And I can't help wondering how she seems to so fully understand my dilemma.

"We'll go in," Dale says, "investigate, and leave. It won't take more than a day or two to look through everything. We'll put everything back in place, and then we'll be done."

"Until we have to look through some other property the Steels own," I say.

"Don, we take this one step at a time," Dale says.

"The lien. How can we get rid of the lien if we don't even know what the Steel Trust is?"

"We'll figure it out," Dale says.

"I'll help," Callie says. "You've already asked me to research. I can find the trust, figure it out."

I sigh. "I'm not sure what I ever did to deserve you, Callie Pike."

She smiles. Sort of. This isn't the kind of thing that anyone wants to smile about. God knows. "I'm not sure what I did to deserve you either."

Dale scoffs. "Get a room."

Ashley grabs his hand again. "If there's nothing else to drop on us, I think this might be our cue to leave."

"You guys sure are taking this better than I imagined," I say. "I was ready to pull out of the whole thing. We still can."

"We can," Dale says. "But we've started now."

Even though the women have taken the news well and Dale wants to go forward, I can't. Already, in my own mind, I've called it off. I don't want to do this. I *can't* do this. I'm an officer of the court. What would Mom think?

"Easy enough to call a halt. Say there was a mistake. Then we don't trespass."

Dale's face goes blank. Seriously unreadable. Finally, "All right, Don. If that's what you want."

Yeah, it's what I want.

Our grandfather may have bent the law. I don't want to be that guy.

"I'll still owe Lambert, but I can deal with that," I say. "But yeah. I want out. I'll tell Murphy I was able to get some research done and the gas line is fine. It was just a precautionary thing anyway. Or a mistake was made. Yeah, that'll fly better. And then..."

"Then what?" Dale asks.

"Then... we pay him. We pay him big, and we go in and find what we need to find. With his permission."

A giant weight has been lifted from my shoulders already. Relief sweeps through me.

My mother trusts me to run her office while she's otherwise engaged. To think I almost really fucked it up.

I can fix it. There's still time. I can make it so this never happened.

Thank God.

Callie smiles weakly. "Are you sure?"

I cock my head. Is she upset with me? No. I must be imagining it. "Yes, I'm sure. Already I feel a thousand times better. I'm not sure I've tasted food since this whole thing started. And then there's Dad on top of the rest of it. Fuck." I thread my fingers through my hair. "What was I thinking?"

"You were thinking you wanted to know what's going on with our family," Dale says. "So do I. But you're the one who'd pay the most dearly if we were ever found out, so this is your call, little brother."

"I'm calling it," I say. "It's over. I'll fix it in the morning."

This is the right thing. My mother didn't raise me to be unethical.

I'll find a way to do this on the up-and-up. Callie's research. Talk to Murphy. He's a good guy. He'll let us do what we need to do.

And if he doesn't?

I can close on the lien.

I hope it won't come to that, but at least I have a remedy that's a hundred percent legal.

CHAPTER TWENTY-FOUR

Callie

I love Donny even more.

He's so in tune with his ethics. Sure, he faltered a bit. Took it a little too far, but he's going to fix it.

And I wonder . . .

What will happen if he finds out what I've done? What I helped to do?

Nothing unlawful, for sure.

But unethical?

It's a fine line.

Rory and I—and the others—had valid reasons for everything we did. Really valid reasons.

Would I change any of it if I could go back?

We didn't have anyone to turn to at the time. Our mother and father didn't have any money to help us, and we weren't close enough to anyone in the Steel family to even ask.

Had we been? We still wouldn't have asked. Just like with the fire. The Pikes don't take charity. We never have, which is why Pat Lamone's assertion that Rory and I are gold diggers will never fly. Still, he has some ulterior motive.

I could be honest with Donny right now. Ashley and Dale are gone. It's just him and me here, and already I see the look of desire in his eyes.

He's feeling so much better now that he's decided not to go through with the breach of ethics that could have turned into a breach of the law.

I'm being pulled in two different directions.

I desire him as much as he desires me.

How tempting it is to follow him to his bedroom. Let him make passionate love to me. Allow myself the beautiful escape.

Yet in reality, escape is impossible for me.

My past has come back to bite me in the ass.

Will Donny still want me? Because he *will* find out.

He *will*.

This won't stay buried forever.

Already someone has dug up my past, stolen the key to it. And it may have been Donny Steel himself.

"Callie," Donny says, his voice low, hypnotic.

He wants me. He wants sex. He wants to fuck.

I know that voice.

I feel it too.

So I'll let myself escape. I'll let Donny take me away where I can leave the past truly behind—even if it's only temporary.

Tomorrow, Donny will fix what he started. Right his wrong.

Perhaps tomorrow I'll figure out how to right mine as well.

For now—

His lips come down on mine.

I open for him, melt into this kiss, into his lips, tongue, teeth.

It's a hungry kiss but not an angry kiss. Donny's no longer angry at himself. It's a kiss of need.

He still has a lot to escape from. His father's in the

hospital. Someone shot him and then poisoned him.

He may need this escape even more than I do.

We're in his bedroom now. How we got here I haven't a clue.

But my clothes . . .

They're being ripped from my body. My work clothes. The tear of fabric hits my ears with a zing. My silk blouse . . . It's not new, but it's my favorite. I won't be able to replace—

Then I don't care.

I don't. He can tear everything I own as long as his lips stay on mine, his hands keep cupping my breasts, his fingers pinching my nipples through the lace of my bra.

Flames skitter across my skin. I'm burning. Burning for this escape.

Burning for Donny Steel.

He rips his lips from mine and gasps a breath. "God, you're beautiful, Callie."

Then his lips take mine once more.

Our tongues tangle. Our teeth clash.

It's a ravishing kiss—one like you read about in romance novels.

And I love every second of it.

My bra is on the floor now. Donny's deft fingers made quick work of it, and then his mouth is on a nipple.

"So beautiful," he murmurs against my flesh.

Beautiful. All those years I envied Rory and Maddie their chest size . . . But none of that matters now.

Donny Steel thinks I'm beautiful.

He tugs on my nipple, and flames curl through me, heating the blood in my veins and causing little explosions all through my body. I'm boiling. Boiling between my legs. On fire.

He slides his fingers through my folds and groans. "God, so wet."

Then he sucks on my nipple again, licking, nipping, until he ungrasps it and then spreads kisses all over the top of my breasts.

Each touch, each flick of his tongue, sends me soaring further into my desire.

It's all-consuming. All-encompassing.

I need him. Need him inside me. Need all of him in all of me.

If I could crawl inside his skin and stay there, I would in this moment.

Next I'm flat on my back on his bed, buck naked, legs spread, his head between them.

At the first stroke of his tongue, I explode.

The climax hits quickly, and I'm nowhere near ready for it. I clutch the covers in my fists, arch my back, and clench my thighs around his cheeks as he continues to lick me.

He groans. I think he says something, but the words jumble in my mind.

I'm flying. Flying and pulsating and heading toward delirium.

Coming, coming, coming...

No. Don't want it to end.

I force it. Force the orgasm. I can almost feel my clit swelling further, my walls throbbing hotter.

Coming, coming, coming....

Then Donny's inside me. When did he undress? I have no idea. Don't care. I only care that his hard cock is drilling into me, easing the ache of emptiness that has been a part of me the last few days.

He looks at me, his hazel eyes smoldering. His lips are slightly parted, and sweat has pasted his hair to his brow.

He says nothing. Just pounds into me, his gaze never wavering from mine.

Thrust, thrust, thrust—

Then a groan as he closes his eyes and releases.

Though my climax is waning, I still clamp around him, take him within me.

And I never want to let him go.

CHAPTER TWENTY-FIVE

Donny

I stay inside Callie for several timeless moments before I withdraw and move to the side, fanning my arm over my forehead.

Once more, I haven't taken care of her to the best of my ability.

She doesn't complain, but I have so much more to show her, to give to her. I want so badly to show her she can have more than one climax.

She turns toward me and snuggles into my shoulder.

I open my eyes and look at her—so beautiful. "I love you."

Her lips curve. "I love you too."

"One day, I swear to you, I'm going to make love to you for hours, the way you deserve."

"I kind of like it this way. That you can't resist me."

"Good thing, since I don't seem to have any control at all around you."

"That's what I like about it. Plus, the feel of you inside me... It's so..."

I widen my eyes. "Yeah?"

"It's not like I haven't had any experience. I have. But with you... Maybe it's because we're in love."

"Or maybe it's my huge cock," I can't help saying.

Callie lifts her head and punches my shoulder. "Yeah, that must be it. Way to ruin a beautiful moment, Donny."

I grab her and pull her to me. "Every moment with you is beautiful." I sweep a lock of hair off her cheek. "And that's no line, baby. I mean every word. Every single moment. Whether we're making love or we're fighting at the Snow Creek Inn. Or working or whatever. Every moment with you ... I cherish every single one."

She sniffles a little, and her eyes glaze over.

"Hey." I stroke her cheek. "That wasn't supposed to make you cry."

"They're good tears," she says. "And I'm not crying. Callie Pike doesn't cry."

I chuckle. "Right. Got it."

"So what now?" she asks.

"Give me a few minutes." I smile lazily.

She swats me again. "I mean what's next? With work and all. And your dad, and the Murphys."

"You really want to talk about that during our afterglow?"

She bites her lower lip.

"Is something bothering you, baby?"

"No. Not really."

Damn. "It's me, isn't it? What I was going to do. I wish I could go back in time and undo every bit of it."

"No, Donny, that's not it. I promise."

"Then what is it?"

"Just ... things." She sighs. "You know. The fire."

"Baby ..."

"Don't." She covers my lips with her soft fingers. "Don't say it. I don't need your help. Your mom already gave me a job. That's all I need right now."

"*All* you need?" I can't help a smile.

"It goes without saying how much I need you." She snuggles back into my shoulder. "I hope I'm worthy of you."

I raise an eyebrow. Strange words coming from Callie. She's always been a little self-deprecating. That's part of her charm. But those last words seem foreign. Very un-Callie-like.

"Of course you are," I say finally.

She stiffens a bit in my arms. Only a bit, but I notice.

Something is definitely bothering her.

I'll make this up to her. Every bit of it. I'm sorry she saw me at my worst, willing to do anything, even go against my ethics.

I'll make it up to her.

★ ★ ★

My alarm rings at six a.m.

Callie is still asleep in my arms, her lips parted. She looks like an angel, her light-brown hair fanned out on my pillow. I hate to disturb her, but I need to get up. First thing to do is undo the whole fake gas leak thing, and I can't start soon enough.

Dale's taking care of our decoys. They'll be compensated for their silence, and now they don't have to work.

I rise, grab a robe, let the dogs out, and start a pot of famous Jade Steel coffee. When I return to the bedroom, Callie is awake and stretching, a yawn splitting her face.

"Morning, beautiful," I say.

"Good morning. Why didn't you wake me?"

"You looked too beautiful to disturb."

"I have a job to get to, you know."

"I hear your boss is a great guy. He won't mind if you're late."

She smiles and wipes some sleep out of her eyes. "He's a tyrant."

I chuckle. "God, you're adorable. I love you so damned much."

She sits up, the covers falling from her and revealing her gorgeous tits. My cock tightens beneath my robe, tenting it.

"Is that a fire hose beneath your robe, or are you just glad to see me?"

I shed the robe quickly and sit down next to her on the bed. "Someday, Callie, I swear to you, I'm going to show you more than one climax."

"But not today?" She raises her brow.

"Not this morning, anyway." I roll on top of her and slide my hard dick between her legs. "God, always so ready for me. Do you have any idea how hot that is?"

"I've heard it's pretty hot."

"You have the sweetest, tastiest, most perfect pussy I've ever—"

"What? You've ever what?"

Not a great move, Don. Talking about all the pussies you've sampled when you're about to dive into the most succulent one ever.

"Nothing, baby. Nothing. Nothing matters except you and me and this moment." I slide into her.

It's a gentle invasion, not like the explosive thrusting of last night.

Classic morning sex, although with Callie, everything's a hundred times better than ever.

Her silky walls glove me, suck me in, sheath me so I

never want to leave this cocoon of pleasure. She wraps her legs around my back, positioning herself at the perfect angle. Her nipples are hard, her breasts rosy. Her heavy-lidded amber eyes sear into mine as I enter her, withdraw, enter her again.

She closes her eyes. "Feels so good, Donny."

"Open your eyes, baby. I want to watch you. You're so sexy, so gorgeous."

Her cheeks are pink, her lips parted. She's an angel. A beautiful angel.

I want to give her a climax. Want to— "God!" I release inside her, give all that I am to her.

Except for that one little thing.

I don't give her a climax.

I sigh.

I have to get to work. Deal with the fallout from my idiotic move, but after that?

I'm focusing on Callie. It's Thursday. Tomorrow night is the night. I can take care of business today and tomorrow, make sure Dad and Mom are doing okay, and then . . .

Callie.

I'll give her what she's deserved all along.

A whole night—hours upon hours—of unadulterated passion and pleasure.

Fuck. My groin tightens just thinking about it.

But first . . .

Work.

"Tomorrow evening," I say to Callie. "Tomorrow evening you're all mine."

CHAPTER TWENTY-SIX

Callie

Smack!
    The hand comes down on my bare ass.
    Smack!
    Again.
    Smack!
    Again.
    I bite my lip against the pain until it morphs into pleasure.
I bite my lip again because it's all so beautiful it hurts.
    I crave the punishment. I crave the pleasure.
    I crave—

★ ★ ★

"Callie?" Something nudges me.

I jerk from my dream. Donny stands above me, gazing at me with those gorgeous hazel eyes.

"You fell back to sleep, baby. I brought you a cup of coffee."

I sit up, my body throbbing all over. I fell back to sleep? I feel like I've just been fucked. Of course, I *was* fucked—I glance at the clock on the night table—a half hour ago.

Then it comes to me—flashes of an image.

Spanking. A spanking. From . . . Was it Donny?

I warm all over. The tops of my breasts are pink with a flush.

I take the mug of coffee Donny holds. "Thank you."

"You okay? You seem a little . . ."

I swallow a sip of coffee and clear my throat, embarrassment flooding through me. "A little what?"

"I don't know. Distracted. But in a good way. You look . . . Damn, Callie, you look like you're ready to fuck."

I smile what I hope to be a flirtatious smile. "Maybe I am."

He chuckles. "God, I love you."

"I love you too."

"Tomorrow, Callie. Tomorrow night is going to be amazing."

"I have no doubt." I take another sip of coffee.

I wonder if Donny might be open to a little experimentation with spanking.

And then I wonder why something like spanking, which I've never given a second thought in my life, is plaguing my thoughts. Making me hot.

I take another sip.

And try to forget the hot dream.

★ ★ ★

At my desk in town, I continue my research while Donny shuts himself in his own office, presumably to fix things with Murphy.

"You mind going for coffee again, Callie?"

I jerk upward at Alyssa's voice. "Oh, sure."

"Thanks. Same order as always."

I collect my purse and take the petty cash Alyssa hands me. Off to Rita's.

Callie the coffee girl.

Somehow, the thought bothers me less now that I have so much more important things invading my mind.

Rory and I haven't talked since we tried—and failed—to retrieve the key to our safe-deposit box in Denver. So much going on.

I head into Rita's and get in the short line. Behind me, at a table near the counter, Sheriff Hardy Solomon is talking to one of his officers.

"Not sure," he says. "Murphy couldn't tell me anything definite. He wasn't home at the time."

"Wasn't he supposed to stay out of the place?"

"Yeah, according to the papers."

"Then we should arrest him."

"For what? Trespassing on his own property?"

"Isn't it an eminent domain kind of thing? The state took possession of his property for a certain length of time?"

"I don't know. I'm going to go see Jade and get her take."

"Jade's still in Grand Junction with Talon. Donny Steel's heading up the office."

"Then I'll go see Donny."

Then rustling, as they presumably rise. From the corner of my eye, I see the sheriff and the officer leave the café.

"Callie?"

I jerk at the voice. Rita herself is working the register this morning.

"Sorry, what?"

"You were a million miles away," Rita says. "What'll it be?"

"I'm sorry. The usual. For the office." I set the cash on the counter.

"Got it. Give me just a minute."

"Thanks. Keep the change."

I walk to the window. The sheriff and the officer are heading toward the courthouse. A minute passes. Another.

"Your order's up, Callie," Rita calls.

I grab the cupholder, neglecting to say goodbye, and walk briskly out the door. I'm tempted to run, but I don't want to spill the coffees.

Screw it. I'm running anyway.

Until—

I jam straight into a hard body.

"I'm sorry, I—"

I freeze.

I've just spilled coffee all over Pat Lamone.

CHAPTER TWENTY-SEVEN

Donny

"Calm down, Murphy. Please."

Brendan has been yelling at the top of his lungs since he steamrolled into my office two minutes ago. I already made the call to Lambert, and he's filing the paperwork as soon as possible. An error was apparently made in the location of the potential gas leak.

Yeah. That's the official party line.

"Calm down? You expect me to calm down? Someone broke into my home, Steel. Ripped everything apart and then left it in tatters."

"You weren't even supposed to be there, which brings me to—"

"It's my fucking home! I needed my medication."

"You left prescription medication? What were you thinking? You know what? It doesn't even matter, because—"

"Doesn't matter? Are you fucking kidding me?"

"For God's sake, Murphy. Let me get a word in edgewise, will you?"

Brendan plunks down on one of the chairs facing my desk. "What? What the fuck is it, Steel?"

He's livid, and I can't blame him. Now I get to give him the party line. It doesn't make me feel any better, and it won't make him feel any better. At least my ethics are intact. Sort of.

"I want to tell you that I took care of the situation like you asked. Okay? I called the energy board, and they looked into the permit. Turns out an error was made in the location of the potential gas leak. They were a hundred miles off."

Murphy stands. "A hundred miles off? What are they? Idiots?"

"It was a mistake. An honest mistake." God, the words taste bitter. Worse than that wine I tried to pretend I liked last night. "The energy board is refiling the paperwork as we speak. You can go back onto your property now. No problem."

"Except that I can't," he says. "Have you heard a word I'm saying? Someone broke in last night. Tore everything apart at my place."

His words finally compute.

"What? The bar?"

"No, the bar's fine. Just my apartment *above* the bar. Every floorboard has been ripped up. The drywall has been opened up. Now who would do a thing like that, Steel? Unless they were looking for something. And I only know one family in town who might be interested in looking for something at my apartment." His blue eyes dart arrows at me.

Family loyalty spears out from me. "You'd better not be accusing me of anything."

"If the shoe fits . . ."

"Fuck off, Murphy. I just took care of this for you. If I hadn't made the call, it would have taken the energy board weeks to figure out their mistake."

God, the lies. Stopping this was supposed to make me feel better.

On the other hand, I'm pretty pissed off that Murphy is accusing my family of coming in and trashing his place. Granted, Dale and I were planning to search it as well, but we would have put everything back in place.

"I'm just as interested in finding out who trashed your place," I say. "I'm the city attorney, remember?"

"*Acting* city attorney," Brendan says snidely.

"For fuck's sake." I walk out from behind my desk to the door and open it. "I'll look into this. Have you called the sheriff?"

"Yeah, and he—"

Speak of the devil. Hardy Solomon appears then, walking swiftly up the hallway. I glance at Callie's desk.

She's gone.

I don't have time to think of the implications. I turn to Hardy. "Good morning, Sheriff."

"Hey, Don. I see you've already talked to Brendan."

I clear my throat. "Got yelled at is more like it."

"Yeah, I got the same," Hardy says. "You need to take it down a notch, Murphy."

"Tell me the same when someone's trashed your home."

"We're going to investigate," Hardy says. "You have my word."

Brendan scoffs.

I shake my head. Hardy's a good guy. He doesn't deserve the treatment he's getting from Brendan.

I, on the other hand, do. I put all this shit in motion. I forced Brendan to leave his home and made it ripe for the picking.

Who did this?

The only people who knew about the coup were Dale and me.

And Uncle Joe. And Brock. And Callie and Ashley.

I can cross Callie off the list right away. She was with me last night. Not that I'd suspect her anyway, but I'm damned glad she has an ironclad alibi.

Ashley was with Dale, I assume, and he wouldn't do this. He can be a hothead, but in the end, he agreed to go my way. To put an end to what had been a bad idea from day one.

Uncle Joe and Brock.

Doubtful. Uncle Joe can be a hothead, but he's far from stupid. Plus, we haven't yet told him and Brock that we reneged on the fake gas leak deal.

No one else knows.

Except John Lambert.

Who's still at his suite at the Carlton. He's a mercenary, but he wouldn't be that much of a moron.

Would he?

"Don?"

I jerk at my name. "Yeah, Sheriff?"

"How do you want to approach this?"

I clear my throat. "I was just telling Brendan. He asked me to look into this when he got the notice, and I got a call back this morning. There was a mistake on the location of the potential gas leak. The updated paperwork is being filed today. The Murphys can go back on their property. There's no danger."

Hardy's eyebrows rise. "Oh?"

"Yeah. Trust me. I worked in Denver for years. This kind of bureaucratic mistake isn't uncommon. I'd like to tell you I'm surprised, but I'm not."

"It's a good thing you looked into it," Hardy says.

"Brendan asked me to. I told him it was probably a

waste of time. I'm glad I was wrong in this case."

"Except my place still got ransacked."

"We'll find who did this, Brendan," Hardy says. "I'll take care of you. Anything for a high school buddy. Plus, it's my job."

"In the meantime, where the hell do I live?" Brendan asks.

"Where were you staying when you thought there might be a gas leak?" I ask.

"With my parents."

"Then stay there," Hardy says.

"I'm thirty-five years old, for God's sake. And it's going to cost a fucking mint to undo the damage these criminals caused."

Hardy shakes his head. "Crime like this just doesn't happen in Snow Creek. First Talon Steel gets shot. Now this. What the hell?"

Brendan shoots me a glare.

Damn. He really thinks the Steels had something to do with this. Even when Hardy mentioned my dad's shooting in the same breath.

Sure, he found documents pertaining to my family under his floor, but this isn't our style. If the Steels want information, we pay for it. We don't trash someone's place to get it.

None of this adds up.

Which means someone else knows what kind of stuff is hidden at Murphy's.

And whoever they are, they're no friends to the Steels.

CHAPTER TWENTY-EIGHT

Callie

I should apologize.

I should tell him fuck off for getting in my way.

I should say *something*.

But I freeze. Rather, my larynx freezes. The rest of me jerks backward, nearly landing on my ass.

"Nice to see you too, Callie."

God, his voice. It's still as reptilian as ever—like a freaking snake in the grass, hissing as it slithers up next to you to fuck you over.

The paper coffee cups lie on the sidewalk, what's left of their contents—what isn't on Pat's shirt—draining out of them.

"Why are you here?" I finally ask.

"I'm heading in for some coffee. To drink, not to wear."

"You know what I mean, Pat. Why are you *here*?"

"I didn't come back to make trouble."

"Right. That's why you told Donny Steel a bunch of lies about Rory and me the other night at the hotel."

"What lies?"

"For God's sake." I kneel down and pick up the empty cups, throwing them in a nearby recycle bin. "You know exactly what lies."

"Maybe I'm not the one lying," he says.

I stand and face him, anger pulsing through me. "Where is it, Pat?"

"Where's what?"

"You know what."

He shakes his head. "You're living in the past, Callie."

"Am I? I'm not the one who told Donny that the Pikes are gold diggers. That the Pike girls are easy. And God, you said Rory slept with you? You're delusional."

"I don't lie, Callie."

"Then you have an interesting definition of lie."

"What if I told you I didn't say any of those things?"

"Then you'd be calling Donny a liar, which he isn't."

"Isn't he?" Pat lifts one eyebrow. "See you around, Callie." He walks by Rita's without entering.

"Thought you were getting coffee," I say.

He doesn't turn around. "Figured I should change first."

I curl my hands into fists. I want to say something. Call him out. But words don't come. Instead, a black cloud settles in my gut. It's full of the words I don't say, the words that stick inside me like a swirling tornado.

Donny didn't lie to me. I know that for a fact.

I have to believe that.

And I realize the depths of what Pat has come home to do.

He's not here to dredge up the past.

He's here to fuck with my future. With Rory's and my future. Did he have something to do with Rory's breakup with Raine? It did seem to come on suddenly. Surprised the heck out of me.

And the Steels.

He knows I'm involved with Donny, so is he messing with the Steels? Surely he's not that stupid. Pat Lamone has no resources, and the Steels have every resource.

He's just one fucked-up man.

The Steels are many, and every one of them is brilliant and richer than God.

Statute of limitations.

I hurry back to the office, ready to run upstairs to research the statute, when I remember the coffee.

Back to Rita's, and this time it's on my own dime.

★ ★ ★

I return with the coffee, only to find Donny's door wide open with Brendan Murphy and the sheriff inside yelling.

I quickly distribute coffee to Alyssa and Troy. Alyssa shrugs when I lift my eyebrows toward Donny's office. Troy doesn't even look up from his computer.

I sigh. I have Donny's coffee. I don't want to interrupt their bitchfest, but I don't want the coffee to get cold either.

I stand next to the open door and knock to get their attention.

No one notices me.

I clear my throat. "Sorry to interrupt."

Again, nothing.

I knock harder.

This time Donny looks toward me and raises his eyebrows.

"Sorry to interrupt," I say again. "I have your coffee."

"Thanks, Callie. I think we're done here anyway. Brendan, Sheriff, I've got work to do."

Brendan sighs and turns toward me. His pale face is red with anger. Of course it is. I heard the sheriff talking earlier about what was going on.

"Hey, Callie."

"Brendan."

"Ms. Pike."

"Sheriff."

They both walk out and down the hallway.

I stand in Donny's now cleared-out office, still holding the paper cup of coffee from Rita's.

"Saved by the bell," Donny says to me. "Or rather by coffee. As much as I love seeing you, I don't think I've ever been gladder to see you than I am at this moment."

"I wasn't sure whether I should interrupt."

"You may always interrupt me. No one is more important to me than you are, Callie."

I warm all over. "That's sweet, but it's just coffee. Nothing important."

"Anything having to do with you is majorly important."

Flames skirt over my skin as I hand him the coffee. "Trouble?"

"Someone trashed Murphy's place—not the bar, but his apartment above—last night."

I nod. "I heard the sheriff talking when I was at Rita's earlier."

"Oh?"

"Yeah. Sorry it took me so long. I ended up ... dropping the first batch of coffees. I had to go back."

He smiles warmly. "Butterfingers."

"It's been that kind of day, I guess." He has no idea. Except he does. He's going through his own hell.

He glances at his watch. "And the day has hardly begun. Shut the door, will you?"

I do as he asks, and he gestures at me to have a seat.

"I guess you know what this all means," he says.

"I'm afraid I don't."

"The only people who knew Murphy's Bar was under investigation for a potential gas leak were you, me, Dale, Ashley . . . and my uncle and cousin."

"What about your energy board guy?"

"Lambert? He was in Grand Junction at his hotel last night. Besides, it wouldn't make sense for him to pull a stunt like this. He's already been well compensated, and I still owe him a favor. He's sitting pretty at the moment."

"Then who? Surely not Brock and your uncle."

"I don't want to think that. But Brock is staying at Uncle Joe's while Aunt Mel is in Grand Junction helping my mom. And man, they're so much alike. Both a couple of hotheads who are prone to acting on impulse."

I cock my head slightly, thinking. "But they wouldn't leave a big mess like that. Would they?"

"Most likely not," Donny says. "Unless they wanted to make it look like it was just someone doing some criminal vandalizing. You know, to throw the spotlight off them."

I drop my mouth into an O. "Are you really accusing them?"

"I'm not accusing anyone, Callie. I'm just looking at what I know. And what I know is that Brock and Uncle Joe are the only two others who knew Brendan wasn't at home last night."

"It could be a random crime."

"Yes, it could be. It's not impossible. But it's highly improbable."

"What does the sheriff know?"

"Nothing yet. They're going to investigate. But..."

"But... you're going to bring in your own team."

He lets out a laugh. Or a scoff. I'm not sure. "Am I that transparent?"

"No. I just know how the Steels operate. You pay to get things done."

"Is that how our family is known in this town?"

"Well... yeah. Kind of."

"Kind of?"

I bite my lower lip. "What do you want me to say, Donny? I love you. I have no problem with any of the Steels. But let's be honest. You guys pay to get things done. It's well known."

Donny musses his hair. "Whatever. I'm not sure I even know my family anymore."

"Sure, you do."

"Dale, yeah. Diana and Brianna. Ava. Henry. But the rest of them?" He shakes his head. "Not so much my cousins, but my parents. My aunts and uncles. All this shit that's being unearthed. They had to know about it. How could they not have?"

"You can't be sure of that."

"I have a hunch."

"A hunch isn't good enough to win a case," I remind him.

"No shit. But a hunch has served me well in the past during discovery. When I have a hunch, I always follow up on it. Sometimes it's nothing. But more often than not..."

My skin chills. "So you think..."

"I think only this," he says. "I have a hunch that my family—my parents and aunts and uncles—know a lot more than they've told my siblings, cousins, and me. It's a hunch, Callie. Nothing more." He pauses a moment. "But my hunches are on target more often than not."

CHAPTER TWENTY-NINE

Donny

I skip out at lunchtime to check out Brendan's apartment. As the city attorney, it's my business.

Of course, my interest is personal as well.

I meet the sheriff as he's coming down the stairs. A surgical mask covers his mouth and nose, and goggles hide his eyes. He wears light-blue rubber gloves.

"Lunch break?" I ask.

"Yeah. I'm heading over to Lorenzo's. Want to join me?"

"I'll take a rain check, Sheriff. I want to take a look around upstairs. Start my own investigation."

"Have at it. Just be sure to wear gloves. We're trying to find some prints." He pulls another surgical mask out of his pocket. "You'll want this. That fiberglass shit will fuck up your breathing. Good thing you're wearing long sleeves. You got goggles?"

What? Does he think I'm an amateur? Granted, I didn't practice criminal law in Denver, but I know the system. Of course I'll wear gloves. I pull the uncomfortable things out of my pocket and slide them on. "I'm always prepared, Sheriff." Except for goggles, apparently. I won't breathe in any fiberglass, but I'm sure my eyes will be a red mess by the time I'm done.

"Good man." Hardy waves and heads toward the door.

I resume walking up the staircase and open the door to Brendan's apartment.

And I have to stop myself from stumbling in shock.

Man, whoever did this left no stone unturned. There's literally no floor. Only the joists holding with a pathway of hardwood here and there. The drywall has been cut and the fiberglass insulation pulled out of the walls. The pink fluff is everywhere. I'm glad for the mask the sheriff gave me. It's not bothering my eyes yet, thank goodness.

Brendan's couch and chairs have been ripped into and the stuffing pulled out. Everything in his cupboards and drawers has been pulled out and thrown into piles that fall between the joists. His clothes are strewn about. Even the contents of the refrigerator are trashed. Did someone really think he'd be hiding something in an egg?

His bookshelf lies on the floor, and pages have been ripped out of his books.

My God...

No wonder he's pissed. In my mind, he isn't even pissed enough.

I'd be gunning for blood.

One thing's for sure. Brock and Uncle Joe did *not* do this. They may be hotheads, but they're good men. They would never destroy a place to get information. They would have gone about it much more methodically.

Call that a hunch, as well.

I'm not sure what I expected to see here, but it wasn't this.

This is the work of a sociopath. Someone who doesn't care how his actions affect others.

That's not Brock or Uncle Joe.

I heave a sigh of relief. Until now, I didn't know how scared

I was that my uncle and cousin would be implicated.

I stand for a few more moments. Should I move some things around? Look for information on my family?

"No," I say aloud.

If any more information about my family were here, it's long gone now. Either stolen or destroyed.

I'm hoping it's destroyed.

If it's stolen, someone else has information that I don't.

And that scares the holy shit out of me.

I turn, and Brendan Murphy stands in the doorway.

"Hey, Murphy. I didn't hear you come in."

"I said hi. You were lost in your thoughts."

"Was I?"

"Yeah. Care to tell me what you were thinking about?"

I sigh. "Just that whoever did this is a fucking sociopath."

"No shit. Is that your legal opinion?"

"Look. I'm sorry, man. If the energy board hadn't screwed up, maybe this wouldn't have happened."

"Damn right it wouldn't have happened. I'd have been here, and I'd have pulled out my Glock."

"Your Glock?"

"I've got it. It's at my parents' place. I never go anywhere without it. I sure as hell wasn't going to leave it here while strangers came in to investigate a fake gas leak."

His words jar me. A *fake* gas leak. Does he know something?

"I mean," he continues, "it turned out to be fake."

"It turned out to be an *error*," I say.

"Dumbass state employees," he mutters.

Guilt eats away at my stomach. I started this. *Me*. Maybe I deserve to lose my law license. What was I thinking?

Just to find out more family secrets? Hell, we Steels were all doing fine before any of this came up. Why didn't I just let a sleeping dog lie?

Now Brendan has to deal with this.

"Have you talked to your insurance company?" I ask.

He nods. "They're paying me about half what it'll take to clean this up and replace everything the assholes destroyed. Next they'll probably cancel my policy."

"Don't worry, Brendan," I say. "I'll make sure the state reimburses you for everything. You get me receipts. I won't let you down."

And by the state, I mean the Steels, of course.

"I'm going to Denver tomorrow," he says. "Someone's going to listen to me."

My heart nearly stops.

"The state won't get away with this," he continues.

Lambert is too smart to leave any kind of trail, but still, I hate the thought of Brendan going off all half-cocked over this. I started something really stupid, and now I have to finish it.

"Tell you what," I say. "I'll go to Denver. It's my place as the Snow Creek City attorney. I'll make sure you get everything you deserve."

"You'd do that?" he asks.

"Of course. I'll have a lot more pull than you do, and besides that, I have all kinds of contacts at the state level from my time in Denver. Let me take care of this for you, Brendan."

"Why? Why would you do this for me?"

"Because you're a friend."

"We're friends now?"

"We've always been friends."

"I'm not buying, Steel. I know what you want. You want

those documents I found, in fact..." He shakes his head. "I bet you had something to do with this. You were looking for something else, and that energy thing gave you and your brother just what you needed to break in here and—"

"I'd stop talking if I were you," I interrupt him. "You're pissed, and rightly so, but if you think my brother and I would do anything like this"—I gesture around the room—"then you don't know us at all."

Anger flows off Brendan in waves. I can almost see it. If Ashley were here, she'd give it a color, I bet. Dark red. Or black, even.

He inhales sharply, appears to hold it, and then exhales.

Silence for a few more seconds, until—

"I'm sorry. I'm sorry, Donny. I know you wouldn't do anything like this."

"Damn right," I say, "but you have my word. I *will* find out who did."

CHAPTER THIRTY

Callie

I stand, shaking, as my brother's voice booms over the loudspeaker on the football field. "Representing the freshman class on the homecoming court, Diana Steel, escorted by Lawson Jericho."

Diana Steel, daughter of Talon and Jade Steel, is gorgeous, of course, as are all the Steels. Why am I here again?

Diana wears a pink minidress that accentuates her shapely legs. Her long dark hair is styled in gentle waves that spill over her shoulders and down her back. She looks over her shoulder and smiles at me.

I smile back. I think, anyway. The butterflies in my stomach are turning into hornets, threatening to sting me from the inside out. The zit on my chin throbs as if it has its own heartbeat.

Applause thunders from the stadium. We have a massive turnout for our football games, even though our town is tiny. Our team always does well, so fans from the nearby counties and even from Grand Junction pour out to watch, especially tonight, the homecoming game.

"And representing the sophomore class of Snow Creek High School, my lovely sister Callie Pike, escorted by Jimmy Dawson."

Jimmy stands next to me, his gaze still trained on

Diana's ass. I feel like a Cabbage Patch doll in my denim skirt and ruffled blouse. Diana's so sleek and gorgeous, and I'm denim and fluff. Pure country girl. At least my ass is as good as hers, even if my face and boobs can't compare. Though Jimmy apparently prefers her ass to mine.

I grip Jimmy's arm as I walk across the fifty-yard line to the center of the field. Every eye from the stadium burns a hole in me, until I realize it must be my imagination. They're all looking at Diana, not at me.

The applause dies down.

Then Jesse again. "Representing the junior class, my gorgeous cousin Jordan Ramsey, escorted by Pat Lamone."

Pat Lamone is a jerk. How he got voted onto the homecoming court is beyond me. Of course, how I got voted on is equally beyond me. I'm only sure of one vote. My own. Yeah, I voted for myself. I couldn't stand the thought of getting no votes at all. The class attendants, except the seniors, are only voted on by their own class, so I know Rory didn't vote for me. She couldn't.

Jordan walks toward the center of the field in a yellow sundress that accentuates her curves and blond hair. Definitely prettier than I am, though the star of the show is still Diana Steel.

Until Rory comes out. She'll outshine Diana.

"And now," Jesse roars, "the homecoming court. Representing the senior class, Carmen Murphy, escorted by Henry Simpson."

Carmen, also gorgeous in green that matches her eyes, her auburn mane pulled on top of her head in loose curls, seems to float toward us on the arm of yet another Steel, Henry Simpson. Blond and blue-eyed, Henry is built like a *lumberjack and is nearly as pretty as Carmen.*

"Laurie Davis, escorted by Stone Huntley."

Laurie and Stone, more Snow Creek beauty, head toward us.

"And Laney Dooley, escorted by DeShawn Phillips."

Yet more applause and it becomes increasingly louder, as we all know what's coming.

"And last but certainly not least, this year's homecoming queen, another one of my gorgeous sisters... Rory Pike, escorted by Jack Cummings!"

Rory.

My sister eclipses even Diana Steel. Dark-brown hair and warm brown eyes, lush figure wrapped in a peach-colored sheath, her cleavage in full view. I resist the urge to look in judgment at my own nonexistent chest. Instead, I stare straight ahead into the stands, my fake smile plastered on my face.

Remembering that old Sesame Street *tune.*

"One of these things is not like the others..."

★ ★ ★

I walk to Rory's studio during lunch, waving to the student who's leaving. "Ror!" I call.

She walks into the waiting area. "Hey, sis. You look... glum."

"Some shit's going down at work. Someone trashed Brendan Murphy's place last night."

"Oh? Wow, I'm sorry. Any news on the Talon Steel case?"

"Not yet. I swear, Donny comes home, and shit totally hits the fan."

Rory nods. "In more ways than one."

I know she's talking about Pat Lamone. "I ran into him this morning."

Her eyes widen.

"Yeah." I force out a laugh. "I spilled four cups of hot coffee on him."

Rory scoffs. "Couldn't have happened to a nicer guy."

"No shit. Anyway, he claims he's not here to make trouble."

She scoffs again. "Right."

"Then he said . . ." I still can't believe it myself.

"What? He said what?"

"He swears he never said those things to Donny."

"Oh? He went into detail?"

I shake my head. "No. I just accused him of telling Donny lies about you and me, and he said maybe he's not the one lying."

"Implying that Donny was?"

"That was what I got out of it."

Rory bites her lower lip. "Do you think Donny's lying?"

A force makes me stand taller. Donny is *not* lying. "No. No, I don't."

"You sound confident. Almost too confident, Cal."

"I love Donny."

"I know. But it was insta-love, Cal. I don't doubt your love for him, but how well do you really *know* him?"

I shake my head, vigorously this time. Am I trying to convince myself? "It was quick. I know that. But it's no less real. I've never felt anything like this before."

"That's the chemistry," she says. "I've been there. But chemistry isn't always forever. Once the passion dies—"

"It won't die," I say bluntly.

"You didn't let me finish."

I huff. "Fine. What?"

"Once the passion dies, you need something else to base the relationship on. That's what happened to Raine and me. We didn't have that foundation."

"Donny and I have a strong foundation. We have a lot in common. Our interest in the law, for example."

"What else?"

"We both like sweet cocktails."

Rory laughs. "That's hardly something to build a relationship on."

"For God's sake, I know that. Geez. He trusts me, and I trust him. You and I know Pat Lamone. We know he's a jerk. We know Donny's not. So which one do *you* think is lying?"

"Pat," she says matter-of-factly.

"Then why the third damned degree?"

"Why not? As a future lawyer, you should appreciate that I want all the facts, and you should appreciate a good debate."

"What do we do now?" I ask. "Our key is gone, so we have no way to get to the box and get the information."

"Did you check out the statute of limitations?"

"Crap. No. Donny's had me busy doing research. But that should be easy enough to find. I'll do it as soon as I get back to the office."

"Okay. What next, then?"

"We go to Denver, I guess. The safe-deposit box is in your name. I was still a minor then, so you have to go. Somehow we get the bank to open it. Maybe our stuff is still there."

"And maybe not," she says.

"And maybe not," I echo, "in which case... You and I didn't do anything wrong. Not legally, anyway. We have nothing to fear."

"Except this whole thing coming out ten years after the fact. I don't like it, Cal. We could be chased out of this town."

I sigh. "Then we'll leave. Start new somewhere else. We'll have each other's backs."

"That would kill Mom and Dad."

She's right. Our parents need us now more than ever after the fire. "He says he's not here to make trouble, but the key to our evidence is gone."

"Right. I mean, if it looks like a duck and quacks like a duck..."

"And he's lying. Lying to Donny. Maybe... Maybe he's just trying to mess things up between Donny and me."

"Why would he do that?"

"I don't know. I'm grasping at straws here. Isn't it odd that you and Raine decided to call it quits right now too?"

"That was a long time coming, Cal."

"Was it, though? You were together for almost two years, living together most of that time, and *now* she's worried about your attraction to men?"

"That always bothered her a little."

"Right. A little. But what if Lamone got to her? Spread those lies about you, about how you loved sex with him." I cringe.

"I think I'm going to be sick," she says.

"See what I mean? What if he told Raine the same things he told Donny? He can't get us arrested or anything, but he can destroy our personal lives. In fact..." My mind races. "How long has he been back in town? What if..."

"What, Callie? What?"

"What if *he* started that fire, Rory? What if this is all related to Pat Lamone?"

CHAPTER THIRTY-ONE

Donny

I call Callie into my office when she returns from lunch. She seems . . . agitated.

"You okay?" I ask.

She nods.

I'm not convinced. She's fidgeting with her hands and having a hard time meeting my gaze.

"What is it?"

"Nothing. I'm fine." She smiles. Sort of.

"I know I said tomorrow was our date night, but some shit has come up. I'm going to Denver tonight. I have some things to attend to tomorrow. I thought you might like to come along. We can still have our dinner."

She twists her lips. "Uh . . . yeah. Sure. Whatever you need."

"I'm leaving as soon as I call Dale. He'll need to take care of the dogs at Mom and Dad's."

"Are you sure you should leave while your dad's still in the hospital?"

"I don't have a choice, Callie. I have to make sure things are okay with the Murphy situation. And I have . . . other things I need to attend to."

I don't want to keep secrets from her. I don't even need to.

"I'm going to make sure no trail was left from my idiotic attempt to commit fraud. Lambert is trustworthy. A snake, but trustworthy, when he's taken care of. He knows I can make his life miserable if he crosses me. But I need to make sure the information didn't leak out anywhere else."

"Okay. Rory and I were actually talking about going to Denver anyway."

Should I ask why? I want to … but I don't. She has to tell me in her own time. "You want her to tag along? I'm happy to get her a room at the hotel I'm booking us at."

"She's as hard up for money as I am right now."

"Callie, I was making the suggestion because I'm happy to pay for it. She can drive down with us tonight if you want."

"I'll text her. Hold on." Callie pulls out her phone.

A few seconds later—

"She's in. What time do we leave?"

"Five. We'll eat on the road."

"Shouldn't I pack something?"

"Sure. Head on home and take care of that now. I want to get on the road right at five. Tell Rory to be ready."

She nods. "I'll pack for her while I'm at home. I'm pretty sure she has students all afternoon."

"Good. And Callie?"

She lifts her eyebrows.

"Whatever's going on, I got your back. Always."

"Donny, nothing—"

"I know. I love you, baby."

The angles of her face soften, finally. "I love you too." She leaves my office, closing the door behind her.

Something's bothering Callie.

I want to help her, but I've got so much of my own stuff

to deal with right now. The secrets and lies of my family.

Someone's out for blood.

Real blood, and my father nearly paid the price.

Murphy paid a price too, though not in blood, and that's on me. I'm the one who started the energy board thing. Damn. I thought I could nip it in the bud before any damage was done.

I was wrong.

Now a stranger has whatever else was hidden in Murphy's apartment.

Maybe it was nothing.

Or maybe it was something ... and maybe it all ties into whoever wants my father—or Uncle Joe—dead.

I look toward the thermostat on the wall near my door.

Seventy degrees.

But it suddenly seems much chillier.

★ ★ ★

We make it to Denver by eleven p.m. Once we check into the hotel and Rory is settled in her room, Callie and I enter our own.

The safe-deposit key I found in my bathroom is burning a hole in my pocket. I called Monarch Security yesterday, and they're finding the requisite footage. Until that arrives, I have no idea how the key got into my bathroom.

Callie picks up her small suitcase and places it on one of the two luggage racks. Her eyes are heavy-lidded. She's tired.

She's frightened.

Frightened, and I'm not sure of what.

I stride toward her, kiss the back of her neck. "What's eating you?"

She sighs softly. "Nothing. I'm fine. Just...exhausted."

"You and Rory didn't talk much on the drive."

"Rory was asleep."

Indeed, Rory had fallen asleep in the back seat. Neither of us wanted to disturb her. "Why do you think *she* was so tired?"

"I don't think she's been sleeping well. The breakup with Raine and all."

"Raine is here in Denver. Maybe they'll work things out."

"Maybe."

I grip Callie's shoulders and turn her around to face me. "Callie, what's wrong?"

She falls into my arms but says nothing.

I kiss the top of her head. "It's okay."

She pulls away, her eyes glazed over as if she's holding back tears. "Nothing's okay, Donny. Your father got shot."

"My dad is going to be fine."

"He still got shot. What if it had been *you* out jogging that morning?"

"I hate jogging."

She punches me lightly on my upper arm. "I'm serious! This is all too close to home. And now Brendan's place. And..."

"And what, baby?"

She burrows her head back into my shoulder. "Nothing. Just...nothing."

She doesn't cry, and although I know in my heart something else is bothering her, I don't push. I'd move heaven and earth to ease whatever Callie's going through, but she's clearly not ready to tell me.

I simply kiss the top of her head. Perhaps she *is* just fatigued. We all are. This is a mess.

I hold her for several minutes, until she finally pulls away.

"Donny?"

"Yeah?"

"Take me to bed. Please. Let's forget about all this crap, at least for a little while."

"Oh, baby," I groan.

Even with everything on my mind, Callie still calls to me. Her body to my body. Her heart to my heart.

I take her lips in a gentle kiss, but within a second it's clear that gentle isn't what she's after.

Fine by me.

She probes my mouth with her tongue, and I respond with my own, until the kiss becomes a raw mass of lips and moans.

She walks forward, pushing me along, until the back of my legs hit the king-size bed. Without breaking the kiss, she pushes me down onto the mattress, our mouths still joined, her lush body on top of mine.

Damn, too many clothes. Already I'm hard and ready. Maybe tonight will be the night I've wanted with her since our recent beginning.

Lovemaking. Worshiping every inch of her body. Orgasm after orgasm after orgasm . . .

She breaks the kiss then. Gasps in a large breath of air.

Her amber eyes have turned into flames.

No, she's not tired. She's on fire.

She kicks off her boots and then sheds her jeans. Still wearing her light-blue socks, she peels off her panties and then straddles me, working my belt.

"Callie—"

HELEN HARDT

"Shut up. I'm in control now. I want to fuck, Donny."

Again... fine by me.

My buckle clinks as she loosens it and then reaches inside my boxer briefs to free my hard cock.

In a flash, I'm inside her, and she's pistoning her hips, fucking me hard and fast.

"Callie... God."

"This is what I want," she grits out. "I want a hard fuck, and then I want something else."

"Whatever you want, baby, but damn... slow down... or I'll—"

"No. Don't want slow. I want this. This is what we are, Donny. You and I. We're passion. We're desire. We're those people who can't keep their hands off each other, and I never want that to change."

"Baby, it won't."

"Quiet! Just let me fuck you."

I zip my lips closed. If this is what she wants—what she needs—I'll do my part. I want what she wants, and having a beautiful woman on top of me riding me like a damned pony works for me as well.

Her pussy grips me so tightly, yet she's wet enough to slide on and off me unencumbered.

She rides, rides, rides...

And my balls scrunch toward my body, and the sizzling begins beneath my skin. The sparks turn to flames as the spasms shoot out my dick and into Callie's warmth.

I close my eyes. Groan. Shout her name.

And she keeps fucking me. Harder, faster, and I swear to God, this climax will go on forever.

Still she slides up and down, milking every last drop out of me.

I'm still hard, and she's still riding me.

She's not looking for an orgasm. If she were, she'd be doing something else.

No, she's . . .

She's . . .

I don't know what she's after. I only know she won't find it this way.

I'm happy to let her keep going. Forever if I had my way.

But this is no longer about me.

Perhaps it never was.

It's about her.

I open my eyes, grit my teeth, and grasp her hips, bringing her down onto my cock and keeping her from rising.

"Callie," I say gently.

"No. I'm not finished."

"You won't get an orgasm this way."

"Who says that's what I'm after?"

I was right. "Callie, baby. What are you after, then?"

She opens her eyes, meets my gaze. Does she even know?

After a few seconds that seem longer, she finally speaks.

"I want you to spank me, Donny. Spank my ass until it's red as a beet."

CHAPTER THIRTY-TWO

Callie

Donny's lips form an O.

And so do my own.

Part of me can't believe what I just asked for.

Is he going to run away screaming? I close my eyes. Maybe if I can't see what's around me, I'll disappear into thin air.

"Callie," he says gently. "Open your eyes. Look at me."

I open one eye slowly. Then the other.

"Are you sure you know what you're asking for?"

"Never mind," I say hastily.

He grabs one of my hands, entwining our fingers together. "I won't say the idea repulses me."

"Have you done it before?"

"Sure. But I never thought of spanking you, Callie."

I wrinkle my forehead. Should I be upset? Grateful? "Oh?"

He pulls me down onto his chest and kisses my lips softly. "You're so very precious to me. The thought of striking you ... It just never entered my mind."

I roll off him and onto my side, still wearing my T-shirt. Though his pants are undone, he's still fully clothed.

"It never occurred to me either, but I had a dream that you spanked me. And it was ... hot." Now I want to bury my head.

Did I truly just tell him about my spanking dream?

He grins. "If it's something you want, I'm happy to oblige."

"Not if you're uncomfortable."

"I want to please you, Callie. I want to give you a thousand orgasms and worship your body the way you want. If you want me to slap your ass . . . I will."

I smile. "You've given me plenty of orgasms."

He shakes his head, chuckling softly. "Oh, baby, no, I haven't. I've wanted to, but I haven't. I don't seem to have any willpower where you're concerned. I get inside you and it's all over."

"I've told you before. I like that. What do you think I was after tonight?"

"A spanking, apparently."

"Well . . . yeah. Eventually. But first I needed you inside me. I needed a hard fucking. I needed to . . ."

To what? Escape?

Yeah, to escape. But that's not fair to Donny.

I curl a lock of his hair between my fingers. "I'm sorry."

"For what? You haven't done anything wrong."

"I think I attacked you for the wrong reasons. I wanted to feel something. Feel you inside me. Lose the emptiness."

"There's nothing wrong with that, baby."

"Isn't there? You don't feel used?"

He chuckles again. "You can use me anytime."

I give him a playful swat on his upper arm. "I don't want to do that. I love you."

"I love you too. And part of loving you is letting you take what you need. God knows you've let me take what I need enough times."

A smile forms on my lips. "And if I need to be spanked?"

"Then I'll give it to you. But first... Why do you need it?"

"Does it matter?"

"To me it does. I'm not going to hurt you, Callie. I love you too much."

He poses a valid question. Why *do* I need it? Is it just because I had a sensual dream about it, or does the reason go deeper?

"You think I'm trying to punish myself," I say softly.

"I don't think anything, but now that you mention it..."

"I don't know. Maybe I am."

"Why? Why would you want to punish yourself?"

For a zillion reasons, none of which I'm ready to discuss with him. "Forget it. It was a silly dream. It's not like I've ever done it before."

"You haven't?"

"No. Never. In fact, until now, I never even imagined wanting such a thing."

"Tell you what," he says. "Let's lie here. Let me kiss those gorgeous lips of yours. Let me undress you, and you undress me. And we'll just see where it goes."

I melt inside. "I love you so much, Donny."

"I love you too, baby." He pulls me back on top of him and our lips meet in a searing kiss.

Then, quick as a flash, he flips me over so I'm on my back, and he lifts my T-shirt, cups one breast, and squeezes it lightly.

I let out a sigh. Just his touch soothes me in a way I've never felt. Never even imagined. He moves his mouth from mine and kisses my jawline, my neck, the top of my chest.

"You're wearing too many clothes," he growls. "We both are."

He pulls my T-shirt over my head, and then he makes quick work of my bra. "I love your breasts. They are *so* beautiful."

He kisses the tops of them, nibbling lightly, until he comes to a nipple. "I haven't gotten to give these the attention I've wanted to. You're so beautiful, Callie. I'll never get enough of you. Never, as long as I live." He tugs on one nipple.

I gasp, the sensation traveling through me at lightning speed. I'm still wet between my legs. I always seem to be when I'm around Donny. Even when I'm not around Donny but because I'm constantly thinking of him. Even when all these other horrid thoughts enter my mind, he's still there—a calming presence.

"I love every part of you. Every single part, and not just because you're the most beautiful woman I know. Because you're you. Because you're Callie Pike."

I close my eyes, revel in the electricity coursing through me. How does he do this? How does his mere presence affect me so?

He pinches my other nipple between his thumb and finger while he tugs on the first with his teeth. Flames erupt around me, covering my body. I'm burning... Burning with fire and passion and love.

He continues to lavish my breasts with attention. As wonderful as it feels, I need more. More of him, more of me. More of both of us to take me away from the images that threaten to invade my mind.

"Donny, please."

I'm not quite sure what I'm asking for. A spanking? Another fuck?

He lets the nipple drop from his mouth then, and while still playing with the other one with his deft fingers, he begins kissing down my abdomen all the way to my navel. He dips his tongue inside once, twice, three times, the tickle inside me nearly unbearable now.

He's on top of me, so I can't spread my legs. Not a worry. He drops my other nipple and with both his hands spreads them for me.

"I can't believe how beautiful you are," he says again. "You dazzle. Every part of you dazzles."

For a moment, I think he's going to lick me, but he doesn't. Instead, he flips me over so I'm lying face down on the bed.

He caresses the cheeks of my ass gently, and his fluttering touch feels like warm silk on my flesh.

"This ass, Callie. So beautiful. Perfect. I'm at a crossroads, to be honest. Part of me wants to smack it silly, make it pink and rosy and beautiful. Part of me wants to treat it tenderly. With the tenderness that it deserves because of its unending beauty."

I sigh against the pillow. How is it possible that I want both things at once? I'm craving the palm of his hand on my ass, but I'm also craving his gentleness. How does this make any sense?

He trails a finger over one cheek of my ass to midway down my thigh. "Your skin is so beautiful. Like fresh cream. Tell me what you want, baby. Tell me, and I'll do it. I'll do anything to make you happy. Anything to see your beautiful smile."

His words are like a warm blanket. They comfort me, and they also arouse me.

Here is a man—a man who loves me so much that he's willing to do something he never thought of doing. He's willing to strike me solely because I've asked him for it. I don't want to take him out of his comfort zone, although this spanking thing is way out of my own comfort zone. Maybe that's what relationships are all about. Going out of each other's comfort zones to make the other happy. Compromise and all.

"Callie? Answer me. Tell me what you want."

"What do *you* want?"

"I don't want this to be about me right now," he says. "This is about you. About the woman I love and about how I can please her."

My eyes are still closed, my cheek embedded in the pillow.

"I want . . ."

"Tell me, Callie. Tell me what you want. And don't ask me what I want. I want to know what you want."

I squeeze my eyes shut. "I want you to do it, Donny. I want you to spank me."

CHAPTER THIRTY-THREE

Donny

This isn't anything new to me. I've slapped many an ass in my day. But this is Callie. The woman I love. The woman who means more to me than anything in the world. The thought of doing her harm... It scares me.

What if I like it?

But this isn't harm. This is sex. It's all part of sex. Just because I've never been in love before doesn't mean I should change things I do in the bedroom. I slide my hand over the left cheek of her ass. I'm tempted to ask her if she's sure, but I resist.

She's sure. She wouldn't have asked otherwise.

I raise my hand and bring it down on her soft flesh.

She gasps, sucking in a breath.

"Okay?" I ask timidly.

She nods against the pillow. "Yes. Do it again."

Slap!

I bring my palm down on her ass again. My hand tingles, and I realize I like the feeling.

"Still okay?"

"Yes," she grits out. "I'll tell you to stop if I want you to stop, Donny. Please. Do it again."

I slap her again and then again. *Smack! Smack! Smack!*

Her ass is a lovely shade of pink now. I move to the other cheek, giving her three quick and consecutive slaps until it's the same rosy hue.

The tingling in my palm sizzles up my forearm, as if tiny needles are prickling my veins.

I open my mouth, ready to ask if she's okay, but then I close it. I'll respect her wishes. She said she'd tell me if she wanted me to stop, so I will give her that power.

Is she punishing herself? Is this sexual for her, or is it something else?

Because I'm finding that it's sexual for me. I've hardened again, like stone.

I slap her twice more, and then I lean down and spread kisses over her pink cheeks. I want to soothe the sting.

She sighs. "Feels good."

"I'm glad. I want you to feel good."

"Is it strange that I wanted this?"

"Not at all." I mean my words. Lots of women enjoy spanking. I just never imagined Callie Pike would be one of them.

I meant what I said to her earlier. The idea of striking her in any way is distasteful to me. Yet I can't deny that I'm enjoying this little interlude. Watching her ass turn from milky white to rosy pink ... It was hot. And the feeling in the palm of my hand. I felt the sting of the slap as much as she did, as if we were feeling it together.

The way it traveled deep into my flesh and up my arm ...

I've spanked women before, but it was never like this.

"Do you want more?"

"I do, Donny. I want so much more."

I lean down and kiss her cheek. "Tell me, Callie. Tell me

what you want. Anything."

"I'm not sure. I've never done anything like this. Like I told you, the spanking came to me in a dream. I loved the idea, and I remember being so turned on in the dream. But I'm even more turned on in real life. Slide your fingers between my legs. See for yourself."

She doesn't have to tell me twice. I glide through her folds. She's soaking. I came in her before, so part of it could be me, but there's no doubt that Callie is very turned on. Slick as a water slide. And damn, her pussy is more than ready.

I'm still wearing clothes. A button-down shirt, a loosened tie, my pants are undone but my boxer briefs are still around my hips. I need to be inside her. Right now.

I get off the bed and disrobe quickly. I throw my clothes on the floor, my belt clattering against a chair. Then I climb on top of Callie, and I don't bother spreading her legs. I dive right into her heat, and she's so tight.

"Fuck," I grit out.

She moans beneath me. It's not lost on me that she hasn't climaxed yet. But she once told me that orgasms aren't that important to her. Perhaps I should take what she says at face value.

That's so difficult for me, though. A woman's pleasure has always been very important to me. I've always prided myself on making sure my partner is satisfied.

But Callie has never seemed unsatisfied. In fact, she likes how hard I am for her all the time.

And now I know she wants to experiment with new things. I won't let her down.

I pump into her pussy. God, so tight, so wet.

She's panting beneath me, her cheeks red, her hair splayed around the pillow in a lovely light-brown curtain of silk.

Will I ever have any resistance with her? I'm still acting like a horny teenager. As soon as I get inside her, I can't wait to come. I have no control at all.

I fuck her. I fuck her hard and fast, the way she seems to like it. And then... I release. I release inside her, contracting and pushing while the shooting stars ricochet throughout my body. Every orgasm with her is intense, so intense, and each one ignites so quickly.

Finally, my arms give out, and I'm forced to pull out of her and roll to my side. My gaze darts straight to her cherry-red ass.

She turns around to face me.

"One day," I say to her. "One day, Caroline Pike, I am going to kiss you all over, lick you all over, touch every inch of you, and caress every sweet spot on your flesh."

She smiles lazily. "I think that's what you've been doing."

I shake my head. "I wish I could. But you know how it is. I have good intentions, and then I can't help sliding inside you. You're so welcoming, always."

"I don't know what you're complaining about, Donny. That was totally amazing."

"The spanking?"

"It was ... I'm not sure I can even explain it."

"Did it hurt?"

"Yeah, it did."

I tense, going rigid. "Callie, I don't want—"

"No," she interrupts me. "It was a good hurt, Donny. It was exactly what I needed. Exactly what I wanted."

"A lot of women enjoy a nice spanking in the bedroom.

For the life of me, I just never thought you would be one of them."

"Like I've told you, I never thought I would be either, until I had that hot dream."

"You tell me whatever you want, baby. I'll try to make all your dreams come true."

"Will you do the same? Will you tell me what you want?"

"Baby, I have what I want."

"You said you wanted to worship my body. Kiss me all over."

"I do. I just can't get to the end of my goal without fucking you."

"Tell you what." She smiles deviously. "Next time, I won't allow you to fuck me. I'll say no. You will not have my consent. Not until you kiss me all over and do what you want to do."

"You can do that?"

She lets out a snorting laugh. "Probably not. I'll probably be begging you to screw me."

"I can't think of one bad thing about that."

CHAPTER THIRTY-FOUR

Callie

Donny's up before the sun in the morning. I wake to hear him thrashing around in the bathroom. He emerges fully dressed.

"You okay?" I ask.

"Couldn't sleep. I may as well get moving on what needs to be done."

"At five thirty a.m.?"

He nods. "Yeah. I have some people I'm seeing for breakfast. From my old firm. Then I have to make sure I minimize the potential fallout from my lack of judgment."

"You were just trying to find out what your family's keeping from you," I say gently.

"Doesn't make it right."

What can I say to that? He's correct.

"What do you and Rory have going on today?"

I want to tell him. I want so badly to confide in him. Just saying the words might help. But Rory and I agreed. Only the two of us. Not even Carmen and Jordan. After all, they don't know what we hid in that safe-deposit box.

The box we no longer have the key to.

"We just have some stuff to take care of. And she wants to see Raine."

He nods. "Think they'll work it out?"

"I doubt it. Raine's moving here to work with a pal from beauty school. Apparently he owns a big salon and spa thing."

"And Rory wants to stay in Snow Creek, huh?"

"Yeah. Rory and I may complain about our family sometimes, but we love them just like you love yours."

"You're talking to the guy who *did* leave his family, Cal."

"And who came back."

"After ten-plus years."

I resist the urge to throw a pillow at him. He's got a lot on his mind, and so do I, but Donny and I can always joke around together.

I love him for that.

And for so many other things.

Donny places his briefcase on top of the bureau and flips it open. He shuffles through a few papers and then places his laptop in the case. He closes it and grabs it, holding it at his side.

"You look like the cover of *Business Weekly*," I say.

"That's me. All business. All the time." He chuckles, but I can tell it's forced. "I hate leaving you here like this. Sometime I'll bring you to Denver and show you all the best places I used to love when I lived here."

"That's okay. I understood from the beginning that this was a business trip, not a pleasure trip."

"Callie, even the most boring business trip is pleasurable if you're along." He leans over and kisses my lips. "Last night was amazing. You sore today?"

"You mean in my pussy or in my ass?"

"I was talking about your ass, but I meant *on* your ass, not *in* your ass. But do you want to be sore in your ass? I can probably make that happen." He grins.

I tingle all over. Anal sex is another thing I've never given a second thought, but when Donny Steel brings it up, I find myself getting really hot.

"I'm not really sore. Maybe just slightly tender."

"You enjoyed it, then?"

"Couldn't you tell? I loved it. It was ... I guess it's just hard to describe. It was painful, yes, but the pain wasn't hurtful pain, if that makes any sense. It was more like something I knew would lead to pleasure, and it did."

"Baby, I will do whatever you want. But at some point, I promise you, I *am* going to worship that body the way it was meant to be worshipped."

"I'll hold you to that."

"Absolutely. I totally want you to hold me to it." He kisses my lips once more and then stands up straight. "I'll probably work through lunch, but I'll make sure that you, Rory, and I have dinner reservations somewhere ... say, around seven?"

"Okay. I'll tell Rory."

"All right. I love you." He walks to the door, opens it, and then looks over his shoulder and puckers his lips in a kiss. Then he closes the door behind him.

I hear his footfalls on the carpeting of the hallway for a few seconds until they die away.

I put my head back on the pillow. Rory's probably still asleep. Oddly, I slept like a baby, despite all my worries. I wish Donny had been able to.

After a few moments of lying still in bed, I wrestle the covers away from me and get up. Maybe I'll go down and hit the gym. The bank won't open until eight o'clock, so Rory and I can't do anything until then anyway.

I throw on some sweat pants, a tank top, and my Brooks running shoes, and then leave the hotel room and head toward the elevators.

To my surprise, Rory stands at the elevator. She's dressed in leggings and a short-sleeved sweat shirt.

I clear my throat.

She turns and meets my gaze. "What are you doing up so early?"

"I was about to ask you the same."

"I can't sleep. I'm antsy."

"You slept on the drive."

"I know. Weird. I sure can't now. I thought maybe I'd get on the treadmill or elliptical or something."

"Exactly where I was heading. Donny already left. Apparently he has an early breakfast meeting with some people."

"At six fifteen?"

"Yeah. He's got a lot on his mind too. The difference is I know about what's going on with him, and before you ask, I can't tell you."

"I wasn't going to ask. Believe me. I don't want anything else on my mind."

"Fair enough. He doesn't know what's going on with me. With us."

"I know you want to tell him, Callie."

"I both do and don't. This was all so long ago. You and I aren't the same people we were then. I mean, what we did . . ."

"We had our reasons," Rory says. "Tell me the truth. If the same thing happened today, would you behave any differently?"

I ponder her question. Would I? Pat Lamone threatened

to destroy us. He brought other people into his vicious little head game. Looking back, even thinking it through, it seems like a bunch of high school drama. But it could have affected our parents' livelihood. And for that reason, I would still attack the way we did then.

"I'm waiting for your answer," Rory prods.

"I would have done the same thing."

"Me too."

The elevator door opens, and we both step in.

"Want some coffee?" she asks.

I nod. "We can have breakfast in the hotel restaurant or just stop for coffee before the gym."

"Just coffee," she says. "For me, anyway. I can't eat."

Just as she says it and I'm about to agree, my stomach lets out a ferocious growl.

"Callie, you are the only person in the world who can be hungry when our lives are nearing ruin."

"First, I'm not hungry. That's my belly, not me. And second of all, Rory, our lives are not in near ruin. We can contain this. We have to," I add more to myself than to Rory.

The elevator jerks to a stop, a little more forcefully than it normally does.

"What the heck was that?" Rory says.

"Who knows? Probably just a finicky elevator." I stare at the doors, waiting for them to open.

They don't.

"You've got to be kidding me." Rory starts pressing buttons like a fanatic.

"Ror, that's not going to help." I grab my phone to call the front desk.

"Hotel Marquee, how may I direct your call?"

"Hi, this is Callie Pike in room 1213. My sister and I are stuck in the elevator."

"Oh, goodness. Can you tell me which elevator?"

"I don't know. The middle one."

"The middle one on the east or west side?"

"I don't freaking know. Check the one that's not moving."

"I'll get someone on it right away. In the meantime, don't panic."

"Don't panic?"

"Yes, please don't panic. Is there anything I can do for you?"

"Uh . . . yeah. Get the elevator moving."

A forced chuckle meets my ear through the phone. "We'll get you out of there as soon as we can. You have my word."

I shove my phone into my pocket with a huff. "She asked if there was anything she could do for us. Sure, a three-course breakfast and some coffee would be great. Just make it appear in the elevator, why don't you?"

"Your sarcasm isn't going to help right now, Callie."

I let my legs give way and drop my ass on the floor of the elevator. Which turns out to be a big mistake. "Ow!" I cry out.

"Are you okay?"

"Yeah." I don't really want to divulge to my sister what Donny and I were up to in bed last night.

"Got a little spanking, huh?"

So much for not divulging anything. "Crap. Is it that obvious?"

"It is to anyone who's done it."

"TMI, Ror."

"To each her own," she says. "I never really enjoyed it that much. Did you?"

Rory and I are very close. I'm closer to her than I am to either Jesse or Maddie. We're the closest in age of all our siblings, so we've always been thick as thieves. But discussing my sex life with her? Yeah. Not going to happen.

"I'm going to pretend you didn't ask me that."

"So you liked it, huh?" She laughs.

"Why are you laughing? You're so freaked about our situation that you can't sleep, and on top of that, we're stuck in a damned elevator."

"Callie, babe, I can laugh or I can cry, I guess."

"I hear you. But I'm not sure my sore ass is something I want you laughing at."

She sits down next to me, minus the ouch. "They'll get us out of here, Callie. It's a good thing neither of us are claustrophobic."

"Right. That's what I'm thankful for right about now."

"Hey. You've always been the strong one. You're the one who tells me this is going to be okay. I need you, Cal."

Strong one? Is she kidding? "You know what? I don't know if it's going to be okay. I have no idea what's going to happen. We don't even know what we're going to find when we open that safe-deposit box. If they'll even let us open it."

"They'll have to open it for us. It's in my name. The problem is that we're going to have to pay for them to saw the lock off."

"Are you kidding me? They don't keep extra keys lying around?"

"It's a security thing. Each box requires two keys to open it. One that stays at the bank, and one that the box renter keeps. That's me. And I no longer have the key."

"What the hell kind of system is that?"

"It's actually a good system, sis. Keeps it more secure."

"Well, it sure as heck doesn't keep it secure when someone steals our freaking key."

"True. But whoever has that key can't open the box. The box is in my name, and I'd have to show ID."

"Are you sure about that?"

"I'm not really sure about anything." Rory sighs. "For all we know, whoever has our key could have gotten a fake ID with my name on it and opened the box."

"Or paid off some bank employee to let them in."

"You've been hanging around the Steels too long. No one else would think about the payoff."

I ponder a moment. Is she correct? She's right. A month ago, I would have never considered a payoff. It would never have crossed my mind. Pat Lamone doesn't have any money. Nobody we know has any money. Except the Steels . . .

And a thought spears into my head.

I thought that I do not like. Not one bit.

But before I can think too much more about it, the elevator jolts, and we're moving.

CHAPTER THIRTY-FIVE

Donny

I'm waiting outside the offices of the energy board when someone finally shows up at eight thirty—a young blond woman wearing jeans and a sequined T-shirt. Must be casual Friday. I didn't have an early breakfast meeting at all. I told Callie a lie, and I feel like shit.

Blondie clinks a ring full of keys. "Good morning. Are you waiting for someone in particular?"

I smile—never hurts to show off the pearly whites. "I'm Donovan Steel, city attorney for the town of Snow Creek on the western slope. One of our residents had some issues with an error that originated out of this office, and I came down to check it out."

She regards me, her head cocked. "You look so familiar to me. Wait a minute. Sure. Donny Steel from Bishop Helms."

"*Used* to be with Bishop Helms. I'm back in my hometown now."

"You did some work with John in the past."

"Lambert. Yes. We're acquainted. Is he in today?"

"He took some personal time, I think. But I'm sure someone in the office can help you."

Right. His personal time. To do my dirty work. I feel about an inch tall right about now. What were Dale and I thinking?

"Can you help me? No one else seems to be in at the moment." I flash the smile again.

"I'm the records administrator, so maybe." She unlocks the door. "Come in. Staffers tend to come in late on Fridays."

I nod. No surprise there. No wonder Lambert can do whatever he wants.

I follow the young woman in and realize I don't yet know her name. I flash the million-dollar smile once more. "I don't think we've properly met. What's your name again?"

"I'm Tasha Sanchez." She holds out her hand.

I take her hand and hold on to it for a little longer than necessary. "Lovely to meet you, Tasha. I'm surprised we haven't met before since you seem to know who I am."

"I'm stuck in the records room. Always drowning in paperwork. I'm not surprised we haven't met face-to-face."

"Well, it's certainly a pleasure."

She blushes. Good. I'm not above using my charm to get what I want. God knows I've been doing it my whole life.

"Coffee?" she asks.

"I'd love a cup."

"It will just be a minute. I need to start a pot. Go ahead and have a seat." She nods to a small waiting area.

I sit on one of the chairs. A reception desk faces me, but of course no receptionist is present. No wonder you can never get a real person when you call a government office. There's no real person here to take your call.

Tasha fumbles with a coffeemaker in the corner, and within a few minutes, the smell of weak coffee wafts toward me. Is my mother the only person on the planet who can make a decent cup of coffee? She's got all four of her kids hooked on a dark, strong brew.

"I'll be with you in a few minutes." Tasha shuffles down the hallway.

A few magazines sit on the coffee table. *Green Energy Digest* and *National Geographic*. I pick one up and find out it's from a year ago. Just like my dentist's office. This place never updates its magazines.

I pull my phone out of my pocket to check messages and emails. Nothing urgent. Good.

So I wait. Since Tasha is in charge of records here, she's a good person to talk to.

A few minutes later, she returns, pours two cups of coffee from the now-full pot, and brings one to me. "Mr. Steel, you can come on back now."

I take the coffee and flash the grin for the fourth or fifth time. "Please, call me Donny."

She blushes again. Good. Very good. I follow her back to a cluttered office. A lone chair sits in front of her desk. "Have a seat."

I sit, barely fitting in the chair.

"Now, Mr.— I mean, Donny, what can I help you with this morning?"

"Papers were served on one of our residents that required him to leave his premises due to a potential gas leak underneath his property. We found out yesterday that the papers were issued in error. The problem is that the resident was forced off his property, and while he was gone, vandals broke in and destroyed the place. I realize that the state isn't responsible for what other people do, but if this hadn't happened, if this error hadn't occurred, Mr. Murphy would have been home, and this wouldn't have happened."

"I'm not sure what you want me to do about it."

"All I'm asking you to do is to check your records. Make sure that this is a closed case at this point. Then I'll speak to Mr. Lambert about any reimbursement that the state might be able to offer Mr. Murphy."

"Yeah, I wouldn't have anything to do with that."

Again with the flashing smile. "I know, Tasha."

Tasha taps on her computer keys. "Our system is so slow." She drums her fingers on the desk.

"That's okay. I don't mind waiting." I smile. Again. I'm going to have facial muscle fatigue.

"For God's sake, come on." Tasha taps furiously at her keys again. "Maybe someday we'll get some funding to actually upgrade this stupid system."

"Take it easy. I'm not in any hurry." Yeah, a little lie. Make that a big lie. I want all of this over.

I sit, trying not to fidget with my fingers, while she continues tapping and swearing at her computer screen.

Finally, "Here we go. Found the permit. Looks like it was expedited by John. Then the next day rescinded, also by John."

"I have John's contact information," I say. "But are there any other names on the permit? Any other signatories?"

She glances across her computer screen, her eyes moving rapidly. "Doesn't look like it. John handled it himself and then found the error himself as well. No harm done. The case is closed."

I don't agree with her "no harm done" comment, but the case is closed and no one else is on the permit, so I'm relieved.

"Is there anything else I can help you with, Mr. Steel?"

I flash the smile again. "Yes, would you like to join me for a cup of coffee?"

"You're holding a cup of coffee."

"There's a shop around the corner."

"You don't like the coffee I made?"

Nice work, Don. Now to weasel out of my faux pas.

"Your coffee is delicious. I was just hoping I could do something to thank you for your cooperation this morning."

She smiles. "The boss frowns on us leaving in the middle of the morning, but I happen to be free for lunch."

"I'm afraid I already have lunch plans. I do appreciate your help this morning, Tasha. I'm glad to know this has all been put to bed and that other than the vandalism in town, nothing else has happened."

"Would you like me to leave a message for John or anyone else in the office?"

"I can get hold of John if I need him. Thank you so much."

"If you can break your lunch date . . ."

I smile. "Unfortunately I can't. It's business. Maybe the next time I'm in town."

"I'll look forward to it."

"Thank you for your time."

"I'll walk you out." Tasha rises.

Employees are streaming in now. I thank Tasha again and leave the city building. A block down the street is the National Bank of Colorado, the bank that houses a safe-deposit box, the key for which is like burning steel in my pocket.

I find myself walking at a slow pace. Right before I reach the building, my phone buzzes. Dale.

"Hey," I say.

"I know you said you'd call when you knew anything, but I'm getting antsy over here."

"I just got done at the energy board. No fallout. Only

Lambert knew about the fake permit. No other signatories, so we should be good."

"And the key?"

"I'm standing outside the bank now. I feel like my feet are glued to the sidewalk. Part of me doesn't want to go in, Dale. We've already opened up a can of worms, and it led to Dad being shot."

"You and I know more than anyone that you can't run away from your troubles," Dale says.

I don't reply. I don't need to. He and I both know he's right.

"Just go in and do it," Dale says. "And call me as soon as you know anything."

"I will."

I check my phone for emails. Texts. Sales at my favorite stores.

Then I mentally smack myself upside the head.

"Fuck," I say aloud. "You've never run away from anything in your freaking life." I grasp the brass door handle and pull it open.

The Colorado National Bank is housed in an old building. I inhale the scent of money and old brick.

A young and bubbly woman accosts me. "It's a beautiful day at the National Bank of Colorado. How may we be of service of you today?"

I can't help but chuckle. "Don't you mean how can you be of service *to* me?"

She blushes and giggles. "I'm sorry. It's only my second day here."

"It's all right." I pull the key out of my pocket. "I need to open this safe-deposit box, please."

"Perfect. I'll get a manager for you."

"Thank you."

The minutes drag. There's a seating area, but I'm too fidgety to actually sit down. My heart beats against my chest. I'm very aware of it.

Th-thump. Th-thump. Th-thump.

Part of me wants to run out the door, but there's no turning back now.

No matter how much I want there to be.

CHAPTER THIRTY-SIX

Callie

We arrive outside the bank after we've been silent for the last several hours. Rory and I both worked out hard at the hotel gym, and now, here we are, about to go in and find out what our future holds.

"Callie," Rory says.

"Yeah?"

"You've had a weird look on your face since the elevator, and it's creeping me out."

I lift my eyebrows. "Do I?"

"Yeah. Ever since we were talking about Pat Lamone having no money. That the only people in Snow Creek who have money are the Steels. What's going on inside your head?"

I let out a breath. I don't want to put the amorphous thought into words. Once I do that, it becomes real.

"Cal..."

"Okay, okay." The door to the bank looms in front of us like a freaking bulwark. Putting off going in for a few moments feels like a gigantic reprieve. If I have to put my thought into words to do that, so be it.

"Cal?" Rory says again.

"It made me wonder if the Steels could have anything to do with this Pat Lamone thing. Do you think... Do you think maybe they don't want Donny and me together? So they're dredging up all this shit to make him fall out of love with me or something?"

Rory raises one eyebrow. I have no idea how she does that, but when she does, I've made her think.

Which freaks me out more than a little.

"Think about it," I continue. "This happened right after Donny and I got together."

"True, but it also happened right when Raine and I split up, which you also thought was weird timing."

I shake my head quickly, nearly whipping my ponytail out of its holder, trying to ease my mind of all the jumbled thoughts, none of which make sense when I put them all together. They only make sense in their isolation. Which means only one of them is probably true, if any.

"Or what if the Steels are behind it anyway? Maybe it has nothing to do with Donny and me?"

"Cal, you're talking nonsense," Rory says. "The Steels have been nothing but generous to us over the years, and especially now, after the fire. Jade gave you a job. Their foundation is helping us out with grants. They hire Jesse's band for all their parties. Come on."

"But why now, Rory? Someone dug up that key. What if it *wasn't* Pat Lamone? What if it was someone else? What if it was . . ." I can't finish the sentence. All I can see is that glasses case in Donny's medicine cabinet in his bathroom. The case holding a key to a safe-deposit box from this very bank.

The freaking case even has a heartbeat in my mind.

I feel like Edgar Allan Poe in *The Tell-Tale Heart*. Any minute now I'm going to go mental and break down the walls of this bank.

"For the record," Rory says, "I don't think Donny is behind any of this. Or any of the Steels. You're grasping, Callie. You're assuming the worst."

"That's kind of what I do."

"I know it is. But you have to be realistic. Donny loves you."

"But what if it's like I said? What if it's not Donny? What if it's his family who doesn't want us together?"

"And like I said, they've been nothing but generous with all of us."

"Being generous and wanting us as part of their family are two very different things."

Rory sighs. "What am I going to do with you?"

"I just need a minute." I lean against the brick building that houses the bank. I breathe in. Breathe out. And again.

Donny was there that night. At homecoming. The bonfire didn't happen until after, but... Did he stick around? Were he and Jesse at the bonfire?

"You look pretty pale," Rory says.

"No shit."

"We've got this, sis."

"Do we?" I question. "Because I truly thought this was all behind us. I mean, the fire and all screwed up my law school plans, but I fell in love. Life was getting good. And now the past—that we thought was dead and buried—is back."

Rory joins me, leaning against the building. "Why do you do this?"

"Do what?"

"Make things worse than they actually are?"

"And how can you be so calm?" I ask.

"You think I'm calm? Are you nuts? I was eighteen when

all of this happened. I was the adult in the room. I should have protected my little sister, not gotten her involved in my mess."

"I was just as involved as you were, Ror. And honestly, biologically speaking, there's not much difference between an eighteen-year-old girl and an almost sixteen-year-old girl."

"But there's a hell of a lot of difference legally."

I say nothing. She's right. She doesn't need me to affirm it.

"Whatever happens," she continues, "this is more on me, Callie."

"No. Please don't do that to yourself. I didn't mean to—"

"I know you didn't, but it's the reality of the situation."

We stand there, both leaning our backs against the brick building, neither speaking for a few minutes.

Finally, "It's early yet," Rory says. "We don't have to do this now."

I nod.

We stand in silence a few more moments.

Then a few more.

Until I take a giant step forward, turn toward the brass door, grasp the handle, and pull it open.

And then I gasp.

Standing inside the bank, his phone in his hand, is none other than Donny Steel.

CHAPTER THIRTY-SEVEN

Donny

I jerk upward at a woman's gasp.

"Callie! What are you doing here?"

Her jaw is dropped, and Rory stands behind her, jaw also dropped. I never realized how much they look alike. Callie's eyes are lighter, and her boobs are smaller, but man, they have the same *What the fuck?* look.

"We...uh..."

"We have a safe-deposit box here," Rory says.

Callie darts her sister a wide-eyed look.

"Small world," I say. "I'm here to open a safe-deposit box as well." Then I berate myself. Should I really be telling Callie—and her sister—about this mysterious key that showed up in my bathroom?

Doesn't matter, really. It's done now.

A gray-haired gentleman approaches me then, his hand out. "Mr. Steel, I apologize for the wait. I'm Michael Keats, the branch manager. I can help you with your safe-deposit box."

"Perhaps you can help these ladies as well," I say. "Rory and Callie Pike are here to open a box too."

"Of course. Only one box owner can be in the room at a time."

"I'm happy to let the ladies go first," I say.

"Oh, no," Callie says hastily. "You were here first."

"I don't mind."

"We insist," Rory adds. "We'll just wait here. Patiently."

Her tone doesn't indicate patience. It indicates—well, I don't know Rory that well, but she sounds pretty on edge.

I follow Mr. Keats behind the tellers to a back room.

He unlocks the door. "I'll need your key, Mr. Steel. And your ID."

I stop my mouth from dropping open. An ID? Of course I'll need an ID. The problem? This isn't my box. Of course, he already knows my name, so—

I pull out my wallet, remove my driver's license, and hand it to him.

He scans it quickly. "Very good. Now if you'll follow me."

I try to remain calm. This box is in my name. My freaking name. Who the hell rented it? Opened it? Put the key in my bathroom?

"Your key?" Keats says.

I hand it to him.

"Box 451. Good." He finds the bank's key and inserts each into the lock. "The keys need to be turned at the same time." He does so and opens the box, pulls it out, and sets it on a table, where a few chairs are set up. "Here you go. Take your time."

I nod. I can't take too much time because Callie and Rory are waiting. Why do they have a safe-deposit box in Denver, anyway? Seems odd.

No odder than my having one I didn't even know about, I guess.

I stare at the long box. What's inside? Documents? Jewels? Money?

Nothing?

It's not a large box. About a foot long, six inches wide, four inches tall, and I'm estimating. Big enough to hold some documents. Not much cash, though, unless it's a lot of large bills. Jewelry, yes.

"Oh, for fuck's sake," I say out loud.

The fact of the matter is, I'm stalling. Callie and Rory are waiting outside to come in here and open their own box. I'm being rude.

I lift the lid.

No cash. No jewels. No piles of documents.

Inside is an envelope. One white letter-sized envelope. My name isn't on it. Nothing is written on it. But someone went to a lot of trouble to give me this key, so I'm damned well opening this envelope. I pick it up. It's heavy, and there's a small object inside, fallen to the corner.

I slide my finger under the flap, and—

"Ouch!" I stick my finger in my mouth.

Damned paper cuts. Whoever put this here should have left a letter opener.

Then I stop. And I freeze.

What if it's got white powder in it? Anthrax? Like the envelopes that sometimes get delivered to politicians' offices?

"For God's sake, Donny, you're being an idiot," I say, again to no one.

Still, I stuff the envelope into my pocket. No need to open it yet. If it contains anthrax or something else deadly, I'm going to be prepared. I check the box once more to make sure nothing else is hidden. I even bang it on the table, thinking I'll loosen any secret compartment.

Nope.

"All right, then." Damn, I've really got to stop talking to myself.

I leave the room. The manager is standing outside the door.

"Are you finished, Mr. Steel?"

"Yes. Thank you."

"Good enough."

I look around, but Callie and her sister are nowhere in sight. "Where are the two women who were waiting?"

"They left, sir."

"Oh? Why?"

"That's not for me to say."

"Of course not. Thank you for your help, and have a good day."

"You too, Mr. Steel."

I head out of the bank, darting my head in each direction. Callie's gone.

She couldn't have gone far. We came to Denver together. I grab my phone and give her a call.

It rings once. Twice. Up to seven times, and just when I'm sure it's going to voicemail, I get a breathless, "Hi, Donny."

"Hey, baby. Where'd you go?"

"Rory and I are at the coffee shop across the street. You can probably see us through the window."

I gaze across the street. Sure enough, Callie and Rory sit at a table.

"I'll be right there." I end the call.

Traffic is far from light, so it takes me nearly five minutes just to get a green light to cross on. I walk inside and toward Callie and Rory's table.

Neither of them looks happy.

I help myself to the chair next to Callie. "Hey, what's wrong?"

"We're fine," Callie says. "We don't have the key to our box, so the bank has to call a locksmith, which means we wait until tomorrow."

"Where's your key?"

"I lost it," Rory says. "You know, ditzy Rory."

Callie glares at her sister.

"And that's why you both look like you just lost your best friend?" I ask.

"Maybe it's time to level with him, Cal," Rory says.

I raise my brows. "Level with me? About what?"

"This is *our* problem, Donny."

"Listen, your problems *are* my problems. Come on now. You probably already know I'm wondering why the two of you have a safe-deposit box in Denver when you live on the western slope."

"You have one here," Callie says.

"I lived here for over ten years." Of course, it's not my safe-deposit box, but who has to know?

Apparently it's in my name, though. Fuck it all. What the hell is going on?

Callie stares at her coffee cup. Her lips tremble. Only slightly, but I'm intimately acquainted with her mouth, so I notice.

"Baby, whatever it is, I'll help."

"No one can help," Callie says softly.

"Cal," Rory says, "maybe *he* can."

"Of course I can. What's going on with you two? Whatever it is, I'll fix it."

"We don't take charity," Callie says.

Callie is clearly distraught, but still, I can't help a flick of anger. I love this woman, and she doesn't trust me. I want to help because I love her. Not to give her charity.

I squeeze my hands into fists, my knuckles whitening.

"Callie," Rory says gently, "let him help. We have to trust someone."

Callie turns to me then, and her eyes—those beautiful amber poppy eyes—glow with an odd mixture of rage and fear.

I've never seen this look on her face, and it nearly sends me over the edge.

"Callie," I finally say, willing my voice not to break, "do you trust me?"

Silence.

"Do you fucking trust me, because if you don't, we may as well end this now."

She drops her mouth open. "In a coffee shop? In front of my sister?"

"What the hell do you want? You don't trust me."

"You guys are getting kind of loud," Rory says.

I stand then. "I need some air." I walk briskly out of the small shop and pace along the sidewalk, nearly taking out a young woman dressed in a black suit.

"Sorry," I mumble.

I rake my fingers through my hair and stare through the window, meeting Callie's gaze.

And I wonder what to do now.

CHAPTER THIRTY-EIGHT

Callie

"Go after him," Rory says.

I let out a sigh. "Maybe it's best not to be involved with someone right now. Until we get this shit settled with Pat Lamone."

"Callie, just because my relationship ended doesn't mean yours has to."

"Again, have you thought about why? We should go see Raine while we're here. Find out if Lamone got to her."

"Raine and I are over," she says. "Let it go, Callie. I have."

"But—"

"No more buts. You have a man out there who adores you, and right now he thinks you don't trust him. I'd say you have about ten more seconds before he leaves forever."

"He can't. He's our ride home."

Rory rubs at her forehead. "My God, you give me a migraine sometimes, Cal. Go get him. You know you want to, and you know he wants you to."

I stand. I do want to. I can't imagine my life without Donny Steel, and I do trust him. I trust him with my life.

"I'll be back."

"Take whatever time you need. I can Uber back to the hotel, or maybe... Maybe I will go see Raine. I keep going back and forth."

"I think you should. Love you, Ror." I dash through the shop and out the door.

Donny stands on the street, smoke curling out of his ears.

Not really, but that's what his tense stance indicates.

Plus, he's glaring at me. Seriously showering me with flaming darts.

"I'm sorry," I say.

"For what? That you don't trust me?"

"I *do* trust you, Donny."

"Do you? I'm not sure you do. I trusted you with some family stuff—after I promised Dale I wouldn't tell anyone. I told you because I trusted you with it."

"Your trust wasn't misplaced," I say. "I haven't said a—"

"For God's sake, Callie, that's not even the point. I don't for a minute think you violated my trust. I'm pissed because you won't give me the same trust I gave you."

I bite my lower lip. He's right. I have no argument. Even if I did, he'd out-argue me. He's a lawyer. I'm only a lawyer wannabe.

"You're right." For a moment, I'm unable to meet his gaze, but then I force myself to look him in the eye.

He's angry. Angry, but also sad.

I can bear anything but his sadness. Even anger is better than that.

"I do trust you, Donny," I continue, "but—"

"No way." He gestures at me to stop talking. "No buts. Either you trust me or you don't, Callie. That's all there is to it."

I gulp. Again, I have no argument. My father once told me that anything that comes before a "but" is all bullshit.

Maybe he's right.

I want to confide in Donny. I want him to make all the mess go away.

But I hate even thinking about that part of my past. Rory and I buried it long ago, made a pact never to discuss it.

And we never did.

Until now.

I inhale. "I want to tell you. But you're going through so much right now. And then Murphy's got vandalized, right after you made the decision to stop the—"

He stops me again with a gesture. "Please, Callie. Not here."

I nod. I get it. He made a huge error in judgment, and Brendan is paying the price. He's not himself. He's going through as much—perhaps more—as I am. It wasn't my father who took a bullet.

"The hotel?" I ask.

He nods. I wave to Rory as we walk back to the hotel.

We don't speak as we walk the block. We don't speak as we enter and tap through the lobby. We don't speak as we wait for and then enter the elevator. We don't speak as the elevator door opens and we walk toward our room.

Donny taps the keycard, opens the door, and holds it for me while I enter.

I turn to him to speak, but—

He grabs me, pushes me against the wall next to the door, and smashes his lips to mine.

The kiss is angry.

Raw and angry, and oh, so delicious.

He growls into my mouth, tangling his tongue with mine, our lips sliding together, our teeth gnashing.

We kiss and we kiss and we kiss, until he rips his mouth away from mine.

"You know that spanking you like? I ought to put you

over my knee and make your ass red for not trusting me, Callie. I could do it."

"God, yes. Please."

He shakes his head. "No way. I won't touch you in anger. Not that way."

God, he really is angry. So angry.

"Donny..."

"No. You don't talk. Get undressed and get on the bed."

I drop my mouth open.

"Did I not speak loudly enough?"

I force my jaw back into place.

"You can say no, Callie, but if you don't, I want you naked on the bed in the next thirty seconds."

Already I'm hot as a flame.

Donny Steel's voice—that commanding voice. It does something to me. Takes me somewhere I never thought I'd go. Or ever want to go.

I'm hardly the submissive type.

But damn...

The flames burning between my legs right now beg to differ.

I shed my clothes in record time, never letting my gaze drop from his. His hazel eyes darken and smolder.

I stand before him, naked and ready.

"On the bed," he growls.

Right. He said to get on the bed. I resist the urge to sprint and slowly stride toward the bed, looking over my shoulder the entire time, my gaze never wavering from his.

"You know what?" He darts me a glare. "Forget on the bed. Get on your knees, Callie."

I hold back a gasp. I'm determined to please him. It has

nothing to do with the fact that he thinks I don't trust him. It's unconditional.

I want to please him. Case closed.

I drop to my knees next to the bed.

He walks toward me slowly. Deliberately. His pants are tenting with his erection.

My mouth waters.

When he stands in front of me, his erection is right at— you guessed it—my mouth.

"Unbuckle my belt, Callie."

I obey. I have no idea why, but something in his voice— his command—makes me want to obey him. If I obey him, I'll please him, and I want to please him more than anything.

Even more than I want law school—God help me.

Even more than I want my next intake of oxygen.

I work his belt slowly, my hands trembling. This is crazy. I'm not nervous. I'm turned on. But I force myself to go slowly, to keep him on edge as well as myself.

"Now unzip my fly," he says.

I comply, again slowly.

"Take out my cock." His voice is gruff. Like sandpaper.

His dick is warm and hard in my hand. Donny often talks about not yet taking the time to worship my body as I deserve. I haven't done that for him either, and I've yearned for it as much as he has.

"Suck me," he says then. "Suck me hard."

I flick my tongue over the head of his cock, savor the pearl of salty fluid at its tip.

"Damn it, Callie. I said suck me *hard*."

I take him into my mouth, applying suction as best I can. He's so big, and he's so hard. I'm not sure how far I can go, but I'm determined to give him what he wants. I suck him deeply until my gag reflex kicks in, and then I ease up.

I look upward. His eyes are closed. He's breathing rapidly.

I must be doing okay.

I take him in again, farther this time, and then back out.

Each time I go a little farther, until I've tamed the reflex and can take him nearly all the way. I add my fist and some saliva to help with the friction. Yeah, not my first time at this horse race, though it's been a while.

He sucks in a breath. "Fuck, yeah."

I increase the speed and the pressure, and he begins moving with me, fucking my mouth.

And I find, to my surprise, that I love it.

I want him to fuck my mouth.

I want him to fuck my pussy, my ass, whatever he wants to do with my body.

I love him, and I want him.

I'm his.

His to use how he pleases.

"Fuck," he grits out again. "Fuck. Want to come." He grabs both sides of my head and takes over my rhythm.

And damn, it turns me on even more.

I've given many a blowjob in my day, but I never let a guy come in my mouth. I never wanted to.

Until now.

If Donny wants me to let him do that, I will. I totally will.

But he has other plans.

He pulls out of my mouth, and in a flash, I'm on the bed, his body over mine, his dick inside me.

He closes his eyes, his hair already slick from

HELEN HARDT

perspiration. He's still clothed, his pants and boxer briefs around his hips.

I raise my hips to accommodate him, wrap my legs up and over his back, pushing him more deeply into me.

Again I won't come, and again, I don't care.

Not even a little bit.

This is what I crave. Donny, taking me. Making me his with his huge cock pounding into me.

"Fuck, Callie," he grinds out again, his voice like a rasp. "Fuck, I can't... I have to— Ah!"

He pushes into me, his pubic hair rubbing my clit.

Just a little more, just a little more ... I arch to meet him, and—

"Yes, Donny. Oh, God!" The orgasm hits me like a tidal wave, crashing into me and pushing me into ecstasy.

I come and I come and I come, until I can't tell the difference between his pulses and my own.

A drummer beats my heart like a conga, and I come. I come. I come.

"Callie, damn it. I fucking love you!"

"I love you too, Donny, so much!"

The words hover around us. He repeats his. I repeat mine.

And together we clash, the cymbals at the end of a symphony.

Until the explosion subsides after a few more moments, and Donny slides off me and lies on his back.

He says nothing.

I say nothing.

Will we go again? Will he worship my body this time? Will he ...

And then I know what I have to do. I have to prove to him

how much I trust him. "Donny," I say.

"Hmm?"

"I want to tell you. I want to tell you what's bothering me."

CHAPTER THIRTY-NINE

Donny

"You have to understand," Callie continues. "I know all the stuff you're going through. I didn't want to burden you with anything else."

I shake my head, my eyes still closed. "You could never be a burden."

My phone buzzes against the back of my thigh.

I adjust my pants and grab it. "It's Dale. I have to answer. It could be about Dad."

"I understand. I'll go over to Rory's room."

"You don't have to leave."

"It's okay. I need to talk to her anyway." She grabs her clothes and heads into the bathroom.

"Hey," I say into the phone while I stand, holding my pants up with the other hand.

"Any news?"

"About what?"

"Right. Geez. I was worried you were calling about Dad."

"And Murphy? His damages?"

"It's not the state's policy to reimburse for damages caused by criminal activity," I say robotically. "I didn't even ask. But it is Steel policy, so I'll tell Murphy I took care of it. Case closed."

Dale heaves a sigh through the phone. "Thank God. I don't know what we were thinking. I can't believe this whole thing was actually my idea."

"So you agree with me now?"

"I do. Ashley helped me see the light. I was so angry that I couldn't think logically."

"Don't blame yourself. I went along with it. It's not worth my law license. Or my sanity, for that matter. It bugged me a whole lot more than I imagined it would."

The door to the bathroom clicks open, and Callie emerges fully dressed. She waves to me and blows me a kiss before leaving. I wave and mouth, "I love you."

"Me too," Dale agrees. "I finally got my life in order, and I risked fucking it up majorly. We'll get the information we need some other way. I guess we have to tell Uncle Joe and Brock, but that can wait until you get back." A pause. "So . . . the safe-deposit box . . ."

I nearly jerk at his mention of it. The envelope. It's still in my suitcoat pocket. Damn. I'd forgotten about it in the heat of passion with Callie.

"Right. Totally weird. The box was actually in my name, and I swear to God, I never opened a box at this bank."

"How close is the bank to your old office?"

"Close. Just a few buildings away."

"Interesting. Someone opened it. And whoever it was had ID and your signature."

"I know. Unless it was someone on the inside."

"Do you know when the box was opened?" Dale asks.

"No. I was so surprised by the whole thing, I didn't ask. I could go back."

"No, never mind all that. What was in the box?"

"An envelope. A plain white envelope with some small object inside."

"And ... ?"

"I didn't open it."

A huge scoffing sigh meets my ears. "For God's sake, Don."

"Get over yourself, Dale. I had this image of white powder coming out of it. You know, anthrax, like is sometimes delivered to politicians' offices. I was freaked."

"All right, all right. Calm down. Do you have the envelope there?"

"Yeah." I grab my suitcoat and pull it out of the pocket. "It's just a white legal-sized envelope. I meant to open it outside, you know, so if there's white powder it won't be concentrated in a room."

"Go outside, then."

"I don't have to. I can go out on the balcony of my room."

"Okay. FaceTime me, and we'll open it together."

I end the call and begin FaceTime. I set the phone on the railing so Dale can watch what I'm doing. "Here goes nothing."

I slide my finger through the envelope, this time being careful not to get a paper cut. The object clatters to the floor of the balcony, and I pick it up.

"What is it?" Dale asks.

"It's a ring. Gold with a big orange stone. God, Dale, it looks like flames." I hold it up to the phone. It's not quite the color of Callie's eyes—it's lighter—but that's what the color reminds me of.

"Whose is that?"

"Do you think I have a clue? It's ... I have no idea what kind of stone this is, but it's white gold or platinum, surrounded by diamonds."

"You sure they're diamonds?"

"Do I look like a jeweler to you? Of course I'm not sure. They're small clear stones. They look like diamonds."

"What else is in the envelope?"

"Good question." I pull out a lone piece of paper. "It looks like GPS coordinates. A few sets. And some phone numbers. Colorado and another area code I'm not familiar with." I hold the paper up so Dale can see.

"Any white powder?"

I tent the envelope over the rail of the balcony. "No," I say sheepishly.

"Okay, then." Dale rakes his fingers through his long, tangled hair. "At least we have something to start with. A ring. And information someone wanted you to have."

"They could have sent me an anonymous note," I say. "Why go to all the trouble of opening a safe-deposit box in my name? And who has my ID? This is freaky, Dale."

"Uncle Joe and Brock have got our guys working on this. They'll come up with something."

"Yeah? Well, get them in on this safe-deposit box bullshit. I want to know who opened this box with my ID and my signature. And for that matter, I want to know who put it in my damned house!"

"Monarch hasn't called you with the footage?"

"No. Not yet."

"We'll get to the bottom of this, Don. Without you breaking the law."

"I hope we can. Maybe we just should have—"

"No, don't go there. It was consuming you. Not worth it."

"I still have to pay off Lambert."

"So what? It's pennies to us. You did the right thing,

Donny. Trust me on that one."

I nod. He's right and I know it. The problem? So much else is still jumbled in my brain. "So what next?"

"Call the numbers. Look up the GPS coordinates."

"I can do all that, but I have to get back to Snow Creek as well. I'm in charge while Mom's not there. I can't let her down."

Dale sighs.

"Don't even start," I say.

"Wasn't going to."

"Sure you were. And you're wrong. Yes, I took the job for Mom, but I also have a responsibility to the city. I need to be there especially while Mom's in Grand Junction with Dad."

"I know that," Dale snaps. "Send me a photo of the document, and I'll make some calls this afternoon."

"Good idea." I snap the photo and text it to him.

"How's your Syrah going?" I ask.

"It's good. Almost ready to move to barrels for aging."

"When do you think that'll happen?"

"Why this sudden interest in my wine?"

"Because, doofus, when the Syrah is done, you'll have more time to spend on this mess."

He scoffs. "You really think all I do is sit around watching grapes ferment?"

"No, of course not. Shit, Dale, I don't mean to belittle what you do."

"It's okay. I don't mean to belittle what you do either. We're both on edge. You're right. You're in charge while Mom's not there. Looks like neither of us have the time we need to devote to this mess."

"I guess we let the experts take care of it, then," I say.

"You mean Uncle Joe and Brock?"

"Of course not. I mean Uncle Joe and Brock's guys. Uncle Joe and Brock run the beef ranch. They can't just stop doing it. Hell, Uncle Joe and Uncle Bryce run this whole damned enterprise."

"True. It's up to us, then. And the experts. The problem is . . . can we trust the experts?"

"I suppose if we trust Uncle Joe, we have to trust the experts."

"Here's the thing," Dale says. "Uncle Joe is one of the people who kept shit from us in the first place."

"Are you saying you don't trust him?"

"No, I'm simply saying that his goal in this may differ from ours."

"What about Dad?"

Dale pauses, as I knew he would. It's still so difficult for Dale to say anything negative about our father. As difficult as it is for me to say anything negative about our mother.

Finally, "Man, I trust Dad. I trust him with my life. Hell, he saved our lives once, and I know he'd do it again. But damn it, Donny. Damn it. I think we need to do this on our own."

"We already brought Uncle Joe in. And Brock."

"Maybe we talk to Brock on the sly."

"He's as devoted to Uncle Joe as you are to Dad, Dale."

"Yeah, yeah. I know. Let me think on this. When are you coming home?"

"Tomorrow, I guess. Or we could drive home tonight. I'd like to take Callie and Rory out to a nice dinner, though."

"Go ahead. Don't take Callie for granted. Family first."

"Callie's not family, bro."

"You love her, man. I can hear it in your voice, see it on your face when you talk about her. She'll be family one day.

As much as I want to get to the bottom of this, I won't sacrifice my relationship with Ashley for it. Not even a little bit."

I nod. "Got it. I'll be in touch. I'm going to give Mom a quick call and check in on Dad."

"I just did," Dale says. "He's good. They think they'll send him home by mid next week." Dale rolls his eyes. "Mom's already planning a welcome home party for him."

I join in the eye roll. I love my mother, but my God, she and Aunt Marj take any excuse to plan one of their legendary events.

"I'll give her a call, anyway. Let her know I'm thinking about both of them. I'll check in with you tomorrow, Dale."

"Good enough."

I end the FaceTime.

Then I stare at the document I'm still holding. GPS coordinates. Three different sets. And five phone numbers. A gentle breeze drifts over my face. We're nearing November, and the weather has become brisk. I scan the coordinates once more. I'm no geographical expert, but I think they're all in western Colorado. Easy enough to look up. I grab my phone as another breeze—

"No!" I scream, as the wind snatches the paper from my hand.

CHAPTER FORTY

Callie

I raise my hand to knock on Rory's door but stop midair when I hear raised voices coming from the room.

I turn to head back to Donny's and my room when the door opens.

"Oh." Raine Cunningham stands before me. "Hi, Callie."

I clear my throat. "Hi, Raine."

"Go ahead in. I'm leaving."

"What's going on?" I ask her.

"Ask your sister. I'm out of here."

"Raine, wait!"

She's already halfway down the hallway to the elevator. I tentatively enter Rory's room. She's sitting on the king-size bed, her head in her hands. I approach her.

"Ror?"

She lifts her head. Her eyes are red and glistening.

"Hey," I say.

She shakes her head. "Raine and I almost never fought while we were together. I mean, we had our disagreements, but a knock-down, drag-out? Never."

"Until now?" I hedge.

She nods. "I'm not sure what I was thinking, calling her, inviting her over here to talk. It's so over."

I sit down next to her. "Tell me."

"It's worse than I could have imagined, Cal. It's Lamone. He *did* get to her."

I rub my temples against a headache that is already threatening to cloud my brain. "Oh, man. What did he do?"

"The same lies he told Donny," she says. "That I slept with him and loved it. That you were next in line. That we're gold diggers."

"And she believed him?"

Rory scoffs softly. "No, she didn't."

"Then what's the problem?"

"It just reinforced her feelings about my bisexuality. She doesn't think I'll ever be able to be in a relationship with a woman without wanting men."

"That's the dumbest thing I've ever heard. I guess she's okay with you being attracted to other women, then?"

"I know, I know. It makes no sense at all. I told her she was being insecure and that maybe she was the one with the problem, and as you can imagine, it escalated from there."

"She *is* the one with the problem, Ror. She has a trust problem."

"Yeah. She does."

"And it's *her* problem," I say. "Not yours."

"Except I lost her."

"A few days ago, you were okay with that."

"I still am, I think. It just hurts, you know?" She sniffles. "I can't be with someone who doesn't trust me. Relationships don't work that way."

My previous conversation with Donny plays over in my mind. I promised to tell him everything. I can't renege on that promise. He has to know I trust him.

"I think," I say, "this has more to do with Raine's lack of trust than it has to do with your bisexuality."

"I know it does, but it still hurts when she accuses me of things that just aren't true. When I'm with a man or a woman, I'm all in. I don't stray. That's not my style. And sure, I'm attracted to others. Of both sexes. But that doesn't mean I'm going to act on that attraction."

"I know, Rory."

"I don't even think about it," she continues.

"If Raine is that insecure, she's not going to find happiness with a lesbian either. She has issues."

"We really had some great times," Rory says. "I do miss her."

"I know. But you said yourself she wasn't your forever."

"No, she wasn't. That's obvious now. Plus, she wasn't interested in children, and I am."

"Really?"

Rory nods. "I never told you because I didn't want to believe it myself. I always thought she'd change her mind. I guess it doesn't matter now. Of course, I'm twenty-eight. My biological clock is ticking."

"Don't be silly. You have all kinds of time."

"Raine is younger," Rory says. "I figured she had all kinds of time to change her mind about kids. She could be the one to have our child. Now I guess it's up to me."

"Not necessarily. You could find someone younger."

"What if I fall in love with a guy next? Then it's all on me."

"You're putting way too much pressure on yourself, Rory."

"Easy for you to say. You've got two more years of fertility than I have, plus a guy who's probably already thinking about impregnating you."

Funny. Donny and I have so much going on that I haven't given the future a thought. I do want kids. I don't think I'm quite the mothering type that Rory is. Just watching her with her students has shown me she'll be a great mom, plus she was a little mother to Maddie when our younger sister was born. Me? I'm a little too sarcastic and abrasive. I do love children, though, and I do want them. Does Donny? Probably. The Steels are all about family.

"I don't know about that."

"Are you kidding? I've seen the way he looks at you. Raine never looked at me like that. No one has."

"That's not true, Ror. You were the homecoming queen."

She scoffs. "High school bullshit. That ended up taking me to a place I never wanted to go that's coming back to kick both our asses. I'm talking about now. We're adults. I've been in several relationships with both men and women, and not one of them has looked at me the way Donny looks at you. He has stars in his eyes whenever he looks at you, Callie. You're one lucky woman."

I can't deny the butterflies I get when Donny gazes at me with those gorgeous hazel eyes. But Rory is the beauty of the Pike family. She's Mom's Mini-Me, and Mom was a beauty queen. Maddie is adorable too, but Rory... She's something special. If she were slightly taller, she'd be walking runways.

"I won't deny I'm lucky," I say.

"So what did he say?" she asks.

"About what?"

"About Lamone. The past. All of it."

I swallow. "I haven't told him yet."

She pops her eyes open. "What?"

"Well...we got back to the room, and one thing led to another..."

She raises a hand to stop me. "Please. Spare me the details. It's bad enough my little sister's getting some and I'm not."

"Ror..."

"I'm sorry. That was uncalled for. But I thought you decided."

"I did. And I will. But we got to the room, and then . . . you know. He was mad. Really mad, Ror, and he took it out on me."

"Lucky girl."

"Yeah." I clear my throat. "Anyway, I was going to tell him after, but he got a phone call from Dale, which he had to take. It could have been about his dad."

"Right."

I look at my watch. "It's been a while. Maybe I should go back and make sure everything's okay."

Rory nods.

"You okay here?"

"I'm fine. I promise. Just having a little pity party for myself. It'll pass."

"Hey, we've been through a lot. I promise you we'll put Pat Lamone and his high school antics behind us. Donny will help."

"I know he will. I just wish . . ."

"What?"

"I wish it had never come to this, Cal. We took care of it back then, but now it's back to haunt us."

"Only if we let it. Lamone's up to something, and I'm pretty sure he wants money, which he thinks we can get because of my relationship with Donny."

"If that's the case, then why did he tell Donny those lies about us? Wouldn't it have made more sense for him to come to you and threaten to tell Donny unless you paid him off?"

Damn. She's right. And why in hell didn't I come up with

that theory? A wannabe lawyer should do better.

"You're right. I'm not sure why I didn't think of that."

"Because you've had other stuff on your mind," she says. "We both have."

"True enough," I agree. "I'm going to go make sure everything's okay with Donny's dad. I'll check in with you later. Before dinner."

"I'll deal with dinner on my own. You and Donny go out and have a nice dinner alone."

"Rory . . ."

"I insist. Please. I'll just be a third wheel, and I'd rather have room service and a pint of Ben & Jerry's."

"You sure?"

"For God's sake, Callie." She grabs one of the pillows from the bed and throws it at me. "I'm sure. Now get out of here."

I smile. "Thanks, Ror. What about the box, though?"

"Crap. That's something else I need to lay on you. The bank's open tomorrow until noon, but the manager called. They can't get a locksmith here until Monday. I have to stay here in Denver."

"But Donny has to be back in Snow Creek by Monday."

"I know. I guess I'll fly back."

"I'll stay with you."

"No, Cal. This is on me. I was the adult back then."

"No argument. I'll talk to Donny. He'll understand."

I leave and walk the few steps to Donny's and my room, when the door bursts open.

"Callie!" His eyes are circles. "Come on. You've got to help me."

CHAPTER FORTY-ONE

Donny

"What? What is it? Is it your dad?" Callie nearly screams.

"No, no. Dad's fine. I ... God, I'm such a moron. Come on." I grab her arms and nearly drag her toward the elevators. I push the down button. Would the stairs be quicker? We're ten flights up. "Come on!" I push the button incessantly.

Finally, an elevator opens. I rush in, Callie behind me.

"Donny," she says. "What's wrong?"

"I just lost a valuable piece of evidence," I say. "It literally blew away."

"What?"

"It's a long story, Cal. Fuck it all. Just come on. I need your help."

"You want me to get Rory?"

"Yeah, actually. That'd be great. Tell her to meet us outside the hotel right under where our rooms are."

She taps on her phone while I berate myself further. If I hadn't been so weirded out about the possibility of anthrax.

If...

If...

If...

My phone buzzes. Dale. "What?" I say, sounding more cross than I mean to.

"I was looking at the coordinates," he says.

"The coordinates?" A wave of calm settles over me. I laugh. I laugh like a maniac. "I sent you a photo. Of the document."

"Uh . . . yeah. You did. I figured you wanted me to—"

"Dale, I swear to God if you were in this elevator with me right now, I'd plant one right on your mouth."

"Dude, you're freaking me out here."

Relief swarms through me. "Man, you know I hate drugs, but right now I could swallow a whole bottle of downers. I'm on edge, man. Fucking on edge. I almost risked my career, and now, because I'm constantly looking over my shoulder, I nearly cost us everything."

"Slow down, Don. What the hell happened?"

Callie's eyes widen as she listens to me tell the story of the paper flying away with the wind. How I was so freaked out I forgot I'd shot a photo of the damned thing.

"Easy," Dale says when I finally pause. "You need a break from all this."

"No shit."

"Let it go, man. Don't carry the weight of all this on your shoulders. That's a big brother's job."

"Stop protecting me, damn it."

"Touché. Try to enjoy the rest of your stay in Denver. You need to relax. Book a massage or something."

I eye Callie. "I don't want a massage, but I know what I do want."

"I don't need the details, dude. But take the time. We'll jump on this Monday. Do you want me to bring Uncle Joe and Brock in on the new info?"

My stomach jolts. Do I? "I don't know, Dale."

"You still having second thoughts about them?"

"Not about Brock."

"I hear you, but if we bring Brock in, there's no leaving out Uncle Joe."

"I know." I inhale deeply. "Let me think about it. Can this wait until tomorrow?"

"Yeah, but I'm going to check out these coordinates."

"I should be with you."

"Don, come on. You need this time. Take it. Have some fun with your woman. You're wound up, man. I've never seen you like this. It's like you're . . . *me*."

A chuckle erupts from my throat, even though what Dale said is far from amusing. In fact, it's so apt it's frightening.

"All of this . . . It's bringing back a lot of things I prefer not to dwell on."

"I know, Don. I know."

"Sometimes . . ."

I jolt as the elevator doors open.

And the past unfurls before my eyes.

★ ★ ★

The doorbell.

Dale and I are latchkey kids. That's what we're called at school. We were in daycare until Dale turned ten. Daycare was okay, but I was always happy when Mommy came to pick us up in the evening. Then we'd go home, and we'd watch TV while she made supper.

But one night was different. Mommy sat us down and talked to us very seriously.

"They're cutting back my hours at work," she said.

"What's that mean?" I asked.

HELEN HARDT

"It means she won't be working as much," Dale explained.

"That's great!" I gave Mommy a hug. "Then you'll be here more."

She smiled. "Yes, I will be, and I love the fact that I'll be spending more time with you two."

She didn't look happy, though, despite her smile. What was wrong?

"The thing is," she said, "we won't have enough money to keep you in daycare."

"So?" Dale said. "I hate it, anyway."

"I know, honey, and now you're such a big boy, I was thinking you two could stay alone after school."

"I vote for that," Dale said.

"Me too!" I said. I didn't care one way or the other, but if Mommy and Dale said it was okay, I was okay too.

"That means you'll both need these." She pulled two shiny golden keys out of her purse. "They open the front door."

"Can't we just use the garage code?" Dale asked.

Mommy shook her head. "You can, but it's old and it doesn't always work. I want you to have these keys so I know you can get inside." She placed a key into each of our little palms.

I gazed down at mine proudly. My own key! "Can I try it out?"

Mommy laughed. "You're so funny, Donny. Of course you can! Go right ahead!"

"Okay! Lock me out!" I scrambled across the living room and out the front door.

Once I heard Mommy lock the door, I slid my key into the hole and turned. Except it didn't turn. I knocked on the door. "It doesn't work!"

"Try again," Mommy said through the door. "Put the key all

243

the way in, and then pull it out just a tiny bit and then turn it."

I followed her instructions, and that time it worked! I turned the key and opened the door.

"Good job!" Mommy kissed the top of my head.

Dale just shook his head and rolled his eyes.

I stuck out my tongue at him.

That was the day I got my own key.

Today, I'm late coming home because I was talking in class and Mrs. Jones kept me after. Dale didn't wait for me. He's already home, so I don't need my key. The door's already unlocked.

Except that's weird.

Mommy always said to keep it locked when we were home by ourselves. When we let ourselves in, we always lock it back up right away.

I push the door open and—

Someone grabs me.

"Dale!" I shriek.

"Shut up, you little cocksucker," a low voice says.

I don't know what he means. "Where's Dale?"

"I said shut up!"

Then a blow to my head that brings tears to my eyes. "Dale! Dale, help me!"

But Dale can't help me.

No one can.

CHAPTER FORTY-TWO

Callie

Donny's eyes are glossed over, his cheeks pale.

"Baby, what's the matter?"

He walks out of the elevator and leans against the wall. "I'm fine."

"You don't look fine."

"I am. I just had a— I'm not sure what you'd call it. I remembered something from a long time ago."

"A flashback? A repressed memory?"

"Not repressed. It's not like I'd forgotten it. It's just something I never think about. I guess it was a flashback."

My own problems melt away in this moment. All I want to do is help Donny. Ease the pain of whatever's troubling him.

It's like I'm back in a damned cage!

God, those words. What has this beautiful man been through?

"Let's sit down."

"I'm fine, Callie."

"You're not fine. You look like you're about to pass out."

He shakes his head. "I'll be fine. This is a good thing. I thought I'd lost something important, but Dale to the rescue once again."

"Once again? What do you mean?"

"Nothing. Geez."

"Come on." I take his arm and lead him into the sitting area of the hotel lobby. I'm thankful no one else is there so Donny and I can speak freely. "Sit."

"Callie . . ."

"Come on. What will it hurt to sit for a moment and collect yourself?"

He sits. "I don't need to collect myself."

"Though you did sit down." I take a seat beside him. "Talk."

He exhales. "I thought I'd lost an important document. The thing I got out of the safe-deposit box this morning."

"And?" I figured as much from listening to his side of the phone call with Dale, but I want Donny to open up to me.

"I did lose it, but I took a photo of it earlier when I was talking to Dale. But . . . Oh, *shit.*"

"What?"

"The original is out there, flying around in the breeze. I have to find it. I don't want that information to fall into the wrong hands."

"Donny, what's on the paper? Why would it fall into the wrong hands? No one's looking for a lone piece of paper flying around in the wind. It's probably on the ground somewhere right now, being trampled by everyone going to lunch."

"You're right. You're right." He stands. "Still, it wouldn't hurt to take a look."

"All right. If it'll make you feel better." I rise as well. "Tell me what we're looking for."

"Just a regular piece of letter-sized white typing paper. With numbers written on it."

"Handwritten? Typed?"

"Handwritten. Fuck! Handwritten!"

"What's the difference?"

"Handwriting. You can tell a lot about someone by handwriting. I used to use handwriting experts all the time."

"Okay. Good. But you have a picture, so you have the handwriting."

"Yeah. I still want to look for it, though. You're right. It's probably fine, but what if... What if someone finds it, someone who..."

Who what? I want to ask. But I don't. He needs me to be calm. "All right. We'll look for it. Where do we start?"

"The wind was blowing to the east, I think, when it blew out of my hand while I was on the balcony in our room."

"Then we walk east."

Donny and I begin our quest, and I look around. There's not a lot of litter in Denver, which is a good thing. So when I see a piece of white paper, I zero in on it. I lean down and pick it up. But it's only a flyer for an upcoming concert. I scrunch it up and throw it in the next wastebasket that we pass. Once we've walked an entire city block, I tug on Donny's hand. "You want to continue?"

"Yeah."

I honestly feel like this is a losing proposition, but if it makes him feel better, I'm all in.

Another city block, and nothing.

Donny sighs then. "It's gone."

"Donny, I wouldn't worry. The chance that the person who finds it will know what those numbers are is one in a zillion. If anyone finds it at all."

"You'd think so, wouldn't you?"

"What's that supposed to mean?"

"It means that when you're a Steel, sometimes things have

a way of finding you and biting you in the ass."

I'm not sure *how* to respond. I've spent so many years thinking the Steels are golden, and now I know they're not. Financially, of course they are. But money isn't everything. And right now, Donny's fighting some kind of demon—a demon that may be more dangerous than the one I'm fighting myself.

Pat Lamone is no one. In the end, he can't really hurt Rory and me. He can make our lives a little more difficult, but what can he really do to us? We didn't commit a crime, and even if he finagles evidence and tries to prove that we did, the statute of limitations will protect us as much as it will protect him. We can't be sent away. So our reputations get a little bit of trashing. We can handle that. We won't have a choice.

So the Steels aren't golden.

Neither are the Pikes.

Unfortunately, none of that makes me feel any better.

"You want to go back to the room?" I ask Donny.

"I suppose."

"Are you hungry? We could stop for lunch somewhere."

He shakes his head. "I couldn't eat, but if you're hungry, sure."

I haven't been hungry since we ran into Pat Lamone. "Let's go back. If we're hungry later, we can call room service."

"Callie?"

"Yeah?"

"Thanks. For helping me try to find it."

"I'll do anything for you, Donny. You know that, right?"

He nods. "I'd do the same for you. You still have to level with me about what's going on."

"I will," I promise. "Will you do the same?"

"I have. You know everything. The mistakes I've made.

How I let my need for information blind me to my ethics."

"For a hot second," I say. "You fixed it."

"Not before Murphy's place got trashed."

"You'll take care of that."

"Yeah, I will. A Steel always cleans up his own mess."

His words are not lost on me. I believe them. I believe a Steel *does* clean up his own mess.

The Pikes should adhere to that same philosophy.

Rory and I didn't create the mess that we're in. Pat Lamone did. But we added to it. We could have let sleeping dogs lie.

But we were young. Hormonal. Full of anxiety and energy. We didn't let the sleeping dog lie.

And now I fear we will pay the price.

CHAPTER FORTY-THREE

Donny

Callie's presence soothes me. Much like Dale's did during those dark days. Much like Mom's did when Dale and I first came to the ranch.

I've always found others comforting, which is probably why I go outward to deal with stuff while Dale goes inward.

He only needs himself.

Until now.

Me? I've always needed others. It's one of my weaknesses.

I don't *want* to need others.

I don't want to put Callie in that position. She deserves better.

Which is why I'm going to have to let her go.

A vise squeezes my heart. It will kill me. My life will be a shadow without her brightness. But I love her that much. Enough to let her go, to have a life free from my mess.

Yet here she is, her touch a comfort to my soul. Just her presence brings me peace.

But I have Mom for that. I have Dale for that.

They can't give me all that Callie gives me, though, and once, before I free her, I'm going to do what I've been promising.

I'm going to worship her the way she deserves to be worshipped.

"Callie…"

"Yeah?"

"I made reservations at Elway's at seven for us. All of us, including Rory."

"That's sweet of you, but Rory already told me she's staying in for dinner. She wants you and me to have some time."

"She's sure?"

"Yeah. She had a knock-down, drag-out with Raine, and she wants to be alone. Says she has a lot of thinking to do. Plus…she's going to stay in town."

"Why?"

"Oh. I guess I didn't tell you. The bank can't get a locksmith to come tomorrow morning, so we have to wait until Monday. In fact…"

"What?"

"I said I'd stay with her."

"Why?"

"It's a long story." She clears her throat. "I'll tell you. I'll keep my promise. When we get back to the room."

"I'll stay too, then."

"You have to get back. Someone has to be in the office Monday since your mom's not coming in."

"Right." Shit. "Tell you what. I'll fly back tomorrow. Dale can pick me up in Grand Junction. You and Rory can have the car."

"Donny, that's not—"

"I insist."

Plus, I just gave myself a reprieve. I can't break things off with Callie until she and Rory return with my car. It'll give me some time with her tonight and tomorrow. Then I'll break her heart when they return to Snow Creek.

I'm such a dick. But it can't be helped.

Callie sighs. "Fine. And thank you."

"Just be really safe driving home."

"Of course."

"Check in with me each time you stop."

"Donny, Rory and I are both perfectly competent drivers. We drive tractors on the ranch, for God's sake."

"Okay, okay. Humor me, though."

She chuckles lightly. "You're totally adorable. I love you so much."

"I love you too, which is why I want you safe."

Which is why I can't be with her.

I lived through literal hell when I was young. But this—letting Callie go—is going to kill me far worse than that horrid part of my life ever could.

"Let's go upstairs," I say.

"All right. And I'll tell you what's bothering Rory and me. I just hope you don't run away screaming when you find out."

"I won't."

I won't scream. And I won't run away.

Not yet.

★ ★ ★

I attack when we hit the room, kissing her with a mad passion, devouring her as if I'll never get enough.

And I won't.

I'll never get enough.

Because I have to let her go.

But devouring her won't lead to what I yearn to do. I want to go slowly, give her the worship I crave, the worship she deserves.

So I break the kiss.

Her lips are parted, glistening from the kiss.

She's so beautiful. So sexy. So completely wonderful.

How can I do this to her?

Am I being selfish, taking her this one last time, the way I've dreamed of taking her?

"God, Callie…"

"It's okay. Whatever you want to do to me, it's okay. I want what you want."

I believe her. But if she knew what was going on inside my mind, she'd be out of here quicker than a lightning strike.

"I love you so much," I say. "I wish there was a word other than love. It doesn't do my feelings justice. I ache for you, Callie. Please tell me you know that."

"I know, Donny. I feel the same way."

"Whatever happens," I continue, "tell me you'll never forget that."

She swallows audibly. "Donny, please… Don't scare me. I want to tell you everything, but—"

I place two fingers over her soft lips to silence her. "Baby, whatever you have to tell me can wait. Whatever it is, I promise it doesn't matter."

"You can't make a promise like that."

"I just did, and I mean it."

I do. I love her. I don't care what silly secret she's keeping. It truly doesn't matter. I'll still love her, and I have to let her go anyway.

My dick is hard as marble, but I'll do this. For Callie, and for me. I'll take her slowly, enjoy her body, show her the pleasures I haven't yet shown her.

I trail a finger down her silky cheek, along her jawline to

her neck, her shoulder. Those sexy shoulders.

"I'm going to undress you, and if it kills me, I'm going to go slowly. I'm going to show you I'm not some kind of sex maniac who can't wait to get inside you."

"I kind of like that sex maniac who can't wait to get inside me. I've told you that before."

I don't reply. I could rip her clothes off now and fuck her. I'm dying to. My dick is aching to be inside her, gloved in her warmth.

I could do it.

Take my comfort. Take what she's offering.

But she deserves to be the center of *my* attention—not of my dick's attention—at least once.

"I love you, Callie," I say, "and I'm going to make love to you."

And as God is my witness, I may never make love to another woman once I end this.

CHAPTER FORTY-FOUR

Callie

I'm nearly breathless from Donny's words alone.

He moves with me, walking us toward the bed, where he gently pushes me so I'm sitting. He removes my boots and socks, discarding them, and then he pulls me into a stand once more.

He kneels before me and unbuttons and unzips my jeans as I suck in yet another breath.

Slowly, he peels the jeans from my legs, trailing his fingers over each inch of my flesh. My thighs quiver, and goose bumps erupt all over me. A chill. Then a warm flame. A chill again.

The tickle in my pussy intensifies. This will be a slow burn. Not what either of us is used to, but as much as I want him inside me, I relish this.

I relish the slowness of it all.

I step out of my jeans when they reach my ankles, and Donny places them next to my boots and socks.

"Your feet are beautiful, Callie," he says, leaning down and kissing the tops of them.

When he said he was going to kiss every inch of me, he clearly wasn't kidding.

I gasp when he slides his tongue up my calf and thigh, until he gets to my pussy, which is still covered by my plain white panties. I brought a thong, but today, to go to the bank and deal with the past, I wore plain cotton panties.

Donny doesn't seem to mind, though.

He places his mouth right on my pussy through my panties and simply breathes. The warmth of his breath, even through the cotton, sends me reeling. A soft sigh escapes my throat. He continues this for a moment, and then he stands and replaces his mouth with his fingers, massaging my clit through my panties. His lips meet mine in a tender kiss. A peck. Another. And then he turns me around, my back to him, and he grabs my ass cheeks, squeezing ever so gently.

He kisses the back of my neck, pushing one sleeve of my T-shirt over to bare one shoulder.

"God, your shoulders, Callie." He gives my shoulder a tender bite and then another. Then he turns me back around and kisses my lips tenderly once more.

So different from our normal kisses. Our kisses are usually raw, not gentle like these. But the passion is still there. All the passion, all the love.

His lips slide over mine, parting them, and then his tongue. Again, so gentle.

My nipples are so hard they ache. My pussy is so wet it's throbbing. I quiver all over, still wearing my T-shirt and panties and bra.

I cup both of his cheeks, trailing my fingers over his blond stubble. I run my hands down his neck, over his broad and beefy shoulders. Then I reach for his collar, start to unbutton his shirt, but he brushes my hand away.

"No. Let me do it all."

His voice is gentle and soft but no less commanding. I drop my arms to my sides, the urge to touch him still so great that I have to will my arms to stay put.

"I want to touch you too," I say.

"I know, baby. Please. Let me do this."

It's the *please* that gets me. He wants me. That much is apparent by the bulge pressing into my belly.

As much as I yearn to pull out his dick, drop to my knees, and suck him, I steel myself. He wants this. And so do I.

He continues to kiss me, still gentle. I'm amazed at his fortitude. So many times our kisses have led to a quick, hard fuck. What is different this time?

I don't dwell on it. Instead, I surrender to the moment. I kiss him back, melting into him. He slides his hands down my neck, chest, squeezing my still clothed breasts and thumbing my nipples, which are already hard as green berries. I deepen the kiss, unable to hold back, and he responds. Our tongues twirl together, our teeth clash, but still his hands stay gentle, cupping my breasts and strumming over my nipples.

He moves one hand then, trails it down my abdomen, and reaches inside my panties to my mound. He slides lower, gliding through my folds.

I break the kiss with a gasp.

"You're so wet, baby."

I simply sigh in response.

Still, he stays gentle, using my own wetness as lubrication as he massages my clit.

I undulate into him, try desperately to ride his fingers, but he stays put, his gentle determination nearly blinding me with lust.

"Please, Donny."

"You'll get everything you need. I promise." He drops to his knees again, removing his fingers from inside my panties and kissing my mound through the cotton. Then he inhales. "You smell like orange blossoms in the summer breeze. God, everything about you, Callie. Everything about you is perfection."

His words make me shiver. Is it possible to orgasm from words alone? I'm beginning to think that it may be.

He grips the sides of my hips gently and then, also slowly, pushes the cotton panties over them. He stops when they're midway down my thighs. Then he leans his nose and mouth into my mound once more and inhales again.

He flicks his tongue over my clit, and I can't help myself. I grab his head of thick blond hair and push him closer into me. He doesn't stop me, thank God. But he doesn't change the speed of his tongue either. Soft and subtle licks over my clit. Gentle and slow . . . and I'm being driven more insane by the second.

"Donny. Please. I need you."

A groan is his response as he licks my clit again, nearly sending me reeling.

I'm in heaven. Or rather . . . right on the edge of heaven. I want to come so badly, but I need more. I need raw Donny. I need feral Donny.

He slides his tongue down my inner thigh, and then he blows on the wetness. My God, so much feeling overwhelms me. The physical feeling, and then the emotional feeling inside me. It's all too much. I'm being slowly driven crazy, slowly driven through a kaleidoscope of flashing colors and lights.

He moves back to my panties then, sliding them the rest of the way down, all the way to my ankles, where I step out of them.

I'm naked from the waist down now, perfect for him to

slide his cock inside me. All he needs to do is lift me in his arms and set me down so I can fill the aching emptiness.

Instead, though, he slides his tongue over the top of my foot, my calf, and then my thigh once more. This time he grips the bottom of my T-shirt and slides it slowly upward until my bra is exposed. He kisses the tops of my breasts. He deftly unclasps my bra in the back. I raise my arms as he pulls the T-shirt off me, and then he removes my bra, discarding both on top of the pile of clothes.

He sighs then. "My God, you're beautiful."

I'm already warm all over, but flames seem to char me. I'm on fire, and my pussy is so ready. So ready for his big cock inside me. So ready for one of his good swift fucks that makes us both complete.

He's got me aching, which is obviously his plan.

"Callie, your body... It's so luscious."

"So is yours," I reply. "Let me see it, Donny. Let me undress you. Please."

He shakes his head before kissing me again. Still gently but still with passion.

He slides one hand over my cheek and down my neck to caress my shoulder. Then to one breast, covering it gently and then giving it a slight squeeze. My nipples ache for him, but damn him, he leaves them alone. Continues the kiss. He begins walking gently back toward the bed until my knees hit the mattress and I sit. His lips slide from mine and over my cheek to my ear, where he nips my lobe.

"Lie down, baby."

I obey. I don't even think about it. I lie on the bed, and I close my eyes and wait.

And I wait.

A moment later, I open my eyes.

He's staring at me. Taking me in. His hazel eyes smolder, and I swear I can see flames in them. Orange flames dancing through the green and gold.

"Please," I say. "I *ache* for you."

"Quiet," he says softly. "Let me look at you, Callie. Let me admire your beauty. Let me imprint it on my memory."

His words confuse me. Imprint it on his memory? Is he planning to . . . ? No, of course not. We're in love.

No one walks away from love.

He continues staring at me, his gaze never wavering from mine, his eyes still burning.

"I'm going to start at your pretty little toes, Callie, and I'm going to kiss you everywhere."

He moves down, near the foot of the bed, still fully clothed, and I wonder . . .

"Donny . . ."

"Yes, my love?"

"Please. Take off your clothes. I want you to do what you want to do to me. I long for it, but I want to look at your body too. I want to . . . imprint it on my memory."

His eyes widen slightly. Only slightly, but I notice. I notice everything about him. That's how in tune I am with him. How in *love* I am with him.

He smiles then. Loosens his tie. Unbuttons his shirt, parting the two halves to expose the tank he wears underneath. He removes his tie, his shirt, the tank. I gawk as I take in his amazing hairless chest, his bronze skin, his perfect abs.

"You're the most beautiful man I've ever seen."

His cheeks pink slightly. He's blushing. Donny Steel is blushing. Because of my words. They're certainly true. All those years I crushed on his older brother, when in reality, Donny is a god among gods.

He unclasps his belt then and slowly removes it. Then the button and zipper on his pants. He slides them down, revealing his huge hard cock.

I gape at him. I can't help myself. Though I've seen it before, it seems more majestic today.

"I want to kiss you all over too," I say.

"Later," he says. "This is *your* time, Callie."

I whimper. "But Donny..."

He kicks off his shoes and then removes his pants, underwear, and socks. "No buts. Let me do this for you. Please."

I moan softly. I have no words for this man. No words for this man who only wants to please me. I love what he's doing. He's got me so on edge. But my pussy... I'm so wet and so ready. So ripe. If I were a tomato, I'd have fallen off the vine by now.

And when I meet his smoldering gaze, I know we've only just begun.

CHAPTER FORTY-FIVE

Donny

I can't stop looking at her.

She's flushed pink all over, her breasts swollen, her inner thighs wet with her cream. My dick is rock-hard, and though I'm dying to plunge inside her and fuck her, I'm determined.

This is what I've wanted all along, what she deserves. Because of my aching need for her, I haven't been able to give it to her.

But I have one last chance to do so now, and I'm not going to blow it.

I sit down on the bed and continue to scan her beautiful body. Her cheeks are rosy, her lips swollen. Her chest rosy as well, and nipples . . . Those luscious nipples. They're dark pink and erect, the areolas scrunched up tightly. Her belly is flat with the perfect amount of curve, and her mound, so neatly trimmed. Just a tiny portion of her pink pussy visible. I resist the urge to yank her legs apart and thrust inside her.

I thread my fingers through my hair, gathering all my willpower. For it will take every last shred. Shall I begin at the top, or shall I begin at the bottom? Does it even matter?

Her toes are still painted red. So very sexy. I glide my fingers over the instep of one foot, and she jerks.

"Ticklish?" I ask.

"A little."

I gentle my caress. I want to tickle her, but more than that, I want to give her the sensual experience of being touched and licked all over. I lean down and swipe my tongue over the instep of her foot.

She shudders. Sighs escape her throat.

I kiss the top of her big toe, and then I kiss each other toe in rapid succession. I move to the other foot, repeat, kissing each toe. Then I massage the arch of each foot with my thumbs.

A soft moan rumbles from her throat.

"Even your feet are pretty, Callie. You're the whole package. The whole perfect package wrapped in beautiful milky flesh, just for me."

"So are you," she pants. "Perfect for me." Then her eyes flutter closed.

I'm tempted to tell her to open them, to watch everything I do to her. But I don't want to make any demands of her right now. All I want to do is worship her body.

I kiss the tops of both her feet and then her ankles, working my way up her calves to her knees. Then her muscular thighs to her glorious mound. So easily could I spread her legs, take that delicious honey between them.

But if I do that, it will all be over too soon. I won't be able to resist the urge to stick my erection in her and take my own pleasure.

So I stay strong. I move past her beautiful pussy and kiss her soft belly.

Her flesh is like silk under my lips and tongue. I look. I kiss. I nip. I nibble. Touching as I go, caressing her curvy belly and then her beautiful breasts.

Those hard nipples beckon. Each breast fits perfectly in

my palm, and then ... finally ... I take one nipple between my lips.

Callie sucks in a breath and arches her back.

"You like that, baby?"

"God, yes. Suck my nipples. Please."

I will. I'll do everything she wants. But I'll do it slowly. I suck lightly on one nipple and gently run my fingers over the other.

"More," she sighs.

I suck harder—but only slightly. Then I release the nipple and kiss it—one, two, three times. I flick my tongue over and around it and then kiss her areola, the top of her breast, all while still very lightly caressing the other nipple.

She arches her back again. Raises her hips. Yes, I know what she wants. I want it too, more than she could possibly imagine.

But damn it, I will be strong.

I take the nipple between my lips once more, this time tugging harder. Her response is a soft gasp. I suck again, again, again. This time I pinch the other nipple lightly.

Another soft gasp and then, "Oh!"

She's so responsive, my Callie. I could spend the whole day on her breasts alone. I continue sucking one nipple, pinching the other, and then ... I can't help myself. I slide my free hand between her legs.

"Oh, yes," she sighs.

I touch her clit only lightly, delving farther beneath to feel her wetness against my fingers. My cock hardens even further. God, I'm as hard as I've ever been. And I ache for release.

No!

No, no, no!

I will not fuck her. Not yet.

I let her nipple drop from my lips, and then I bring my fingers to my mouth. Just a tiny lick. A taste of her sweet cream. That's all I need. Then I'll resume.

She opens her eyes then, just in time to see me swirl my tongue around my fingers.

"That's hot," she says softly.

"And delicious," I reply. And God, it is. Peaches, apples, oranges. I love them all, but none are as sweet as Callie's pussy.

"There's a lot more where that came from." She smiles.

"We'll get there, baby. I promise, we'll get there."

I steel myself once more. Her words make me want to be inside her, to feel her heat around me.

But instead, I go back to her breasts. I switch to her other nipple, kissing it, sucking it, while working the first with my fingers.

Again her back arches, her hips rise.

She's so ready for me. Even now, I smell her musk, her sweet citrus tang. It lingers on my tongue.

I could kiss these nipples forever.

"God, you're beautiful," I rasp out against her sweet flesh.

She sighs. I drop her nipple then and kiss my way up to those beautiful lips. Again, I kiss her softly. Even though I want to shove my tongue in her mouth and take her in one of those raw kisses we're both used to.

I have to keep it soft and gentle. Otherwise I'll end up fucking her.

She swirls her tongue with mine, and I love every bit of it. The taste of her mouth, the texture of her tongue, and the inside of her cheeks, all of it. All of this kiss is everything. Everything I ever wanted, everything I ever needed, everything

I ever dreamed of I find in this kiss with Callie.

I can't help myself. I maneuver my hard cock between her thighs, let it dangle against her wet folds. It takes every ounce of strength I possess not to shove it inside her, but I don't. I simply slide it through the wetness, relish this foretaste of the feast to come.

Then I move it away and break the gentle kiss. "I'm going to turn you over," I tell her. "There's a whole other side to your body I haven't worshipped yet."

She moans. With her help, I gently move her over so she's facedown, her cheek against the pillow, her hair splayed into a glorious light-brown curtain.

I gaze at her then. Feasting on her with my eyes as I did when she was lying on her back. Her lovely milky shoulders, her sexy back, her gorgeous and perfectly shaped ass, and finally, those long and shapely legs.

If I didn't have the urges of my cock driving me, I could gaze at her for hours upon hours and never grow tired of the sight. But my physical body takes over, and I fist my dick and give it a couple of good pulls.

Damn. Not the best idea I ever had. I could so easily slide between those beautiful ass cheeks, take her from behind.

And damn, I'll do it, but—I gnash my gums and grit my teeth—not before I'm done worshipping her amazing body.

I want to slide my tongue between her cheeks. Give her that rimming that's been on my mind since we first met. But if I go near her sweet pussy, this will all be over within seconds. So I climb on top of her, slide my lips down the curve of her neck.

And I push my cock into the small of her back.

It doesn't satisfy me, but it staves off the most primal of my urges.

Her neck, oh yes, her neck. Soft and silky and milky. I kiss her, lick her, give her tiny nips with my teeth. Then I move upward slightly, tug on her earlobe, nibble on the outer shell of her ear.

Then I dip inside, fuck her ear with my tongue.

And that gets her roused.

She sighs beneath me, moves her hips upward, searching...

Searching for what I so want to give her at this moment.

I clamp my lips to her shoulder and suck, trying to ease the ache in my cock.

I suck hard.

Yeah, I'll mark her. Mark her as mine. The idea overwhelms with yearning. I want to mark her.

Always.

She'll always be mine.

Even when she's not.

No. Can't go there right now. Need to remain calm. Need to focus.

Make slow, sweet love to her. To Callie. To my Callie. My life.

I let go of her shoulder. Yes, that will leave a mark. I can't bring myself to be sorry.

I kiss her lightly across both shoulders while I caress her sides, running my hands up and down her hips, the cheeks of her ass.

I slide my fingers between her crack, massage her tight little hole.

God...

I'll never get to take that ass. I can't do it today. She's not ready.

Damn.

Damn it all to hell.

Someone else will—

I whip the thought from my mind.

Can't go there now. Concentrate on the task at hand.

And what a sensational task it is.

I kiss down to the small of her back. I imagine a tramp stamp there, identifying her as mine.

Property of Donny Steel.

I've never been a tattoo freak, but man, I want those words tattooed on Callie's body. Even now, knowing I can't keep her, I want my mark there.

I kiss the cheeks of her ass, give her little nips.

I know what I want. I know what I need. I know what she needs.

"Move your knees forward," I tell her. "I want that ass in the air."

She obeys me without question. I didn't want to make any demands of her today, but I need to do this. I've been aching to give her a good ass licking since I noticed her.

I stare for a moment—that milky ass in the air. Then I grip her hips, spread her cheeks, and I slide my tongue between them.

My dick is throbbing now. If only I could slide it into that tight little hole.

Can't think about that now. Can't.

I slither my tongue between her cheeks again, and then once more. She moans beneath me. And I wonder . . . I wonder if anyone has ever been inside this heaven.

No. Can't go there.

I make my tongue rigid then, into a point, and I slightly nudge into her hole.

She gasps beneath me, but she doesn't stop me. So I continue. Massage the hole with my tongue and then slightly probe the center. Yes, good rimming. Damn good rimming. I'm good at it, and I like doing it.

I'll come back to her ass when I'm done kissing the rest of her. Definitely come back.

She may be able to take a finger, and if she can take a finger . . .

Perhaps I'll get my deepest desire after all.

CHAPTER FORTY-SIX

Callie

Donny's tongue is in my ass. But oddly, I'm not embarrassed. In fact, I want him there. I want him everywhere. All over my body. Kissing me, licking me, taking me.

I yearn for his dick inside me. Every other time we've done this, he hasn't been able to wait. I've loved that. So I feel a strange loss. The fact that he can resist me—does that mean he's getting tired of me?

Every other time, when he swore he'd worship my body like this, he couldn't help himself. He got inside me quickly, thrusted, took me hard and fast.

I loved it every time. Every. Single. Time.

But his soft tongue...gliding slowly between my ass cheeks. Poking my hole. Probing it. No one's ever done that to me before, and it feels...

It feels...

Heavenly.

I wouldn't have thought so. In fact, I'm not sure the thought ever occurred to me. But it's hot. Very, very hot.

"You're so beautiful, Callie," he says against my flesh.

Those words. He says them a lot, yet I never tire of hearing them. I never tire of the rasp of his voice, his groan, his growl.

Then his tongue is at it again, licking, probing. He stops every couple of seconds, nibbles on the flesh of my ass. Then he goes back to work.

Amazing. Such an amazing feeling that I never thought possible.

Time to stop thinking, Callie. Time to start feeling. Enjoying. Don't worry that he isn't fucking you hard and fast. Just enjoy the slow buildup. The slow tease. The slow burn.

The jabbing. The silkiness of his tongue sliding in my most intimate place. I feel ... I want ... I ... wonder ...

What would his cock feel like inside my ass?

And I want it. I want it more than anything. Something that's never been on my radar before now, and I want it as much as I want my next breath.

"Donny ..."

"Yeah, baby?"

"I want you to ..."

"Hmm?"

"Put your ... You know ..."

"Mmm." He nibbles on the flesh right next to my asshole. "I'm afraid I don't know, Callie. You're going to have to say it."

"I want you to fuck me there. I never thought I'd want it, but I do, Donny. I want it."

He gives my cheek a quick nip. "I would like that very much."

"Then do it. Please."

"I wish I could. But we're not set up for that, Callie. I didn't bring any lubricant with me."

"So? Your saliva or something."

"God ..." His voice is a growling rasp. "How I wish I could. But it can be tough the first time, and I don't want to hurt you."

"Please. Hurt me."

Even *I* don't believe the words that just came out of me. Hurt me? Seriously? Of course I don't want him to hurt me. Though the spanking hurt…in a deliciously amazing way. I want this so badly. And I trust him. I trust Donny. Which means…

I have to trust that he knows what's best for me. He's clearly much more experienced with anal sex than I am. Not difficult, since I'm not experienced at all.

"I'm sorry, Callie. You have no idea how much I wish I could."

"It's okay."

"I need to prepare you, and I don't have the tools to do that."

"Tools?"

"Let's not talk about this now. I'm not done worshipping this body." He slides his tongue between my ass cheeks once more.

I quiver beneath his touch. "I never thought this could feel so amazing."

His reply is a growl.

He continues licking me, and with each swipe of his tongue, I become more on edge, more ready, more and more in love.

I'm lost inside myself. Lost in the fantasy of tongues and teeth. But my eyes shoot open when something more rigid pushes against my asshole.

"See what I mean?" Donny says. "That's my finger. I'd love to slide it inside you right now."

"Do it." I grit my teeth.

"Not yet. Not yet, baby."

He moves forward then, away from my ass, kissing the small of my back and then upward, to my shoulder blades. He sucks on my neck again, and I know he's leaving a bruise. I want the bruise. I don't care if I look like a schoolgirl who spent the afternoon necking under the bleachers. I need those marks on me. Donny's marks. He's making me his.

"Are you ready?" he whispers against my ear.

"Always," I say on a sigh.

He slides onto his side and pulls me against him, spoon style. His cock is between my legs, its warm length sliding through my folds. I'm so wet. So wet and ready.

"Please, Donny. Please."

"I'm going to go slowly. I'm going to fuck you slowly, Callie. This time, you're going to feel every part of me touch every part of you."

I already do feel every part of him inside me when he takes me. But I understand what he means. He's going to go slowly, inch by inch, so I can take in every tiny nuance.

As much as I ache for a hard fuck, I brace myself for his leisurely invasion. I already know I will love it.

He pulls me into him, lifting one thigh slightly and then . . .

He glides inside me in a slow hard thrust.

Pleasure erupts out of my throat. And I understand. I understand why he wanted to do this.

It's so different. Such a new and vibrant sensation. He holds himself inside me for a moment, as time seems to suspend itself. I feel so complete, even more complete than I have in our previous lovemaking sessions. Because right now, as he's deep inside me, he's touching my heart. He's touching my soul. This goes so far beyond the physical. It's spiritual. Ethereal.

It's everything and nothing all at once, all wrapped into our bodies joined as one.

I could stay this way forever. The world can go on around us, as Donny and I just lie here on the bed, his cock embedded so fully into my body. Let the world go on, but let us stay here trapped in the time warp. The time warp of love and peace, desire and tranquility.

I push my ass backward, trying to embed him in me farther, deeper. If only his entire body could take in my entire body. I want to crawl into his skin with him, truly *become* him.

I let out a long sigh, and then he withdraws. I cry out at the loss, but then he's inside me again after another long slow thrust.

And I'm back. Back in that wondrous place of completion. Stars burst before my eyes. I haven't climaxed, but I don't care. Nothing is better than this. Nothing. Nothing in the whole world.

He pulls out again slowly. Slides back in.

Sounds come from my throat. Maybe some words too. I make no sense of any of it. I don't have to. Sense isn't necessary here. Only desire, emotion, raw feeling. Logic doesn't matter. Nothing matters. Only this wave of emotion and sweetness and pure, pure love.

I'm floating now. Floating above the bed, or so it seems. The comfort of the mattress has wrapped around us, cloaking us in warmth and love.

Again he pulls out, and again he pushes back in.

Slowly, slowly, slowly . . .

"God, Callie. How have we missed out on this before?"

"I don't know. It's amazing, Donny. Pure rapture."

He embeds himself inside me once more. "I want so much

to take you. To jam my cock inside you and release. But this . . .
I've never . . ."

"Never . . . what?"

"I've never felt like this before. It's never been like this.
Not with anyone. And it never will be again." He kisses my
shoulder, the side of my neck. "God, Callie, I never thought I
could love like this."

I sigh into him.

And I love him all the more.

CHAPTER FORTY-SEVEN

Donny

I grit my teeth. I'm lost. So lost. Lost inside Callie's body, and I don't want to be found.

An image expands in my mind—Callie and me, alone. Somewhere far from Colorado, where there are no mysteries, no secrets.

Only the two of us. The two of us and our love.

I wish. I wish so hard.

I'm not ready for this to be over. Not even slightly ready.

Quickly I withdraw from her body.

"Donny?"

"It's okay, baby. Let me love you."

"I think that's what you were doing."

"Remember when I promised you you're not a one-orgasm woman?"

"You did. I hate to have to prove you wrong."

"I hate to have to prove *you* wrong."

I move on top of her and crush my lips to hers. This time it's not a gentle kiss. It's a raw and taking kiss, like our normal kisses. I relish the inside of her mouth, her silky tongue, her sugary flavor. I could kiss her forever, but despite that, I break the kiss and move down her body, stopping briefly at her nipples to suck each one, but then down her belly to her mound, where I spread her legs.

"I'm going to eat you. I'm going to eat you and suck every ounce of juice out of you, Callie. I'm going to make you come. And then I'm going to make you come again. And again. And I won't stop until you beg me to."

"Donny, I'm just not—"

"Shh. We'll see about that." I close my eyes for a moment and inhale her citrusy musk. She's so wet, so ready, and my dick—still hard as a rock, of course—throbs between my legs. So easy . . . It would be so easy to cram it back inside her and take my own pleasure.

But I made a promise. A promise I'm going to fulfill.

I may never get the chance to take Callie's sweet ass, but I do have the chance to prove to her that she's capable of more than one orgasm.

I inhale again and then open my eyes. I gaze at the sweet pink pussy before me. So beautiful and so perfect. I could stare at her forever.

I slowly slide my tongue between her folds, lap up some cream. Savor it on my tongue.

Then I close my lips around her clit and suck softly, gently. She undulates beneath me, arching her back, raising her hips. I kiss her inner thighs, give her a few quick love bites. Resisting the urge to mark her again.

Then I decide to mark her anyway. I've already marked her neck, and no one will see her inner thighs. I suck her flesh hard into my mouth. She sighs, grabbing the bedcovers in her fists.

Then I return to her pussy. I shove my tongue into her heat, withdraw, and then again. Her cream slides over my tongue, down my throat. When I return to her clit, I suck on it again softly, flick my tongue over it, caress it with tiny kisses.

"God, Donny, please."

"All in good time, baby."

I begin again. I lick her and lick her and lick her, paying only minimal attention to her clit, until finally . . . finally . . . it's time. I shove two fingers inside her and suck her clit hard.

Her orgasm is immediate, and she clamps over my fingers, squeezes her thighs around my head.

Her moans, her soft sighs, her unintelligible words—all of it swirls around us in heated bliss. I move my fingers in and out of her, finding her rhythm and cadence, swirling them, scissoring them, making sure I pay a lot of attention to that soft spot on the anterior.

I wait for the orgasm to subside so I can begin again, but the contractions don't stop. As I work her, she continues to come.

She may not be multiply orgasmic, but her orgasm can last forever.

This is what I'll show her today.

I suck on her clit, and she convulses again. She's so wet now that I can add a third finger, forcing her open, taking her body with mine.

My dick is itching to get back inside her, but if I do that, her orgasm will eventually stop.

As her contractions start to wane once more, I flip her over like a pancake. She gasps.

But before she can say anything, my tongue is sliding through her pussy folds from behind. And then I jab my fingers back into her.

The explosion increases again, and this time, as I

massage her clit, I lick her asshole as well.

"Donny. Oh my God."

Moments pass, moments of unending harmony, until I flip her back over onto her back and take care of her clit once more. The nerve center of the female body. The only body part that was fashioned solely for pleasure. It's a magic button that can take a woman into the throes of ecstasy.

She's still going. That orgasm. That unending, beautiful orgasm.

"Please."

"Keep going," I say between her legs.

"But I'm not… I can't…"

"You are… and you can…" I move back to her pussy.

Her thighs clamp around my head again, but I wonder…

She's so, so turned on, so… I move my fingers out of her for a moment, lubricate the index finger of my other hand with the cream—

I push her thighs forward, suck on her clit, massage her G-spot… and probe my lubed finger over her tight little asshole.

She gasps. I stop. I wait for her to tell me no as I continue to eat her. She doesn't say no. I push slowly again, this time breaching her tight rim. She gasps again. And again, I wait.

She doesn't say no. Should I ask?

Asking would make me move my mouth away from her pussy. But I owe her this. I need to hear her say it.

I lift my head. "Callie?"

"It's okay. Do what you want."

"All I needed."

I push my tongue back into her pussy and slide my finger past the tight rim of her hole.

"Oh my God!" Her contractions increase.

Nice. So nice. She's responding to the new stimulation. I knew she would. Makes me want her all the more . . . want what I'll never have.

Callie Pike. My soul mate.

The woman who means the world to me.

The woman I have to let go.

God, no!

Can't go there. Not right now. Not while this incredible woman is coming under my mouth and hands and fingers.

She continues grasping the comforter, lifting her hips, grinding against my mouth, my fingers.

And I know.

I know she's had just about all she can take.

Which means I want to give her more.

And I can give her that now. I remove my finger from her ass, swipe her pussy with my tongue, give her clit a quick kiss, and then, in a flash, I'm on top of her with my cock inside her warm and inviting pussy.

Sweet, sweet heaven.

I meet her gaze. Her amber eyes are flaming.

The color of flames.

The color of . . .

The ring from the safe-deposit box.

I don't know where it came from. I don't know whose it was or is. But I know one thing.

It belongs to Callie. It was forged for her. No one else could ever wear it.

It will be my gift to her.

My goodbye gift.

Emotions overtake me. This can't be. No, it can't be our last time.

I slow down my thrusts.

As she whimpers. "Donny, please."

But I must go slowly. I must savor this. I must savor *her*. "I love you," I say softly. "I love you so much."

"I love you too," she gasps. "Always. Always, Donny. There's no one else for me. No one else in the world."

Her words spike into my heart. The truth of them. The utter truth of them. She means them with all her heart, and they're no less true for me.

I can't be with this woman, but I know there will never be anyone else for me. Not ever. My womanizing days are over. I'll never be a husband. A father.

None of that matters anymore. Without Callie, it's all meaningless.

I open my mouth to profess my love once more, but my climax sneaks up on me, and I release, emptying into her body. Emptying into her soul.

This orgasm is so complete, so necessary, that for a moment, I almost feel like I've been propelled out of my own body. My spirit looks down from above the room. I see myself, the tan of my skin, the muscles of my thighs and back. And I see Callie. Beneath me, her eyes open and meeting my gaze. The utter trust in her eyes. Trust and love and eternal devotion.

Then I'm back in my body with a forceful *thud*, easing out of her and moving to one side.

She turns toward me, her gaze questioning. "Donny?"

"God, I love you," I say, my arm over my forehead. Sweat pours out of me.

"I love you too. That was...amazing. Except it was so much more than that. It was...spectacular. It was..."

"Doesn't exist," I say absently.

"What? What do you mean by that?"

"Sorry. A word. A word to describe it doesn't exist. It was . . . kaleidoscopic. Except that's not right either. It connotes only visual. Euphoric. Still not right. It means intense excitement and happiness. Not enough."

"You could invent a word." She smiles. "Like lawyers do, as you told me."

God, she's fucking adorable. The joking we shared, when life was a little less complicated. Before my father was shot, before I breached my ethics, before I brought Callie into this mess . . . Before everything.

How can I get along without her now?

I clutch her to me, our bodies as close as two can be without actually being joined by the act itself. I inhale the sweet fragrance of her hair, slide my lips over the silk of her neck.

I imprint it all on my mind—all that is Callie Pike—and I make a silent vow.

I'll fix whatever's worrying her. I'll make it all go away. I'll secretly fund her family's ranch and winery. Rory and Jesse's music. Maddie's college.

And Callie's law school.

I'll do it all.

I can't have her, but I'll make sure she has everything she deserves.

CHAPTER FORTY-EIGHT

Callie

We miss our dinner engagement and spend the evening and night in each other's arms, falling in and out of slumber.

When I finally open my eyes to a light streaming in, I turn toward Donny. He's awake. Staring at me.

"Hey, you," I say.

"Hey, baby." He trails his finger over my cheek and threads his fingers through my hair.

My body is used up. So beautifully used up. "Donny..."

"Yeah?"

"I'd like to try..."

"Try what, baby?"

"You know. From behind."

He smiles, his eyes crinkling in that adorable way, yet something in their hazel depths seems almost... sad.

"You mean anal sex?"

Have I upset him? Why does he look so sad? "I'm sorry I brought it up."

"Why? I already told you I'd love that, Callie."

"Then why do you look so..." *Sad.* I can't say the word. I'm afraid of what it might mean.

"I just... I don't want to leave you."

I touch his cheek. It's slightly chilled, which I find odd.

"You don't have to. I'll drive back with you. Rory can—"

He places two fingers over my lips. "No. Rory needs you here."

"Donny, I should tell you—"

This time his lips stop my words. He presses them against mine in a soft kiss. "Not yet. Let's not ruin what we have left of today with all of our other problems. I can promise you this, Callie. Whatever they are, they don't matter to me."

"I know that. I trust you. But I—"

Again with his fingers. "Shh."

Then he leans forward and replaces his fingers with his lips, kissing me slowly. It's gentle again, like it was last night. Gentle and sweet, yet so full of passion.

I revel in it, melt into him, until—

My stomach lets out a loud growl.

Donny breaks the kiss and chuckles. "I didn't feed you last night."

"You didn't hear me complaining."

"Nor was I. In fact, I haven't been all that hungry lately."

"Neither have I. Although my stomach seems to disagree."

"Tell you what. Let's jump in the shower and get dressed. Then you and I will go get Rory, and I'll take you out to a fabulous breakfast."

"I still don't feel very hungry."

"Your stomach obviously does. You and I both need to eat, no matter what else is happening in our lives. Without food, we won't be able to keep up our strength."

I nod, slide off the bed, and pad into the bathroom. I take care of business quickly and then start the shower. I run a brush through my long hair and can't help a giggle at my reflection in the mirror. Those hickeys on my neck from

Donny. No one ever gave me hickeys back in high school. Now I'm really too old to be having them, but I don't care. I love them. I'll know that he was there. I'll cherish the damned things.

I hop into the shower and let the warmth flow over my hair and down my back. A few minutes later, Donny joins me. He pulls me toward him, and we stand under the rain, the water sloshing over our slick bodies.

His dick is hard, but he doesn't attempt to do anything. He seems satisfied to just hold me, and frankly, it's working for me as well. Last night was amazing. Twelve hours of on and off lovemaking. And though I can't say he was right about me being multiply orgasmic, he did make my orgasm last for what seemed like forever. Then, after I dozed off for an hour or minutes—I don't even know—he brought me to another orgasm. And then another. All slow and sweet, just like he promised.

Did I miss the fast, hard fucks? Yes, but there's no reason to. We'll have it again. Just like we'll have slow again. I have so much to look forward to.

None of it matters to me, Callie. His words . . . and I believe him. I have nothing to fear. No matter what Rory and I did in the past, I know it won't have any bearing on Donny's and my love.

Donny and I finally unclench after about ten minutes, and we gently scrub each other clean. I leave the shower first, wrapping my hair in a towel and then folding another towel around my body. Donny turns off the faucet, and I hand him a towel.

His eyes still look so sad. I kiss his stubbled cheek. "You okay?"

He pulls me to him, only our two towels separating us. He kisses the top of my head. "Everything's fine, my love."

CHAPTER FORTY-NINE

Donny

Except the words are a lie.
Everything's *not* fine.
Everything will never be fine again.

CHAPTER FIFTY

Callie

Monday morning, Rory and I leave the hotel and walk to the bank. Rory talks to the manager we saw Friday, Mr. Keats. When he returns, he looks glum.

"It'll be another few minutes. The locksmith is on her way."

I nod, suppressing a shiver.

I miss Donny. Sleeping without him in the hotel bed the last two nights seemed all wrong. We never made it to the breakfast he had planned, and each time I tried to tell him about Pat Lamone, he shushed me. Said he wanted just me until he had to leave for Denver. So after our shower, we headed back to bed and held each other. He couldn't get a flight for Sunday, so a few hours later, I drove him to the airport, and Rory and I made it through the rest of the weekend in a tidal wave of anxiety.

"Nervous?" Rory asks.

I nod again. The effort required to eke out a *yes* seems too great.

"What do we do if it's not there?"

"It has to be there, Ror. It has to. You had to show your ID to get near the box."

"Yeah, but so what?"

For the third time, I nod. I know exactly what she's thinking, because it's the same thing I'm thinking. Anyone with enough money—for example, the Steels—could get into that box. Flash enough green, and you can get anything.

Time moves slowly. My skin feels clammy, and my throat has a lump forming in it that's the size of Kansas. I take my phone out of my purse, fiddle with it, and then shove it back in. I don't care about emails right now. I don't care about anything.

I'm missing a day of work, but since Donny is my boss and he knows where I am, I guess that doesn't matter.

Except that it matters to me.

All of this matters to me.

Donny was weird when he left Saturday afternoon. We hardly talked. He gave me a searing kiss before he left, and he told me he loved me.

But his eyes—those beautiful golden-green eyes... They still looked sad. They still looked sunken. They still looked... all wrong.

Despite our amazing time in bed, things aren't right between us.

I feel it.

And so does he.

What will become of us?

Too much to think about. Too damned much! *Concentrate on one thing, Callie. We're here. At the bank. The locksmith will be here soon, and we'll find out if the stuff is still in the box.*

I clasp my hands in front of me. God, they're sweaty. Clammy and disgusting.

Rory sits next to me, wringing her hands as well. Her lips tremble.

I want to ask if she's okay. I want to be here for my sister.

But my larynx seems to have stopped working.

A few more minutes pass, and then—

"Ms. Pike?" the same manager asks.

Rory clears her throat. "Yes?"

"It will be a few more minutes. I'm so sorry. We just got word from the locksmith that she's running a little bit late on her previous job."

I stand then, my hands curled into fists. "Her previous job? It's nine o'clock in the morning."

"I'm sorry, but sometimes locksmiths have emergencies."

"This is an emergency!"

"I'm sorry, ma'am, but this is not an emergency. A young woman inadvertently trapped her baby in a locked car. *That's* an emergency."

"That's a neglectful mother," Rory says calmly.

My sister's right. She'll make the most amazing mother. I'd like to have children too someday. Beautiful little people with blond hair and amazing hazel eyes.

But I can't think about that now.

"The locksmith will be here as soon as she can," Mr. Keats says. "We're all very sorry. Would you like to reschedule?"

"No, I would not like to reschedule," Rory says. "We don't live here. We live in Snow Creek."

"Then why do you have a safe-deposit box here?"

Rory does not answer. She simply glares.

My sister is getting angry. Really angry. Rory is a kind and gentle soul, an artist and a musician, but even she can get pushed too far.

She settles down a bit, though. "I apologize," she says to Mr. Keats. "I'm sure it was a terrible thing for that mother to lock her baby in the car. Accidents happen. I shouldn't have said she was neglectful. I don't have all the facts."

"I understand, Ms. Pike," Keats says. "If you'll excuse me, I have some work to do while we wait."

Rory nods as Mr. Keats returns to his cubicle.

Then we wait.

And we wait.

If only Donny were here. Why was he acting so strange? How will we get through this?

The door of the bank opens then, and a woman wearing jeans and a red T-shirt walks through. The shirt reads *Karen's Locks*.

Rory and I abruptly stand.

"You're the locksmith?" Rory asks.

"Yes, I am. I'm here to see Michael Keats."

Mr. Keats approaches us quickly. "Karen Bates?"

"Yes, I'm sorry I'm late."

"Wait a minute," Rory says. "Is the baby okay? The one who was locked in the car?"

Karen smiles. "She's fine. She slept through the whole thing. The poor mother cried like a baby, but the little one was just fine."

Rory lets out a relieved sigh. "Thank goodness."

Yes, my sister will be a hell of a mother. I hope she gets that chance.

"Come on back, all of you," Mr. Keats says.

I inhale a deep breath, gathering all my courage.

In a moment, we'll find out.

We'll find out if our property was stolen.

And if it was . . . I don't know what we'll do.

The four of us—Keats, Karen, Rory, and I—crowd into the room. The walls are lined with locked boxes of various sizes. I cast a glance around. Which one of these is Donny's? My gaze falls on Box 451.

That's it. That's the number that was on the key inside the glasses case. Funny that I only now remember. How did I think, for one minute, that Donny had taken our key?

Karen opens up her toolkit and pulls out a drill. Keats nods to a plug on the wall. Several minutes pass while Karen readies her tools. The boxes on the wall seem to move in closer. The room is shrinking, closing in on us.

Then the piercing shriek as she drills into the lock.

EPILOGUE

Donny

It's Monday morning, and I have a Callie-sized hole in my heart. But I push it into the back of my mind. I can't dwell on what I can't have. I have a job to do.

I'm in court, standing in front of the judge, when my phone vibrates in my pocket.

I ignore it, of course. Judges don't take it kindly when you blow them off to look at your phone.

Already, though, I know it's not good news.

Call it instinct. Call it a gut feeling.

Call it one of my hunches.

Call it whatever you'd like.

I drone on about the speeding ticket I'm prosecuting. I can do this in my sleep. I've defended multimillion-dollar clients. This is nothing. I'm on autopilot.

Inside my body, my guts are twisting. An invisible black cloud forms above me.

When I look at the phone after I'm finished in court, I'll know. I'll deal with it.

I'm Donovan Talon Steel, and I *will* find out who shot my father.

And whoever it is will pay.

CONTINUE THE STEEL BROTHERS SAGA
WITH BOOK TWENTY-ONE

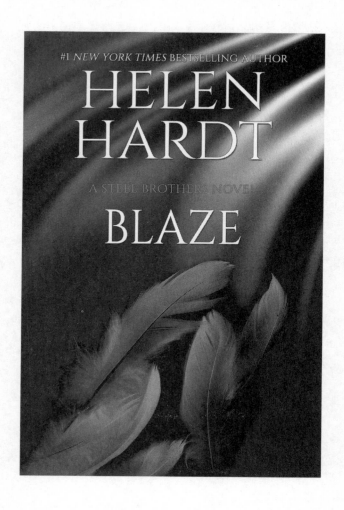

MESSAGE FROM HELEN HARDT

Dear Reader,

Thank you for reading *Flame*. If you want to find out about my current backlist and future releases, please like my Facebook page and join my mailing list. I often do giveaways. If you're a fan and would like to join my street team to help spread the word about my books, please see the web addresses below. I regularly do awesome giveaways for my street team members.

If you enjoyed the story, please take the time to leave a review on a site like Amazon or Goodreads. I welcome all feedback. I wish you all the best!

Helen

Facebook
Facebook.com/HelenHardt

Newsletter
HelenHardt.com/SignUp

Street Team
Facebook.com/Groups/HardtAndSoul

ALSO BY HELEN HARDT

ACKNOWLEDGMENTS

The differences between Donny and Dale—as well as the differences between Callie and her sister Rory—are front and center in *Flame*. We learn so much more about Donny and Callie as people this time. I hope you've enjoyed their character development as much as I have. I'm writing *Blaze* now, and let me tell you, things are heating up! And I'm not talking solely about Donny and Callie's relationship.

Huge thanks to the always brilliant team at Waterhouse Press: Jennifer Becker, Audrey Bobak, Haley Boudreaux, Keli Jo Chen, Yvonne Ellis, Jesse Kench, Robyn Lee, Jon Mac, Amber Maxwell, Dave McInerney, Michele Hamner Moore, Chrissie Saunders, Scott Saunders, Kurt Vachon, and Meredith Wild.

Thanks also to the women and men of Hardt and Soul. Your endless and unwavering support keeps me going.

To my family and friends, thank you for your encouragement. Special shout out to Dean—aka Mr. Hardt—and to our amazing sons, Eric and Grant.

Thank you most of all to my readers. Without you, none of this would be possible. I am grateful every day that I'm able to do what I love—write stories for you!

On to book twenty-one in the Steel Brothers Saga!

ABOUT THE AUTHOR

#1 *New York Times*, #1 *USA Today*, and #1 *Wall Street Journal* bestselling author Helen Hardt's passion for the written word began with the books her mother read to her at bedtime. She wrote her first story at age six and hasn't stopped since. In addition to being an award-winning author of romantic fiction, she's a mother, an attorney, a black belt in Taekwondo, a grammar geek, an appreciator of fine red wine, and a lover of Ben & Jerry's ice cream. She writes from her home in Colorado, where she lives with her family. Helen loves to hear from readers.

Visit her at HelenHardt.com